SALT IN THE WOUNDS

MICHAEL BRADY BOOK 1

MARK RICHARDS

AUTHOR'S NOTE

Salt in the Wounds is set in Whitby, on the North East coast of England. As I'm British and the book's set in the UK, I've used British English. The dialogue is realistic for the characters, which means that they occasionally swear.

This is a novel. I've taken some slight liberties with the number of police officers there would be in Whitby. Other than that I have tried to stay faithful to the town and its history.

As it's a work of fiction names, characters, organisations, some places, events and incidents are either products of the author's imagination or used fictionally. All the characters in this book are fictitious. Any resemblance to actual persons, living or dead, is purely coincidental.

www.markrichards.co.uk

SPRING 2015: SCATTERING THE ASHES

The top of this hill then.

Just the two of them.

Together. One last time.

It was the right decision. Ash had been through enough.

The right place as well. High on the cliff top, where Grace could watch the sun rise out of the sea every morning. Look south to Whitby and north towards the hills. See the gorse bloom in the spring.

Where a seagull could float up to her on a thermal.

And where he could talk to her. Look up from the beach as he walked Archie. Tell her everything was alright. That Ash was doing well at school. That they were coping. His book was taking shape...

He stood on the cliff edge. Or as close to the cliff edge as someone who was afraid of heights could stand.

There were two small boats out at sea, one stationary, the other – red and white, low at the back with a fishing party – chugging round in circles.

He looked 200 feet down to the grey water of the North Sea. Then he pulled the blue/green tube out of his pocket. Unscrewed the lid. Held it in his right hand. Raised his arm and tilted his wrist.

"You're sure, Michael?"

"You know I am, Dilip. We've discussed it. I've thought about it. I've walked the dog and thought about it some more. What can we do? It's the only decision we can take."

"You know that... Once we do this there's no going back?"

"Dilip... Dilip, you've explained everything. A hundred times."

"I'm sorry, Michael. I have to ask."

"We're ready."

At first nothing happened. Very gently, he shook the tube.

And the last of his wife's ashes – held back so he could have one final moment with her – slid out into the pale spring sunshine. For an instant the wind dropped and they hung in the air in front of him. Almost a cloud, he thought.

He gazed into it. Trying to see her face in a cloud of ash.

The cloud drifted slowly away to the north. To the hills, to the gorse bushes burning yellow.

He tried to watch it. Follow its journey. But the wind picked up and it was gone.

A single tear rolled down Michael Brady's cheek.

"Take care, sweetheart," he whispered. "Take good care on your travels."

And then he turned and walked back down the cliff path to his car.

Time to drive into Whitby. Time to collect the keys to the house. Time to drive across the Pennines and finish packing. And in a few days, time to drive back with his daughter.

Time to start a new life.

But there'd never be enough time to heal...

1

"This is a cool town, Dad. Two garden centres and a garage."

"This is Pickering, Ashley, not Whitby."

"Oh, and a Chinese takeaway. And a car park. I'll certainly be coming here with my friends. If I make any, that is."

Was he supposed to reply? He drove across the roundabout by the Forest and Vale and started up the road to Whitby.

"Twenty miles to go," he said. "Thirty minutes. Forty at the most."

"You know I don't want to move to Whitby, don't you?"

"You have told me, yes. Once or twice."

"OK, just so you know."

Brady sighed. What else could he do? They couldn't live in Manchester any more. And they'd discussed it a hundred times...

"Look, Ash, Whitby will be fine."

"Dad, Whitby is the other side of the country. And it's fine for a holiday. As long as you're there for three days and you want to eat fish and chips and walk on the beach. But no-one could want to live there. No-one who's not your age. Or dead."

Pickering gave way to the North York Moors. He'd wanted a sunny day to welcome them. A good omen for their new life. But the clouds were dark grey, the Moors bleak and foreboding.

There was a whine from the back of the Tiguan. "Archie needs a wee," Ash said.

"OK, there's a car park just up here on the right."

Brady indicated and turned in. He parked the car facing the Hole of Horcum, a huge bowl in the Moors, formed – legend had it – when Wade the Giant scooped up a handful of earth to throw at his wife.

"You coming?"

"As if." Ash was already busy on her phone.

"OK. Five minutes. I'll just walk Archie across the road."

Brady lifted the tailgate. A black and white Springer Spaniel did his best to jump out. "Patience, Archie. Just wait a minute. You need your lead on."

They walked across the road. A path led through a gap in the fence to the edge of the giant's bowl. Archie had a wee, sniffed the heather, decided this was a good place for a long walk. Brady looked down into the hole Wade had made and saw the paths winding across the hillside. Archie was right.

"But not today," he said. "We need to unpack. But

we'll be back, I promise. And there's a beach waiting for you as well."

Archie reluctantly jumped back into the car. An expectant look produced the obligatory biscuit.

"You OK?" he asked, getting back into the car.

"Yeah, I'm good." Her mood had lightened. He still couldn't get used to how quickly it changed.

'Teenage girls, Mike,' someone had said to him. 'I say something to mine one day, she's fine. Say the same thing the next day and I'm the worst father in the world. Take my advice, mate. Day she turns 13, fly to Argentina. Come back when she goes to university.'

"Let's go," he said. "Or the removal van'll overtake us."

He drove out of the car park. The road bent round to the left and started to dip downhill. "Fylingdales," he said, pointing to the right. "It used to be three giant golf balls when I was your age."

"What is it then?"

"Early warning system. Part of the RAF. Supposed to give us four minutes' warning if Vladimir Putin wakes up in a bad mood."

"You mean if someone tells him he has to live in Whitby?"

He laughed. "Very good," he said.

He glanced across at her. She was her mother. The same mouth, the same dark brown hair. Maybe a shade or two lighter. The hint of green in her eyes. Sassy, argumentative, assertive. All the qualities that had attracted him to Grace. But which might make her teenage years an interesting challenge...

He reached across and squeezed her hand. Surprisingly, she squeezed back.

"We'll be fine," he said. "You, me, Archie... And we're here, the top of Blue Bank."

Whitby was spread out below them, squeezed between the Moors and the sea, the ruins of the Abbey guarding the town.

"Are you looking forward to this, Dad?"

She surprised him with the question. *Was* he looking forward to it?

Yes, some days he was. Some days the thought of getting up, dropping her at school, coming home, writing, looking out of his window at the sea, walking Archie on the beach, more writing in the afternoon, cooking dinner for the two of them, talking over the meal, doing some research at night, offering to help Ash with her homework while he still could.

Yes, some days he was looking forward to it.

And some days it terrified him.

Dropping Ash at school, coming home to an empty house, looking at the rain lashing horizontally off the North Sea, trudging along a sodden beach with an equally sodden dog, coming back to an empty house, cooking a meal he ate on his own because Ash was going out and had forgotten to tell him. Another early night as he tried to escape the pain...

"Of course I am," he said.

And he drove down Blue Bank, through Sleights and into Whitby.

2

"You sure you'll be OK?"

"I'll be fine, Dad. I'm going to watch a film. And encourage Archie to sleep on the sofa."

"Don't you dare..."

"What time will you be back?"

"Ten. No later. Trust me, Ash, I don't want to go. You know I hate parties. Especially birthday parties for middle-aged men."

"Have you got a key?"

"Who's the parent here? Yes, I have. I'll see you at ten. Do you want me to say 'happy birthday?' to your Uncle Bill for you?"

"No. You know I don't like him."

"He's your uncle."

"He gives me the creeps."

Brady turned to go. "Dad," Ash said. "One last thing..."

"What?"

"Don't get in a car with anyone that's been drinking."

He smiled. So far so good then. She'd listened to something he'd told her. Something based on bitter experience...

He walked past the park, down the hill and up the other side. Why was he worrying about getting himself fit again? Rule out the seafront and it was impossible to walk anywhere in Whitby without walking up a hill.

Brady rang the bell of his sister's house. Four bedrooms, detached, two cars in the drive. Did a detective really need a personalised number plate? He could think of better ways to spend £500. Just the middle aged equivalent of having your name on a t-shirt.

He hadn't been lying. He hated parties. People round for dinner? A perfect evening. Well, it had been, once upon a time.

Parties where he had to make small talk with a lot of people he didn't know? He'd rather take Archie for a walk. He'd rather take Archie for a walk in the rain.

Kate answered the door. His big sister. If three years older still counted as a big sister. "Michael. Come in."

They hugged. The hug of a brother and sister who'd always been friends.

Kate stepped back and looked at him. "Are you growing a beard? And letting your hair grow?"

"I thought I might. Now I'm a writer..."

"You know your beard's got a touch of grey don't you?"

"My daughter is 13. She's told me. Several times a day."

"It definitely makes you look... I'm not sure... A bit Chris Hemsworth."

"Who?"

"*Thor*, Michael. But older. And without the hammer. And the six pack..."

She took his coat. "Ash didn't want to come then?"

"She's watching a film. And giving Archie too many biscuits. You know how it is at that age: grown-up parties where they don't know anyone..."

"I do. We've all been there. How's she doing?"

"OK, I think. But she's a teenager now: I'm the last one to know."

"Both mine have gone out," Kate said. "Maddie's got a new boyfriend." Her tone of voice suggested she wasn't impressed.

"Is Bill alright with that? The girls missing his party?"

"He's delighted. Anything to avoid Maddie's boyfriend. And we're going out tomorrow. Just the four of us."

She took him into the lounge. Maybe 20 people. Ten o'clock couldn't come soon enough.

Let's get this over and done with.

First stop, the birthday boy. Detective Chief Inspector William Calvert. Pink faced, slightly overweight. A man who'd be a lot happier when he didn't have a police medical to worry about.

What was that word Ash had started using? Gammon? Yep, it worked for Bill.

They shook hands. "Happy birthday, Bill. I didn't bother with a card. Thought this might look better on the mantelpiece."

His brother-in-law laughed. "Thanks, Mike. I'm in need of reinforcements. Kate's gin shelf is taking over." He glanced down at the bottle. "Laphroaig. Thank you."

"How's it feel then? Five years to go?"

"Bloody brilliant. Whitby can just behave itself for the next five years. No crime. Nothing happening. Then I can do my duty and take Kate on a cruise."

"No crime? That's optimistic…"

Bill shook his head. "We're on top of it. We know who the villains are."

Until there are new ones.

But he was out of it now. Whatever happened, it was someone else's problem.

"Kate says you're going to write a book. Story of the investigation."

"That's the plan."

Bill looked sceptical. "I don't see the point. It's not going to change anything."

Because the story needs to be told. Because I owe it to Grace.

"Besides," he added. "You've always been a copper. That's all you've ever wanted to do. That's what you told me, first time I came round to your house when I started seeing Kate. Three months of tapping away at your laptop and you'll be itching to nick someone."

Brady shook his head. "Not any longer. That part of my life's over."

"So why haven't you retired? Kate said you were still on leave – "

"A year's sabbatical, technically…"

"You should do what I'm going to do. It's all planned. One last piss-up with the lads, take my pension and sod off to the golf course. You could have played the mental health card. Early retirement…"

Brady shook his head. "It's too final. I'm 95% there. But only 95%. And I don't play golf."

"You'll change your mind. Getting a drink would be a good start. You want a beer?"

"Yeah, sure. Thank you."

"There's a few in the fridge keeping cold. Go and help yourself."

Brady walked into the kitchen. The fridge door was already open.

"Is the selection as good as Bill says then?"

She turned round. Dark hair pinned up. Grey eyes. His first impression was how determined she looked. The sort of girl that ignored her father's pleas and buckled on armour in *Lord of the Rings*.

"It's what you'd call a Bill selection," she said. "Bud, Estrella, San Miguel. Bill Calvert goes to Benidorm. There'll be an Amstel and a bowl of peanuts if you look hard enough."

Brady laughed. "Michael Brady," he said, holding out his hand.

"Frankie Thomson. And I know."

"You know what?"

"Know who you are. Everyone knows you've come to live in Whitby. And as you're Kate's brother and still look like a cop. Well," she added, "A cop who's growing his hair..."

"It didn't take much working out."

"No. Sorry." She turned back to the fridge and grabbed two bottles of beer. "I'll leave you to find the Amstel and the peanuts. My boyfriend gets thirsty when we're taking a taxi."

Brady settled for a bottle of Estrella. There was a buffet laid out and he was hungry. But he was a man who played by the rules. He'd wait for Kate to say something.

He looked at his watch. 7:50. Ten minutes to walk home. Two hours then. He went reluctantly back into the lounge. And came face to face with Bill's boss.

Brady recognised him. A conference on drug trafficking.

He held out a well-manicured hand. "Alan Kershaw."

What little silver hair he had left was cropped close. A smooth face. A man who was carefully climbing up the ladders. Who made sure the snakes were delegated to someone else.

"Michael Brady. We met - "

"At the conference in Birmingham," Kershaw finished for him. "You gave a presentation on drugs. County lines."

Brady remembered. He'd asked a question. A reasonably intelligent one. "I hope you haven't needed the information?"

"In some places. Whitby? No, not yet."

Kershaw glanced at a woman across the room. Very evidently his wife. 'Two minutes,' he mouthed. "You must excuse us," he said. "Another engagement. But you're not 50 every day."

He turned to go. Then he changed his mind and turned back to Brady. "I hope you're happy in Whitby, Mr Brady. Someone said you were writing a book. I'll put it on my Christmas list. But remember you're Michael Brady, writer. A civilian. You left DCI Brady in Manchester. We don't need him in North Yorkshire."

Brady didn't know how to reply.

Just play a dead bat.

"I've no intention of doing anything else. And being a father to my daughter."

Kershaw nodded. "The best way. And now, if you'll excuse me..."

The evening wore on. Kate finally declared the buffet open, he had another beer and found that he didn't dislike quiche as much as he thought he did. Dutifully clapped when Bill had stumbled through a self-congratulatory speech. Learned that the neighbour had a problem with slugs. "Are you a gardener, Mike? Good soil in Whitby. You'll be surprised what you can grow, despite the wind off the sea."

He couldn't wait.

He found Bill, told him to be careful now he was old and went looking for his sister. "I promised Ash I'd be back."

"You can't go."

"Why not? I've got to, Kate. I promised her."

"Five minutes, Mike. I've a surprise for you."

"It's Bill's birthday, not mine."

"And you're my brother. Just be patient. I'm re-introducing you to Whitby society."

The doorbell rang. "Go ahead," Kate said. "Answer it."

"What is this? Some prank call?"

"No. Do as you're told. Open the door."

What else can you do when your big sister gives you an order? He opened the front door. And looked at a face he hadn't seen for nearly five years.

"Bloody hell. Patrick."

"How are you doing, Mike? Hell's teeth, what's that on your face? You're going grey."

THE LIGHT WAS STILL on in her bedroom. Brady put his head round the door. "Hi, sweetheart. Sorry I'm a bit late. Everything been OK?"

"Yeah. Sure, I let Archie out before I came to bed."

"Everyone sends their love."

"OK, that's cool."

"And I met Patrick."

"Who's Patrick?"

"I talked about him once. He was my best friend at school. He's got a business in Whitby now. Really successful. And he's got a new wife. Tall, really good looking. Looks like a model."

"If you say so."

She was tired. He tiptoed over and kissed her.

"Ugh, you've been drinking. Late home *and* you're drunk."

"Two beers, Ash. You sleep tight. Love you."

"Love you too, Dad. And Dad..."

"What, love?"

"Don't be late again. You don't want to be grounded."

3

This was the moment he'd been dreading. Ever since he'd made the decision to move. As they'd driven across the M62. As he'd stood in the shower that morning.

"You're sure you don't want me to come in with you?"

Ash shook her head. "Year 8? It's not going to look good if I walk in holding hands with my daddy."

She was right. Obviously. They'd been to the school. Met the headteacher. Met the head of year. Met everyone they needed to meet.

"I'll be fine, Dad."

He still thought she looked nervous. But what else could he do?

"OK. Have a good day. I'll collect you at four."

"You too. Don't waste all morning talking to your friend. Go home and get writing."

She opened the door and climbed out. Walked into school in her all-too-clearly brand new uniform.

"She's strong. She'll be fine," Brady said out loud. He

didn't know if he was trying to reassure himself – or sending a message to Grace.

He'd met Grace from work. Ash was in the school play. The first night. Front row seats. He'd kissed her. 'I've always liked you in that jacket. Brings out the colour in your eyes.' Held her hand as they walked across the road to the car park. 'Do you want a drink before we go up to school? I'm sure a day saving the NHS merits a gin.' He hadn't heard the car accelerating. Maybe he had. He wasn't concentrating. Suddenly an engine was screaming. He turned round. A black car. Felt his wife's hands punch into his back. He stumbled forward. Three steps. Four steps. Tripped. Fell. Put his left hand out to break his fall. Broke his wrist. But knew she'd saved his life...

An hour later Brady finally dragged a very wet, very reluctant dog off the beach. 'The bacon sandwich stall opposite the amusement arcade' Patrick had said. And there he was. Jeans, black jacket and still the half puzzled, half amused look he'd had even as a 12 year old.

"Morning," Brady said as they shook hands. "And sorry again for having to dash off the other night."

"No problem. Kate told me about Ash. No problem at all."

Patrick turned to his right. He made a theatrical gesture of introduction.

"Michael, I would like you to meet my good friend, Dave. The man who makes the best bacon sandwiches in Whitby. Possibly in the world. David, Michael Brady. One time detective, now another writer to add to Whitby's growing collection."

Dave looked about 60. Maybe slightly younger. His face had all the battle scars of a long career in the front row of a rugby scrum. He leaned over the counter and stuck out a ridiculously large hand. "Pleased to meet you," he said in a broad Geordie accent. "What'll it be?"

Brady smiled. One of those people you liked immediately. "Patrick told me I had no choice in the matter. Two mugs of tea, please. And two bacon sandwiches."

Dave started laying bacon on the griddle. "What are you then? Local or tourist?"

"Local, I guess. I grew up here. I've just come back. Rented a house for 12 months."

"So I'll be seeing yous again then?"

Brady looked up at the sun. "If every morning's like this and the bacon sandwiches are as good as he says, then yes."

"They're not. They're better."

Dave flipped half a dozen rashers of bacon over and turned round. "I'd best get to know you if you're local. Oven bottom or baguette?"

"Oven bottom," Brady answered. "Providing it's this morning's."

"Cheeky sod. I'm at the bakery by six. Bacon? As it comes or crispy?"

"Crispy. No question."

"Two out of two so far. But now we come to it..."

Dave turned and faced him. "Tomato sauce? Brown sauce? No sauce?"

The question hung in the air.

"Take care," Patrick said. "This is how he judges people. So as the good Inspector Callahan would say, 'What's it gonna be, punk?' Red sauce or brown sauce?"

Why not? Red sauce or brown sauce? It seemed a

reasonable way of judging people. It had to be at least as accurate as the psychometric tests at his last promotion board.

"None of the above," Brady said. "There's a pan on the hob. I'm willing to bet it's got plum tomatoes in it. And not from the cash and carry either."

Dave leaned forward and high-fived him over the counter. "Welcome to Whitby, young man. Gold star. Just don't bugger it up by asking for Earl Grey."

They took their sandwiches and mugs of tea and walked 50 yards up the road. The slipway went down to the beach, the pier – long, curved, punctuated by the lighthouse – stretched out into the North Sea. "Over here," Patrick said, gesturing to a bench by the bandstand. He took his backpack off his shoulder and sat down.

Brady looked out across the harbour. Let his eyes drift up to St Hilda's Church and the Abbey on top of the hill.

"Pleased to be back?" Patrick asked. Then, "I'm sorry. That was a stupid question. We all heard what happened. And I'm truly sorry I couldn't be at the funeral. Let me start again. How are you doing? How's Ash doing?"

"Can I come back to you at four o'clock? See how her first day's gone?"

"She'll be fine."

"I hope so. She seems to make friends easily. She's good at sport. We both know what a difference that makes."

Brady took a bite of his bacon sandwich. "You weren't lying were you? The secret of success in life. Do one thing and do it bloody well."

There was a whine from near his feet. He looked down. "Play fair, Archie, you've had your breakfast. Maybe a bit of bread if there's some left…"

"What made you leave Manchester?" Patrick asked.

He was conscious of something as he fell. Something flying over him. Something green. The colour of her jacket…

There'd been a bang. Impact. Someone had screamed. Then silence. A moment of silence. Then a noise. A noise he'd never stop hearing. The noise of his wife landing. Half on the road, half on the pavement.

Three noises.

And a fourth.

A car accelerating into the distance.

Brady looks up. A grey Merc brakes sharply, swerves to avoid her. A mini stops on the other side of the road. A young woman climbs out, phone already to her ear.

A second person screams.

"Grace? Grace!" Brady stumbles towards her. Suddenly aware of a pain in his left arm. Shoulder as well. Where he fell on the road.

More cars backing up now. Someone directing the traffic. The young woman running across the road. "I've phoned the police," she says. "And the ambulance."

"I am the police," Brady says uselessly.

He's bending over her now. Takes his jacket off, wincing with the pain. Put it under her head, he thinks. Make her comfortable. He remembers the first aid training just in time. 'Don't ever move someone's head.' His wife's head stays resting on the kerb.

A crowd is gathering. He glances up. Two people recording

it on their phones. When did that take over from offering to help?

"Grace," he says. "Grace. Look at me. Talk to me."

Her eyes flicker. Move towards Brady. Don't focus on him. "Ash..." she whispers. "Ash?" It sounds like a question.

"She's fine, sweetheart. She's at school. I'll phone. She'll be fine."

Grace sighs. Seems to relax. There's a small trickle of blood on the road. From the back of her head. A cut, Brady tells himself. Just cuts and bruises.

He turns his head. Sees Grace's right leg. Her trousers are ripped. Her leg ridiculously bent. Doesn't want to look. Forces himself to look. Sees the bone, clearly visible.

He hears someone in the crowd throwing up.

There are sirens. An ambulance. Two paramedics. Then police sirens. Two lads in uniform. One of them vaguely familiar.

Now he's just a spectator. Watching as the paramedics stabilise Grace's head. Gently, oh so gently, manoeuvre her onto the stretcher.

Someone has draped a blanket round his shoulders.

"You alright, boss?" the vaguely familiar one says.

"I'm fine. I need... I must go with her."

A uniform helps him into the ambulance. A different uniform tells him to sit down. Grace is within touching distance. Brady tries to reach out to her. Aware of the pain in his wrist. Grits his teeth. Touches his wife. Whispers, "I love you."

Brady shook his head. "There was no alternative. Ash passed the place every day on the way to school. I'd have done the same if I'd gone back. We didn't get anyone for it. People pussyfooting round the station, not daring to talk in front of me. We had no choice."

"So you came home?"

"What else could I do? How much longer was I going to sit by her bed? Six months? A year? Two years? I had to make a decision."

"What did they say?"

"Said there was no hope. So I *had* to make the decision. For Ash. The kid's life was on hold. And she needs someone. At least I've got a sister here. God knows she isn't going to ask me if she has a problem with her periods."

A seagull flew down and landed a few feet away. Archie growled: it ignored him and stared at the bacon sandwiches. "I swear to God," Patrick said, "The bastards get bigger and more aggressive every year. If evolution means anything the seagulls will conquer Whitby in the next 500 years."

"The other thing about Ash," Brady said. "It wasn't just having Kate nearby. She's all I've got now. I sort of felt – I don't know, maybe this sounds stupid – I sort of felt I'd be closer to her in a small town. She's reached that age now. 'Where are you going?' 'Out.' 'Where?' 'Nowhere special.' 'Who with?' 'Just friends.' I remember Kate saying exactly the same to Dad. Next thing she's bringing Bill home."

Patrick's face clouded. "Did you ever say anything to her? About that night? Or to your dad?"

Brady shook his head. "What was the point? She was in love. Keeping quiet was the only option."

There was another whine. More pitiful than the last.

Brady looked down. A pair of brown eyes stared back at him. He admitted defeat. "Once," he said. "Just this once. Not every morning, OK? You understand? It's *definitely* not happening."

He stood up – "Give me a minute, Pat" – and walked back to Dave's stall.

He was back two minutes later. Archie was close to smiling. "A cooked sausage," Brady said. "Left over from yesterday. Rescued from the bin. But he's a Springer. He'll eat an abandoned barbecue. Anyway, enough of this serious talk. We're men. We only talk about football or sex. How bad are Middlesbrough this year? And Kara. Bloody hell. Congratulations. A whole new meaning to punching above your weight."

Patrick laughed. "Not bad to your first question. They'll make the play-offs. I'll take you to the next game if you're free. And in answer to the second, I'm still not sure..."

"How did you meet her?"

"On holiday. I was in Marbella. I've got a house there. It was just after Sofia and I divorced. It was all a bit bloody. Well, a lot bloody. I wanted some time away."

Brady looked at a man who clearly couldn't believe his luck. "I'm still in shock. I went round to some friends for drinks. She was there. She'd been doing some work with a photographer out there. Six months later we're married."

Brady smiled at him. "That's good. I'm pleased for you. Really pleased."

"Hang on," Patrick said. "There's more... She's pregnant."

"Ah, Patrick. Fuck. That is brilliant. Just brilliant. Does Dave sell champagne?"

Patrick shook his head. "Don't say anything. I'm not supposed to know."

"What? Why not?"

"I don't know. Maybe she's waiting until she's sure. I'm not going to say anything. You know, spoil her moment..."

"So how did you find out?"

"By accident. I found the test. Two blue lines. She'd dropped it in the bathroom bin, safe in the knowledge that I never go anywhere near the bathroom bin."

"Except..."

"Except I'd thrown my last razor blade away. Not that you'll know what razor blades are any more... I needed a shave. I thought there were some in the cupboard. There weren't." Patrick shrugged. "So I went through the bin for the one I'd thrown away."

"Textbook detective work. All the best clues are discovered by accident."

They'd tried for another one. A brother or sister for Ash. But his job, Grace's job... It just never happened. "I think the window's closed," Grace had said one day. In truth, they'd both known it for a while. "Shall I have a vasectomy?" he'd said. But he'd never got round to it. Then Ash had come home and said she was in the school play...

"It's going to cause trouble," Patrick said.

"The pregnancy? Why? Kara must be healthy. If looks are anything to go by. And a baby is hardly going to stop you working."

"No." Patrick nodded across the road, "Sofia's family..."

A man in his mid-thirties was walking towards them. He was speaking on his mobile. Perfect teeth. Perfect designer stubble. Perfect cashmere coat draped over his shoulders. A shame he was two stone overweight. And rapidly going bald.

He nodded at Patrick and stopped. "Enzo," Patrick said. "How are you?"

"Good." He was clearly Italian. But his accent was local, overlaid with English boarding school. "And maybe better this afternoon. I bought a new horse at the weekend. She's running at Thirsk."

"Well, good luck with that," Patrick said, clearly not meaning it. "Enzo, this is - "

Brady stood up. "I don't need introducing. Michael Brady. And I remember you, Enzo. I used to work for your dad in the summer holidays. A misspent youth as a bingo caller." What he remembered was a little boy of seven or eight. Running round the amusement arcade like he owned it. "How is your dad?" he asked. "I always liked him."

Enzo shrugged. He clearly didn't remember Brady. "Old. He had a fall. But he still thinks he's in charge."

"Give him my best will you? Tell him I said hello."

Enzo clearly wouldn't. He nodded at them both, tapped a number into his phone and walked towards the town.

"No love lost there," Brady said.

"Enzo thinks I dishonoured his sister. You know his dad's values. Family, loyalty. Enzo takes them to extremes."

"What happened?"

"Bluntly, we couldn't have children. Endless IVF. We threw any amount of money at it. Sofia started drinking. Marriage bloody guidance. Counselling. Then it was more than drinking. In the end it was all too much for me."

"So when Enzo finds out about Kara..."

"Right. He's not going to be telling me when his horse is due to win."

Patrick stood up. "I'm sorry, Mike. I'm going to have to get back to work. Got a call with an architect and a planning officer at eleven. Look, why don't you come round to dinner? And bring Ash. Maybe she'd see Kara as a big sister?" He laughed. "What am I saying? What the hell do we know about how women relate to each other? Anyway, come round on Saturday."

"Yeah, I'd like that. And Pat - "

"What?"

"Thank you. That's the first time I've really talked about it."

"What about all those police psychologists?"

Brady shook his head. "I couldn't, just couldn't. They were just... strangers. Doing a job."

"I know what you mean. Same as marriage guidance. Every psychologist I've ever met has been bloody useless. All that training and they haven't grasped the simple importance of fresh air and a bacon sandwich."

He screwed the sandwich bag into a ball and threw it towards the rubbish bin. It arced gracefully through the air and fell three feet short. "Bugger," Pat said as he walked forward to pick it up. "Didn't allow for the wind off the sea." He put the bag in the bin, picked his back-pack up and held out his hand.

"Thanks again," Brady said. "I'm grateful."

"No problem. That's what best friends are for."

"Even after five years?"

"Especially after five years. See you Saturday. And hope Ash's first day has gone well."

"Me too," Brady said. "No news is good news."

"Hello. This is Michael Brady. Ashley's father. I need to speak to Mrs Clarke."

"I don't know if she's available, Mr Brady. It's the first night of the school play tonight."

Sheila? Shirley? What the hell was the school secretary called?

"Shirley. It is Shirley isn't it? I thought I recognised your voice."

"Sheila."

"Sheila, I'm so sorry. I'm at the hospital..."

He'd noticed it when his father died. Auto-pilot. However much grief you're feeling, however much pain you're in, it doesn't matter. Something inside you takes over. Does what needs doing.

"...It's an emergency," the auto-pilot said. "My wife, Ashley's mum. She's had an accident. I really need to speak to Mrs Clarke."

Sheila put the phone down. There was a long silence while she walked down the corridor to the school hall.

"Hello?" Sheila had found Mrs Clarke.

Brady explained. Accident. Hospital. Neither of them would be at the play.

"I don't know, Mr Brady. Maybe I should tell Ashley after the play?"

"But then she's going to come on stage and see two empty chairs isn't she?"

"Oh. Of course. I'm sorry. What shall I say to her?"

"Say…"

Say what? 'Oh, Ashley, there's nothing to worry about but someone tried to kill your dad and hit your mum instead.'

Say that Grace saved my life? That she's badly hurt but I don't know how badly?

The truth would have to wait.

"Tell her that her mum's had an accident. A fall. She might have broken her leg. I'm at the hospital with her. Tell her I'm sorry."

The auto-pilot made a second phone call.

"Maria? Hi, this is Michael Brady. Maria, I need to ask you a favour if I can. Grace has had a fall. She might have broken her leg. I'm at the hospital with her. No, I won't be able to make it to the play. That's why I'm phoning. I don't think I'll be able to collect Ash afterwards. I might be here a while. Would you, could you, take her home with you? Let her stay with Connie tonight?"

And now Grace's mother. But supposing Ash phoned her Grandmother?

The auto-pilot told some more lies…

Brady picked up the mugs and walked back to Dave's. "Thanks," he said, putting them on the counter.

"Alright were they?"

He smiled. "Not bad. Fair to middlin' as they say in Yorkshire."

"So I'll see you every morning?"

"Looks like it. And looks like all I need to do is sit on the seafront for a week and I'll meet everyone I know in the town."

"Aye? Who was it this morning then?"

"Enzo Barella? You must know him? I worked for his dad when I was a teenager."

"Enzo? Everyone in Whitby knows Enzo." Dave paused. "There's more there than meets the eye."

Something in his tone of voice told Brady not to reply. It was one of the most important lessons he'd learned about detective work. There were times when the best way to ask a question was to keep quiet.

"Two children at a posh school. Two flash cars. Two racehorses - "

Maybe three, Brady thought.

" – All paid for by one amusement arcade. You do the maths."

Brady felt it. The old, familiar flicker of interest. He snuffed it out. Time to do as he'd been told. "Don't waste all morning talking to your friend" presumably also meant 'don't waste all morning talking to the bacon sandwich man.'

"Thanks, Dave. You take care, I'll see you tomorrow."

"You n' all," Dave said. "Oven bottom, crispy bacon, plum tomatoes and a left-over sausage for the boss." He tapped his head. "You're in the database now."

BRADY WAS GETTING into the car when his phone rang. Patrick. "Don't tell me Enzo's relented? We all need to back his horse this afternoon?"

"Very funny. No. I've cocked up. Sorry. This weekend is Whitby Goth Festival. So next Saturday for dinner if that's OK?"

"Sure. No problem. What's happened?"

"Nothing's happened," Patrick said. "I'm a Goth. Don't laugh, you bastard. Kara spent a year in black leather and ripped stockings as a teenager. She gets nostalgic. And share your wife's interests. That's what they told me in marriage guidance. So twice a year I have to dress up like a Victorian gentleman and listen to Siouxsie and the fucking Banshees."

"I might have to see that..."

"You should. Whitby at its most spectacular. And maddest. You'll enjoy it."

4

It was Saturday night. "Dad," Ash said. "Is it alright if I go out?"

"Sure. Where are you going?"

Please, not 'nowhere special.' We've only been here a fortnight...

"Into town? To see the Goths?"

"I guess so. Who are you going with?"

"Two girls from school. Immy and Bean."

"OK, so one of them's called Imogen. I'm still young enough to work that out. Who on earth is 'Bean?'"

"Her name's Jessica. But everyone calls her Bean. Don't ask me why. I've only been – ha, ha, joke, Dad – there a week."

And – as far as he could tell – the week had gone reasonably well. The work she'd been doing in Manchester seemed to have translated to Whitby. There hadn't been any dramas. So far so good. "What time are you going to be back?" Brady asked.

"Nine-thirty?"

He nodded. "That's fine. No later."

"Says the man who promised his lovely daughter he'd be in at ten and was half an hour late."

"OK, I can't argue with that. You alright for money?"

She was. The doorbell rang. Ash went to open the front door. "Bye, Dad," she called.

"Look after yourself," he called back. "Remember your key."

The door closed behind her. He glanced out of the window. Three teenage girls walking down the road. All in jeans, almost identical from the back.

"Just you and me, mate," he said to Archie. "Maybe we should go and start the book."

An hour later he conceded defeat. 'Writing is easy,' he'd read somewhere. 'You just stare at a blank screen until your forehead starts to bleed.'

If tonight was any guide blood would be dripping onto his keyboard on a regular basis.

"I'll be an hour, Archie," he said. "And no is the answer to your next question. It'll be too crowded."

He walked down the hill and turned left into town.

Whitby Goth Festival had started in 1994. Brady had been dimly aware of it in a couple of holidays. But this was on a different scale. It was like stepping back into the 19th Century – with the odd medieval jester and visitor from outer space thrown in for good measure.

Along the sea front or over the swing bridge? It

looked marginally less crowded on the other side of the bridge. He crossed the bridge, overtook Count Dracula and his bride and turned left into Church Street. He walked along the cobbled street. And there it was...

The jet shop. They'd painted the outside. But it was the same shop. The first time he'd brought her to Whitby. He'd wanted to buy her something.

"What is it?" Grace asked.

"Jet? Technically it's decaying wood that's been under extreme pressure. About 200 million years old. It's supposed to give you spiritual guidance. And inner harmony..."

Grace held the black earrings up and looked in the mirror. "They're beautiful. Thank you."

"You have to promise to wear your hair up. You know I'm powerless when you pin your hair up."

She laughed and fluttered her eyelashes at him. "Whatever you command, sir..."

The shop assistant wrapped the jet black teardrop earrings and held the package out.

Brady took it. "Later," he said. "In the hotel. And next time we come to Whitby I'll buy you the necklace to go with them. But only if you behave yourself, Miss Miller..."

Whitby had split into three. Goths, photographers and – standing outside the pubs with their pints – the spectators. "Best free cabaret on Earth," he heard one of them say.

No question, black was the dominant colour. As far as the Goths were concerned, black was the new black.

Plenty of red as well – or maybe a reddish orange. Was that blood? Or did it just go well with black?

Red hair everywhere. Dark eyeliner. One girl with

barbed wire drawn across her face. Plenty of white make-up. Long black coats.

Top hats and skeletons. Victorian wedding dresses. And aviator goggles and leather jackets. 'You'll see a lot of steampunk,' someone had said to him. Not that he knew what steampunk was...

There was a battalion of men in uniform. If he'd been asked to guess he'd have said the Prussian army. Whatever it was, it had invaded Whitby.

Ostrich feathers were in plentiful supply. And so were families. "We thought little 'un would've been frightened," he heard one mother say. "She's been good as gold."

'Little 'un' – complete with curly black hair and fangs – looked about 18 months old.

Small Victorian sunglasses. A man wearing a studded gas mask. His wife wearing a face mask. Looking like the dentist from your nightmares. Black, stretched from ear to ear, sharp spikes protruding outwards. 'Open wide now...'

Plenty of people with horns. *The Devil Rides Out* in Whitby.

"Mike. I wondered if we'd see you."

It was Patrick. He hardly knew anyone in Whitby. So it *had* to be Patrick. The diffident teenager who'd gone to a fancy dress party with a piece of wire round his ankle and claimed to be a homing pigeon...

...And who was now wearing a Victorian top hat. A red and black patterned frock coat. A matching waistcoat. White ruffled shirt. Black silk cravat. Black pinstripe trousers. Boots that a butler could have spent all morning polishing...

"Patrick. Wow. You look - " Brady couldn't find the right word. He could. He just didn't know if you could say it to someone you'd played football with. Someone you'd thrown up with at teenage parties.

"Wow, Patrick. You look stunning."

But not as stunning as Kara.

White blonde hair tumbled over her shoulders. One half of her face was covered in white make up. Her cheek was decorated with cobwebs. Black lipstick. A black basque decorated with red bows. Black leather mini-skirt. Thigh-length black boots. A black cloak around her shoulders, the red lining matching the bows on her basque. A black leather cat o'nine tails in her right hand.

Brady didn't know what to do. What was the correct form of greeting? Shake hands? Kiss her on the cheek? Lick the bottom of her boot?

None of the above. "You're wasted in Whitby, Kara. You should take that outfit to Westminster. MPs and all their kinks? You'd make a fortune."

She laughed. "Only twice a year, Michael." She flicked her husband lightly with the cat. "And it keeps Patrick young."

Brady frowned. "Are you sure? That looks like a walking stick to me. How long have you needed that, Patrick?"

"Not just a walking stick," Patrick said. He lifted the stick up. The handle was black lacquer, inlaid with an intricate white pattern. He pulled it gently: an elegant blade slid out.

"Here." Patrick passed it to him. Brady slid it all the way out. Tested the point against his thumb. "That's a serious weapon," he said. "You do realise possessing it is an offence, sir? Or it would have been in my previous life."

"You'd have to arrest half of Whitby, officer. There's enough swordsticks at a Goth weekend to re-run the Charge of the Light Brigade."

Brady passed it back to him. "Have a good night. I've got to get back."

"You don't want to come for a drink with us?"

He shook his head. "No. I'm not dressed for it am I? Besides, I told Ash to be in for 9:30. My standing as a good dad depends on being back before her. And I'm still in trouble for the other night. You two take care."

He watched them disappear down Church Street. Then he turned to walk home. It was even more crowded now. The first really good weather this year and the world and his wife had come to Whitby. And most of them wearing black to celebrate...

HE'D BEEN HOME for half an hour when Ash came in. 9:29 – she'd clearly inherited her mother's punctuality gene.

"Everything OK?" he called out as he heard the door open.

"Sure," she said, putting her head round the door. "We met Maddie."

"Yeah? Your cousin? How's she doing?"

Ash shrugged. "OK, I guess. She's got a new boyfriend."

"Kate said. What's he like?"

"He's older," Ash said. "Twenty? Something like that. He's got a beard. Not grey though. Goodnight, Dad."

"Ash?" Brady called after her.

"What?"

"Put your dirty washing on the landing will you? I need to go full domestic goddess in the morning."

5

Mark Smeaton had just confessed. Thomas Cromwell had everything he wanted. Proof positive of Anne Boleyn's adultery. It had been easy.

But confessions probably were a lot easier in 1536. No such thing as the duty solicitor. The rack waiting impatiently in the next room...

He put his book on the bedside table – if he could write one-tenth as well as Hilary Mantel he'd be happy – and turned the light out.

Tomorrow morning. Take Archie on the beach, make some scrambled eggs for Ash, start the book.

He rolled over onto his left hand side. Put his right hand out, just as he'd put his right hand out for 20 years. But she wasn't there.

You can put your hand out as many times as you like. It won't bring her back...

It was going to be another one of those nights. An hour before he went to sleep. Awake at two, awake at four.

Finally dropping off into a deep sleep. And half an hour later the alarm goes off.

"I can give you something," his doctor had said. "Help you get to sleep."

There'd never been any chance of that. What was he going to do, take sleeping pills for the rest of his life? He was on his back now, gazing at the ceiling.

Just under two weeks to go. Then it would be a year.

Then three more days... And it would be six months since they'd turned the machine off. "Fuck," he said out loud. "Just fuck."

Sometimes it was easier to get up. Admit defeat at three in the morning, turn the laptop on and do an hour's work. Sorting the details out, the house, her pension. Replying to the solicitors. All the paperwork that went with someone dying. He'd done nearly all of it at three in the morning. Switched on to auto-pilot. And finally fallen asleep an hour later.

He knew what the stats said. The stats were insistent. He'd re-marry. The vast majority of men who are divorced or widowed at 42 re-marry.

But they were wrong. He didn't want to re-marry. "Time will heal, Michael," his uncle had said at the funeral. "You'll meet someone else."

No, he wouldn't. All those nights sitting on her bed. Watching the red line go endlessly across the monitor. Watching her. Praying to a God he didn't believe in. Did her eyelid twitch just then? No, it didn't. Just the red line, running across the monitor until someone made a decision.

And in one of those nights something inside him had

simply turned itself off. He'd reached out. Taken her hand. Lifted it to his lips. "Only you," he'd whispered. "There'll only ever be you."

His phone rang. He'd finally fallen asleep and now his bloody phone was ringing. Phone calls at ten to midnight. They were exactly like phone calls from school.

Sorry to wake you, sir. There's been a shooting.

We're sorry to disturb you, Mr Brady. There's been an incident at school.

Never good news.

It was Kate. What did she want at this hour? Was it Bill? Had his heart attack come early?

"Michael."

One word. That was all she needed to say.

It was bad news. Very bad news. He'd never heard Kate use that tone of voice. But he'd heard it plenty of times before. An equal mixture of panic, shock and fear.

Sarah Cooke. He'd been a detective for six months. Given her his card. "Anything I can do," he'd said. "If you think of anything. If anything happens. Day or night. Call me."

Something had happened. "Get here now. Please. He's back." She'd been whispering. But it was still the same tone of voice.

He was there in ten minutes. Five minutes too late.

"Kate. What's the matter?"

"It's Pat."

Maybe he was still asleep. Maybe he hadn't been back in Whitby long enough. "Pat?" he said stupidly.

"Patrick. Patrick, your friend. My friend. Our friend."

"What about him?"

"He's been stabbed."

Twenty years of training took over. He knew better than to say 'he can't have been' or 'are you sure?'

"How badly?"

"I don't know. Bill rang me. He's there."

At the crime scene. Ducking under the blue tape. Talking to witnesses. Trying to make sense of it all. Saying, 'where are bloody forensics?'

Doing everything he used to do.

"Where have they taken him?"

"I don't know. James Cook probably. The hospital in Middlesbrough."

How far was that? Thirty miles? Thirty-five minutes on a blue light?

"Are you alright?" Brady said. "Do you want me to come round?"

"You can't. You've got Ash. Besides, I've got the girls. Well, Lucy. Maddie's not back yet."

He looked up. Ash was standing in the doorway. "Dad? What's happened? I heard your phone. Who are you talking to?"

"I'm talking to Kate, love. Go back to bed. I'll come through in a minute. I promise."

What should he do? What should he say to her? "Kate, I need to go. Ash has just come in. Just... just let me know if you hear anything."

"Of course. Try to get some sleep."

He sat on the side of the bed.

Stabbed. OK, think rationally. Despite the headlines the overwhelming majority of stabbings are not fatal. Just a drunken argument. A fight. Mistaken identity. What had

Patrick said? "Enough swordsticks at a Goth weekend to re-run the Charge of the Light Brigade..."

He walked through to Ash's bedroom. With Archie, who'd heard someone moving about and bounded upstairs.

Ash was sitting up in bed, her knees pulled up to her chest. "What's happened, Dad?"

He'd decided to tell her the truth. When he'd finally come to terms with being a single parent he'd realised the only option was to be honest with her. He'd been walking Archie. A day on the Pennines. A brief respite from his ghosts. And he'd realised that all he could do was tell her the truth.

And now he was going to lie to her...

But she was entitled to sleep. One of them being awake all night was enough.

"You remember Patrick? I met him the other morning. After I dropped you at school. My best friend when I was growing up?"

"What about him?"

"He's... he's had an accident. A fall. Somewhere in town. That was Kate on the phone. She thought I should know."

Ash stared at him. "Why is Kate phoning you?"

"Because... because the police are involved. Bill's there."

"So is it serious?"

"I don't know. Maybe. They've taken him to hospital. Probably just a precaution."

She wasn't convinced. She had her mother's ability to know when he was lying.

"I thought you said nothing happened in Whitby?"

"I did. It's true. Nothing does happen."

"Can Archie stay with me?"

"I've just persuaded him to sleep downstairs."

His daughter and his dog both stared at him. Impossible odds. "Of course he can." He bent over and kissed her. "Go to sleep, sweetheart." And went back to bed, knowing he'd need a new book well before sunrise.

6

Brady scribbled a note – *Taken Archie to the beach: back for 8:30* – left it on the floor where Ash couldn't miss it and quietly closed her bedroom door. He needed to do something physical. Couldn't just sit by the phone waiting for news.

"Come on then, pal. Let's go and get wet."

TEN MINUTES later he was on the beach. And being rewarded by the Gods. For five minutes the rain stopped, the clouds parted and he watched the sun rise out of the sea, turning from pink to red to orange to yellow.

He loved sunrise. He loved the fact that it was different every morning. He loved the way the sun climbed out of the sea. The way the light shone through the clouds. How it bounced across the sea and reflected off the wet beach. You watched the sunrise and it was hard not to feel optimistic.

A flock of seagulls – well, six. Was that a flock? – flew

south across the face of the sun. "Did you see that, Archie? If I'd been a Roman emperor I'd have taken that as an omen and invaded Gaul."

Archie dropped a wet tennis ball at Brady's feet. There were more important things than invading Gaul...

FORTY MINUTES later he drop-kicked Archie's ball for the last time. "That's it, OK? I'm wet through. And my hand stinks." He made a useless attempt to clean it on a hand-kerchief.

The answer – what any sane, rational person would have done – was a whippy stick. Everyone else had one for their dog. But Brady liked drop-kicking the ball, catching it on the half-volley. He'd been a good foot-baller: he liked to think he wasn't completely past it.

Getting Archie's saliva all over his fingers was a small price to pay. And he loved seeing Archie jump and catch the ball as it bounced. "Awesome mouth/eye co-ordina-tion," he said. "You're showing off, Arch."

He looked at his watch. Time to go home and cook breakfast. Archie dropped the ball at his feet. "Good boy. Thank you. But it's time to go. Come on."

He clipped the lead onto a clearly disappointed Springer and headed back to the slipway. Up the Khyber Pass and back to the car.

Or maybe not.

Somehow he'd pushed it out of his mind. Persuaded himself that it was nothing. Some minor skirmish. A Goth with one too many pints of Theakston's. Or stoned. He'd smelt it a couple of times last night. The faintly musky, faintly burnt rope, completely unmistakeable smell of pot.

Patrick would be back home later today. A week taking it easy and he'd be back to normal.

He walked over to where they'd eaten their bacon sandwiches. Looked across the harbour to the back of Sandside.

The dark blue and orange lifeboat, two small weekend boats, the buildings crowding down to the water.

And the police incident tape.

Brady had seen his share of crime scenes. But never from across a harbour. But there it was. The incident tape, the copper on duty to make sure no-one wandered up – accidently or otherwise – from the small strip of beach. He could just make out the blue and white tent over the crime scene. Was that an alley leading up from the beach?

This was more than a skirmish.

All his fears from last night flooded back. He had to go and see what was happening.

'Remember you're a civilian.'

Maybe. But even civilians were allowed to walk into town. "Come on," he said to Archie, "Let's see how far they'll let us get."

He started walking past the arcades, towards the swing bridge.

"Hey! Plum tomato man!" The broad Geordie accent cut through the cries of the seagulls.

Brady turned. "You want a tea?" Dave said. "On the house?"

A man who clearly wanted to talk.

"I was just going to walk up there. But yes, sure. Thank you."

Dave passed him a mug of tea and stepped out of the kiosk. They stood behind it, looking across the harbour.

"Doesn't look like they're letting anyone get very close."

"Half the bloody town's closed off," Dave said.

"What've you heard?"

"You sure you want to know?"

"Yes. Whatever you tell me, I've heard it before."

"About eleven last night. Single stab wound. Your boy's in James Cook at Middlesbrough. And he's poorly."

Brady nodded. Carried on staring across the harbour.

"Why?" he asked.

Dave shrugged. "No-one knows. The best guess right now is mistaken identity. One Victorian gentleman looks pretty much like another on a dark night."

"I thought Goths were a peaceful bunch?"

Dave nodded. "From what I've seen they are. They're the kids who didn't fit in. The ones who were picked on in school. The ones that were slightly different. An' I can hardly bring myself to say the word, but a lot of 'em are vegans."

"So you're sceptical?"

"Mistaken identity? How long were you a detective? How many cases of mistaken identity did you come across?"

"A long time," Brady said. "And one a year? Maybe two?" He paused. There was a lot more to Dave than the best bacon sandwich he'd ever eaten. "How come you're so well informed?"

"Change of shift. They all need something before they start. Or when they finish. And the police canteen's being renovated. Coppers are like teenage girls. They never go anywhere on their own. So I make bacon sandwiches and listen."

Brady put his mug down. "I'm going for a walk," he said.

"You look like you've just done that."

"I'm going to investigate. See how far I can get."

"Old habits die hard, eh?"

He walked up the seafront. Past the Magpie Café, past Gypsy Sara's. *A true born Romany. Consulted by royalty.* Maybe she knew what was going on.

He turned left across the swing bridge. Shortened Archie's lead to give him more control. "Stay on the footpath, Arch. I'll walk on the road."

He tried to walk down Sandside. The incident tape was stretched across the street. He almost ducked under it by instinct. But...

"I'm sorry, sir. Can I ask you to turn round? This is a police incident."

"What's happened?"

"I'm sorry, sir. I can't say anything to members of the general public. But we'll be here all day. Might be best to walk your dog somewhere else. Leave us to do our job."

There was nothing he could do. Kershaw's words hit home. 'Remember you're a civilian. You left DCI Brady in Manchester.'

That was exactly what he was. On the outside looking

in. Relying on other people for information. With no idea how accurate the information was.

All he could do was go home and wait for news.

He glanced at his watch. Nine o'clock. "Shit," he said out loud. "Not again." He'd promised to be back for 8:30. Maybe he'd get away with it. Maybe Ash had slept in.

7

He made it. Just. He'd been in ten minutes when Ash wandered sleepily downstairs.

"Hi, sweetheart. You sleep OK?"

"Yeah. I heard you go out with Archie. But I guess I fell asleep again."

"You want me to do you some breakfast?"

"Yeah. Sure. Have I got time to have a shower first?"

"Of course. Just do me a favour will you? Bring your washing down? I'll sort it all out while you're in the shower. Then I'll put it on."

"Here you go," she said a minute later. "Remember not to mix stuff up. My white blouse has to stay white."

A year on and Brady still wasn't sure what to do with anything that wasn't standard wash. He'd had a favourite jumper. One failure to read the label and it had made the journey from large to small in less than an hour. But everything this morning looked reassuringly straightforward.

He picked his phone up. 9:40. Bill must be home by now. He opened recent calls. Pressed Kate's number. Waited for her to answer. Started absentmindedly separating the washing with his other hand.

"Michael. Hi." Calmer this time. But tired. Someone else who hadn't slept much.

"How are you? I just wondered if you knew anything. Bill must be back by now?"

"He came in about seven. Swore a couple of times, drank a whisky and went to bed." She paused. "I think it's a bit of a mess. You know how many people must have been in the area."

"Has he heard anything?"

"I'm not sure. And if he did he didn't say."

Ash's pale pink sweatshirt. The one she'd worn last night. Surely that was close enough? He threw it in the whites pile.

He decided not to tell Kate what Dave had said. No point in two of them worrying. Well... worrying more. "So we're no further forward?"

"I'm sorry, Mike, no."

Brady bent down and picked Ash's sweatshirt up. He'd thought... when she came in last night...

"Mike? Are you there?"

"Sorry, Kate. Just trying to fix breakfast at the same time."

He held the sweatshirt to his nose. Breathed in.

"Maybe, I'll phone the hospital. You take care, love. I'll let you know."

"You too, Mike. Do that."

Brady breathed in again. What he'd smelt last night. The faintly musky, faintly burnt rope, completely unmistakeable smell of pot.

"Jesus Christ. Not again."

"Mike?"

"Sorry, Kate. I've... I've burnt the toast. Twice. You know what they say about men and multi-tasking. I'll talk to you later. Try and have a good day. Say hi to Bill when he wakes up."

He held the sweatshirt to his face again. There was no mistake. Fuck. He didn't need this. He'd had some suspicions about one of her friends in Manchester. He didn't need them following him to Whitby.

He cracked five eggs into a bowl. Milk, salt and pepper. Started to whisk. Ash, looking freshly scrubbed and younger than her 13 years, walked in.

Should he say something? No. Definitely no. Don't over react. Smell does not equal use. And besides, he had other things on his mind. He needed to tell her about Patrick.

"Ash?"

"What's up?"

"Could you just put your phone down and do us some toast?"

He should teach himself to make bread. How good would that be? The smell of fresh bread every morning? He poured the eggs into the wok. Yes, sure you could use the microwave. But how much time did you spend cleaning the plastic jug? Besides, you never saw anyone use a plastic jug in a film.

What was that line from Macbeth? If it were done, 'twere best it were done quickly.

"Ash, I need to say something to you."

"What's that?"

"Please put your phone down. It's important."

She sighed but did as she was asked.

"I didn't tell you the truth last night. About Patrick. I'm sorry."

"Well, duh, Dad. That was hard to work out."

Really? Could she see through him that easily?

"When I told you that Patrick had a fall. That's not true."

"So what happened? And you've stopped stirring the eggs, Dad."

Christ, they were sticking to the wok. He scraped furiously with the wooden spatula.

"He was stabbed."

"Stabbed?" Her eyes widened. "Here? In Whitby? You *promised* me nothing happened in Whitby. Why?"

"I'm sorry, Ash. I don't know anything else. I wish I did. I tried to get close to where it happened this morning, but - " He shrugged. It felt like he was admitting defeat. "I couldn't. I'm just a normal person now."

Ash looked shaken. "Is he? I mean, will he... What's happening?"

Brady shook his head. "Sweetheart, I just don't know. I've phoned Kate. She doesn't know anything. Bill's come in and gone to sleep."

"Maybe you should phone the hospital, Dad?"

"Yeah, I thought about that. But I'm not a relative.

They're not going to tell me anything. Especially... well, especially with the police being involved."

The toast popped up. Ash buttered it and Brady ladled the eggs on to it while Ash poured herself a glass of milk.

"Ash," he said, as they sat down to eat. "I'm really sorry about last night. I just wanted you to sleep."

"It's OK, I understand."

"No, it's not OK. And I won't do it again. Whatever happens, I'll be honest with you."

He hadn't meant this. Just tell her about Patrick. But he'd started the conversation. He couldn't stop now. "And I want you to do the same with me. Whatever happens, tell me the truth. No matter how bad it is, tell me the truth. I can deal with the truth, so long as I know about it."

She was silent for a while. She checked her phone. "So I'm alright to go into town with Bean again? She wants to be a photographer when she's older. She says the Goths are too good to miss."

He smiled. "Yeah, of course you are. And if you want to have Bean – Jessica – for a sleepover one night, that's fine as well."

Ash disappeared upstairs to get ready. Brady stacked the plates in the dishwasher, washed the wok – maybe the microwave would've been easier after all – and fought the urge to phone the hospital.

He lost.

"Hi. Good morning. I was wondering if you could help me? My..." He hesitated. 'Friend' wouldn't get him anywhere. But there was no reason he couldn't be a relative on the phone…

"My brother was admitted last night. I was hoping to get some news on his condition."

"Do you know what ward he's in?"

"I don't. I'm sorry."

"What's his name?"

"Smith." How useless was that? "Patrick Smith."

The line went quiet. Then the receptionist was back. "Could I just ask you to confirm his date of birth?"

Shit. The same year as me, that's easy. When the hell was Patrick's birthday? It was close to Christmas. Just before or just after? Play for time.

"Ouch! That's a tough one. We're not big on sending each other birthday cards. Brothers are nowhere near as important as wives and girlfriends."

She laughed. Thank you. An extra five seconds of thinking time. All he needed. The first day of winter. "December 21st, 1972."

"He's in men's surgical. I'll put you through."

"Thank you so much."

The line clicked. Then it started ringing, presumably in men's surgical. It carried on ringing. Brady had seen plenty of nurses' stations in the middle of the night. And answering the phone to enquiring relatives wasn't always top of the priority list. Sunday morning would be the same. Especially if there was an emergency.

The phone carried on ringing. And ringing.

"Sod it," Brady said.

Then, "Ash," he shouted upstairs. "I'm going to see

Patrick. Take a key when you go out. And take care. I'll be a couple of hours."

"'Kay, Dad," floated back downstairs.

Why not? Being Patrick's brother had worked on the phone. No reason it wouldn't work in person.

Brady grabbed his car keys.

8

It was a beautiful spring morning. Brady kept glancing to his right, catching occasional glimpses of the sea as he drove across the Moors. Thirty miles. Thirty-five minutes on a blue light. Maybe 45 for someone without one. Maybe longer if these damn caravans didn't go any faster...

He'd walk into reception. 'Hi, good morning. I've come to see my brother. Patrick Smith? He's in men's surgical, I think.'

'It's not visiting time, sir. Not for another two hours.'

'I've driven up from London. Through the night. I have to go straight back. Just five minutes?'

Or just walk in and go straight to the ward. He'd always been amazed at how lax security was in hospitals. Not lax, non-existent. Wear a white coat, carry a clipboard, go wherever you wanted. Or a pair of scrubs.

'What did the killer look like?'

'He was wearing a pair of scrubs and a face mask. Had a stethoscope...'

So it could be anyone. Just like a Goth dressed as a

Victorian gentleman could be anyone. But he still didn't believe in mistaken identity.

I'm on my way, Patrick. We'll soon be back on the seafront eating bacon sandwiches.

His phone rang. Brady had a moment of surprise. The last time he'd driven across the Moors he'd lost the connection about six times. Clearly a farmer had finally decided that a mobile phone mast was a more profitable crop than winter wheat.

Kate. Again.

And for the second time in 24 hours she only needed to say his name.

"When?" Brady said.

"Some time around ten? They didn't tell Bill the exact time. I'm so sorry, Michael."

So just after they'd finished breakfast. When he'd been trying to get through on the phone.

"Are you OK?" he asked.

"Not really. Are you driving? Where are you?"

"I'm..." Brady looked out of the window. Another place he'd never be able to drive past without remembering. "I'm at Ugthorpe. Just going past the pub. Or the hotel. Or whatever it is."

"Maybe you should pull over."

"Maybe I should."

There was a picnic area off to the left. He stopped the car and got out. Stood on the side of the hill, looking out to the Moors. The hill fell away in front of him. Then climbed up the other side in a patchwork quilt of fields.

A wave of anger swept through him.

Denial, anger, bargaining, depression, acceptance.

He'd been through them all with Grace. Discovered that they weren't stages of grief but layers of grief. That they ebbed and flowed like the tide. That there were false dawns. That when he thought he was finally over bargaining – anything, just anything, to talk to her one last time, to say goodbye properly – suddenly it was back.

That depression had hovered over him like a cloud. Always there to tap him on the shoulder. 'You thought I'd gone away? You thought you were finished with me? Think again.'

This time it was different. He looked towards the Moors and realised he'd skipped straight through denial. What was the point? Denial was a waste of time. Besides, dealing with the reality of death was what he did for a living. Used to do for a living. There'd be no bargaining either. And he'd had enough depression to last a lifetime.

So just two. Anger and acceptance. And maybe a third. Frustration. Because his best friend was dead and there was nothing he could do about it. Nothing. Except watch someone else handle the investigation.

His brother-in-law. Bill Calvert. A man who'd never changed.

He should go and see Kara. Where was she now? At the hospital. In shock. Sitting with a blanket round her. Drinking tea. Waiting for news. He knew the feeling...

Brady was a spectator again. Someone waiting for news. It had always been this way. He'd always been a spectator.

A young detective, sitting in a hospital corridor, waiting impatiently. 'I just need a few words. It's important.' 'It might be important, Detective, but his health's important as well. And he's nowhere near well enough to speak to you.'

Then when Ash was ill. Children always want their mum. Your job is simple. Run up and down the stairs with drinks. Wait until your wife delivers the verdict. 'She's not as hot as she was. But she still feels sick. So leave the bucket where it is. Try and get some sleep.'

And now it was Grace. And here he was again. Waiting for news. A spectator. Helpless.

His phone buzzed. Maria. 'Ash is fine. Play was a big success. Ash was lovely. They're just getting changed.'

And Ash, ten minutes later. 'Tell Mum how much I love her. Hope she's not in too much pain. Three red hearts. A head with a bandage round it. A face with a single tear.'

Brady knew he should walk down to A&E. Knew he'd probably broken a bone in his wrist. But how could he? So he stayed in the corridor. Reading the same three posters on the wall until he knew them by heart. Wondering how the gap between five past and ten past could possibly be half an hour. And knowing he wouldn't move from his seat in the corridor.

"Are you alright there?"

"I'm waiting for news of my wife," he answered for the tenth time.

And finally he had it.

The doctor was Brady's age. Slight, balding, visibly tired.

"Mr Brady? I'm Doctor Sharma. I know you've been waiting a long time..."

I should have put the phone on record, he thought afterwards. So I could listen again. He hadn't taken it in. Just a collection of assorted phrases.

'Badly broken leg. Set it as best we can. For now. Need to operate. Sorry to tell you this. Fractured skull. The brain is floating. Inside of the skull is sharp. Jagged. Damage. Swelling.

The brain swells. Relieved the pressure. Induced coma. Won't know for three or four days. While the swelling goes down.'

"You should go home and rest, Mr Brady. Try and get some sleep."

"Can I see her?"

"Very briefly. And I should warn you..."

That it won't be your wife.

He looked through the window into the room. Tubes and monitors, a head swathed in bandages. There was a heart in one corner of the window. Clearly drawn by someone's child. How long ago? I hope mum or dad made it.

"You should go home and get some rest, Mr Brady," Dr Sharma said again.

He nodded. Did as he was told. Walked past A&E on his way out of the hospital. Decided to see how his wrist was in the morning.

Brady carried on staring out across the Moors. He'd barely been in Whitby five minutes and his best friend was dead. Grace had been murdered. And Patrick? He'd seen the tent, the incident tape. Right now murder was at least fifty-fifty.

Brady knew he was responsible for his wife's death. If he hadn't asked for the case. If he hadn't been obsessed with it. If he'd been prepared to turn a blind eye...

Was Patrick's death his fault as well?

"You don't want to come for a drink with us?"

Supposing he'd said yes? Then Patrick wouldn't have been wherever he was at whatever time it happened. He hadn't needed a butterfly to flap its wings somewhere. Just his best friend to go for a drink with him.

Then...

But that assumed it was mistaken identity.

"Mistaken identity? How long were you a detective? How many cases of mistaken identity did you come across?"

"One a year. Maybe two?"

It couldn't be mistaken identity. Someone had murdered his best friend. And he couldn't do anything about it. Except watch.

Another wave of anger washed over him.

"Grand day," a voice said behind him. Brady turned. He hadn't even heard the caravan pull in.

"Yes, lovely," he said.

The man continued walking past him, down to the bushes. "Old bladder's not what it once was," he said ruefully. "Can't do long drives any more. Not without a pit stop."

There was no point standing here. It was a Sunday morning. A beautiful day. A week before the bank holiday. He wouldn't be the last incontinent tourist.

9

Ash was still out when he got home.

I'm back, he texted

OK. In town with Bean. Going to get something to eat.

No problem. What time will you be back?

3?

Fine. Take care. See you then.

Should he ask her to come home? So he could tell her? There was no point. "Just you and me, Archie, then." Brady needed some physical contact. He sat down on the floor, his back against the settee. "Come here, pal. I need a hug."

Archie obediently flopped down at his side. Brady put his hand on the dog's head. "Two weeks, Archie," he said. "We've been in Whitby two weeks and this happens. And we can't do anything about it. I'm supposed to sit upstairs writing a book while my halfwit brother-in-law tramples his size 11s through the investigation. I tell you something, pal, he'd better get it right."

. . .

ASH HAD COME in at three. She'd brought Bean in with her. "We were just going to listen to some music." Then they'd seen his expression. Bean had said, "I'll text you." He'd told Ash. He'd hugged her. She'd hugged him back. He'd let Archie sleep in her room again. Two nights in a row. That was a battle he'd lost.

NOW IT WAS MONDAY. And it was raining. Correction, it was pouring. The first time since they'd been back. Brady remembered it all too well. The rain horizontal off the North Sea. Almost always when there was a school cross-country.

When even Count Dracula would have had second thoughts about landing in Whitby.

He ruffled the top of Archie's head. "Sorry, mate, the walk's going to have to wait. Look." He opened the back door. "Stick your nose out if you don't believe me. And there's something I have to do."

Patrick's house was impressive. Beyond impressive. A garden the size of a small county. An uninterrupted view across the fields and out to sea.

He rang the bell.

A woman in her late 20s answered it. Long black hair falling in curls. A pale peach jumper, jeans. Perfect teeth.

She looked past him at the rain. "You're clearly not cold calling. How can I help you?"

"My name's Michael Brady. I've come to see Kara."

"I'm not sure that right now is a good time."

"I was a friend of Patrick's," Brady answered. "I was

with him and Kara on Saturday night. I know what happened."

"You'd better come in then."

She opened the door and Brady walked into the hall. The inside was as impressive as the view from the garden.

Kara must have heard him. She stepped out of a doorway. Hair pinned up. A pale blue dressing gown over her jeans. No make-up. Puffed up eyes from the tears. A completely different woman to the one he'd seen on Saturday night. Not even a distant relation.

"Michael," she said.

Brady didn't know what to do. Six months and physical contact with any woman other than Kate still made him uncomfortable. Did he kiss her? Put his arms round her? He couldn't possibly shake hands. But he had to make some physical gesture. Awkwardly, stiffly, he put his hand on her arm.

"It's good of you to come."

"No, it's no problem. I wanted to. I thought yesterday... I thought you'd probably have someone here with you."

She nodded. The other woman was hovering behind Brady. "This is Rebecca. Becky. We've known each other since we were children. She makes tea and orders sleeping pills off Amazon."

"You haven't seen a doctor?"

Kara shook her head. "What's the point? He'd only do what Becky's doing."

She led the way into the kitchen. Pulled a stool out on either side of the breakfast bar.

"You want coffee?" Becky asked.

Brady didn't. But it would occupy his hands. "I was driving up to the hospital," he said awkwardly. "Kate phoned me."

Kara nodded. "He was stable. They thought he was going to make it. Suddenly – "

She looked down at the floor. Shook her head. Looked back up at him. Pulled the collar of her dressing gown round her head. Talked to him from inside the cocoon. "Suddenly every monitor he's hooked up to is off the scale. Nurses running everywhere. Two minutes later he's gone."

Brady didn't reply. He let her talk.

"Something they hadn't noticed. Saturday night in A&E. The worst time to be there. Internal bleeding they said. Something ruptured. Burst. I didn't really take it in..."

There'd be a post-mortem. And several hours with the police. How much should he tell her? How much did she want to know?

Becky put his coffee down in front of him. Walked round and sat next to Kara. Took her hand.

"What happens now?" Kara asked.

So she did want to know. "There'll be a post-mortem," Brady said. "To determine the exact cause of death."

"It was a stab wound. In his back. Someone... Someone stabbed my husband in the back."

Tears rolled down her cheeks.

"Look, I can come back. I only wanted to come and – "

"No. I'm glad you're here. The police will be next, won't they?"

"Inevitably. Whatever it is..." Brady didn't want to say

the word 'murder.' "...Whatever it is the police will want to ask you questions."

And lots of questions. Because you're a suspect.

Brady knew the stats. Two-thirds of women that are murdered are murdered by their partners or by their ex. The other way round was lower. But it was still a high enough starting point for Bill. And Kara was tall. Athletic. Could she stab someone? Yes. Could she have concealed a weapon in what she was wearing on Saturday night? Brady's first instinct was 'no.'

But he was hardly an expert on basques...

"What should I tell them?"

"The truth. That's all you can do."

"Supposing the truth makes her a suspect?" Becky said.

So he had to say it out loud. "Kara's already a suspect."

Brady looked around him. Move this house to Manchester and it was worth seven figures. Easily. Add in Patrick's other property. There'd be shares, investments, life cover. Kara would be a wealthy woman. Motive and opportunity. She had both. Yes, Bill would have a lot of questions.

"I should go," he said.

"You haven't finished your coffee..."

"Yeah, sorry. I've left Ash at home. I only wanted to say how sorry I was, Look – " There was a notepad on the table. 'Collect dry cleaning' was scrawled on it. Presumably in Patrick's handwriting. Presumably a Victorian gentleman's outfit that hadn't been worn since the last Goth festival.

Brady wrote his mobile number down.

"Anything I can do," he said. "If you think of anything. If anything happens. Day or night. Call me."

Exactly what he'd said to Sarah Cooke.

Fifteen years ago.

And it hadn't ended well.

10

He pulled his chair up to his desk. Turned his laptop on. Tapped the code in. Not Grace's birthday. That would have been too painful.

Six days behind schedule but which writer wasn't six days behind schedule? He'd already got the framework of the book in his head. Time to get it down on paper. Or screen.

His phone rang. A number he didn't recognise. Like most people he'd given up answering numbers he didn't recognise. But...

"Michael Brady."

"Michael, it's Kara."

Call me. She had.

"How are you doing?"

"I'm OK. Well, no, I'm not. Michael..." She hesitated. "The police have been. I need to talk to you."

"OK. Of course. Do you want to meet me for coffee?"

"Can I come to your house?"

"Yes, sure, if you want to. When were you thinking of?"

"Now. If that's alright with you."

"Yes, of course."

Twenty minutes later she was knocking on the door. Jeans, a huge yellow raincoat. Hair tied back in a pony tail. Some make-up today.

"Come through to the kitchen." He hadn't cleared up after breakfast. Ash had left the cereal box out.

"Would you like a drink? Tea? Coffee? And I'm sorry about the mess."

"Nothing. Water. Water's fine."

She was perched on one of the kitchen stools. If she only wanted water she had something serious to say. People who were happy to waste your time – or who wanted something from you – let you make tea and coffee. People that had something to say drank water.

"OK. What can I do to help?"

"Patrick said to me – after we'd met you at the party." She sipped her water. A strand of hair escaped and fell forward over her eye. "He said, if I was ever in trouble and he wasn't there, I should ask you for help."

"We hadn't seen each other for five years…"

"People don't change. If you've a problem, go and see Michael. That's what he said."

Brady walked across to the sink and filled the water jug. "I'm sorry," he said. "This sounds like I'm going to need a coffee."

"They came this morning. First thing. Two detectives. A man and a woman. The guy whose party it was. Your brother-in-law."

"Inevitably. What did he ask you?"

She pushed the stray strand of hair back into place. "He said he was trying to build a picture. Of what happened."

A textbook starting point. But he knew Bill. He would have arrived with a theory already half-formed.

Don't get drawn in. You think you owe it to Patrick. You do. So give her advice, say goodbye. Leave it to someone else. Not being involved will be frustrating. But it'll fade. You've got a new life to live.

Don't say, 'So what did you say?' Because she'll tell you. And you'll be hooked.

The water had dripped through the filter. He poured it into the kettle. "So what did you say?"

"I told him what happened."

"Tell me. From after you left me."

Because what happened before is irrelevant, Bill. What happened before is that they got ready – which took a long time in Kara's case – and called a taxi. Which is easy enough to prove. And if this girl with a ponytail slipped a knife into what little she was wearing she won't tell you and she won't tell me.

"We went for a drink."

"Where?"

"The White Horse."

"Did you speak to anyone you knew?"

"Patrick did."

So far, so good if you were Bill. A clear picture. "Then what?"

"We walked around a bit. Like you do. Looked at the

costumes. Bumped into a couple we met the year before. Then..."

And here we come to it. Brady knew he didn't need to say anything. All he had to do was listen.

"We went into an alley. The one where... Where it happened."

"Which alley?"

"By the Rowing Club. It leads down to the sea."

"Why?"

"Because – "

She was silent.

"Patrick told you I'd help," Brady said. "I will. But you've got to tell me the truth."

What had he said to Ash? Tell me the truth. If you tell me the truth I can deal with it.

"Patrick was horny. He wanted a blowjob."

"In an alley? With hundreds of people walking past?"

She looked straight at him. "It turned him on. And me. The idea that someone might see us."

"So not the first time?"

"No. It was something... we found out we shared. Patrick was... He said he was making up for lost time after his first marriage."

'The ring of truth.' He could hear Fitz saying it now. Jim Fitzpatrick, the man who'd taught him how to be a real detective. 'Sometimes, DC Brady, you just hear it. They tell you something. It makes them look stupid, foolish, naïve. But it has the ring of truth.' Yep, you'd have enjoyed this one, guv.

"Is that what you told Bill Calvert?"

"No. I told him I felt sick. That I thought I was going to throw up."

"Why didn't you tell him?"

"Because... You're not a woman. There are some men... They feed off things like that."

"So you went in the alley..."

"But I needed the loo. There was a side entrance to the bar. I went in. When I came out... When I came out Patrick wasn't there."

"Where was he?"

"I thought... That alley goes down to the beach. I thought he was down there. I thought maybe... Maybe he wanted to do it on the beach."

I'll get someone to check the tide tables.

No. Now it was Bill's job to check the tide tables. Assuming he believes her.

"But he wasn't there?"

"No. I turned round. I took two or three steps. That's when I saw him. Saw the blood."

'I thought I'd been punched.' He remembered a boy in a hospital bed saying it to him. 'Like a really hard punch. Then you realise it's not a punch. Just a deep, deep pain. Throbbing. Coming and going in waves. Like I could never escape it.'

Was that what Patrick felt? In the ten or twenty seconds before he lost consciousness? A sudden punch in his back. What's his first thought? Why has someone punched me? Then something tells him it's not a punch. He staggers forward. One pace, maybe two. Puts his hand out on the wall of the alley. Now he knows it's serious. Tries to turn round to find his wife. Instead he slides down the wall. Is that the last thing he sees? The wall of an alleyway? Maybe he smells the sea one last time. Maybe he hears Kara scream.

"Patrick's lying on the paving stones? Or on the cobbles or whatever's in the alley? Face down?"

Kara shook her head. "No. There were some bin bags. I'd guess they'd been put out for the morning. That's why I didn't see him."

He doesn't slide down the wall. He falls forward onto left over fish and chips. Patrick didn't smell the sea one last time. Just vinegar and tomato sauce.

"So you bend down. You get covered in blood. You shout for help."

She nodded. "I tried to pull him up. See his face. I couldn't. Then someone came running. All of a sudden there was a crowd. Someone must have phoned for help – "

"While half a dozen people were filming it on their phones..."

"How did you know?"

"Because they always do. Because going viral is more important than getting help."

The kettle had boiled. Brady spooned some coffee into the cafetiere. Carried it to the table with the mugs. "I'm sorry," he said. "Do you want a sandwich or anything?"

She shook her head. "And then – "

Brady held his hand up to stop her. "I don't need any more," he said. "The ambulance, the hospital. You don't need to say any more. I don't need to hear any more. Leave that to my imagination." He poured the coffee.

"The police will be back," he said.

"Because I'm a suspect?"

Do I need to spell it out? Does she need me to spell it out?

"Because right now you're the *only* suspect. Have they looked at CCTV? Maybe. Does it show the alley? Maybe. Was it working? Probably not. So..."

"He's going to come back and arrest me," she said flatly. "He thinks I did it."

"Not necessarily."

"Yes he does. He just looked at me. He thought, 'She's done it. I don't need to look any further.'"

Brady didn't say anything.

Bill would be under pressure. An unsolved murder in Whitby? Just as the summer season was about to start? It wasn't *Jaws* but Kershaw would want it clearing up. And quickly.

Bill would start with motive and opportunity. She ticked both boxes. Was Kara physically capable of stabbing her husband? She clearly kept herself fit. Was she strong enough? He remembered asking a pathologist a question. 'How much effort does it take to stab someone?' 'Not much,' he'd replied. 'About the same as lifting a bag of flour.'

So the answer was 'yes.' Even Bill could work that out.

"So will you help me?"

He owed it to Patrick to help her. He owed it to himself to say 'no.'

"You know I will. Whatever I can do. Whatever advice you need."

She wanted more than advice. He could see it in her face. "So you'll find the killer?" she said.

Shit.

Her husband had just been murdered. She was asking for his help. "It's difficult, Kara. I'm a civilian. Just like anyone else. I can't run round Whitby interviewing people."

He left the rest unsaid. He didn't want to go back. Not to that world.

It had happened last week. Maybe the day after he'd met Patrick. He'd taken Ash to school. Walked Archie on the beach. Realised that he felt... 'Clean' had been the only word he could find.

He didn't want to feel dirty again.

"I understand," she said. But she didn't.

"Look," he said. "It's really difficult. But leave it with me. Let me think."

"Thank you." Then, "What should I do now?"

"Go home," Brady said. "Go home and rest. Drink tea. They'll be knocking on your door soon enough. But here..." For the second time he scribbled something down on a piece of paper. "If the shit hits the fan this is the guy you need. He's in Leeds. The best solicitor I know. Expensive. But you can afford to pay him. And phone me."

She stood up and reached for her coat.

"Did you drive here? Do you need a lift home?"

Kara shook her head. "Becky dropped me. Then went shopping. She'll be outside in the car."

She turned to go.

"Wait," Brady said. He wanted to give her some good news. See her smile. "There's something I need to say to you."

"What's that?"

Straight out. There was no other way to say it. "Are you pregnant?"

She stared at him. "No-one knows."

"Patrick knew."

She sat back down on the stool. Reached for her luke-warm coffee. "How? How did he know?"

"He told me when we met last week. Said he found the test you'd taken in the bathroom bin. He swore me to secrecy. But now…"

She pulled her coat around her. "Yes," she said. "I am. I didn't want to tell him. Not straightaway."

"Why not?"

She took a deep breath. "Because I found out I was pregnant when I was a teenager. I never told Patrick. I was pretty wild for a couple of years. I was going to have a termination. We'd made the appointment. But I lost the baby, before… Well, before the appointment."

"So you wanted to be certain?"

She nodded.

"Well, he knew. And he was delighted. Beyond delighted."

So maybe that was Patrick's last thought. Not his wife. Not the smell of fish and chips. The child he'd never see.

"So he knew," she said. She stood up and walked over to the window. Gazed up at the sky. "He knew I was pregnant." She was talking to herself more than to Brady. "He thought, 'I'm going to be a father.'"

"Yes. And like I said, he was delighted."

She turned back to him, holding out her hands. Tears were rolling down her cheeks again. Different tears, Brady thought. "He died thinking I was having his child?"

Brady nodded.

"Thank you," she said. "Thank you so much."

He took both her hands in his. "No problem. I hope I did the right thing."

"Yes, you did. You really did."

For once he knew how to react. He pulled her closer and hugged her. "And if it's a boy," he said, "Call him Patrick."

11

Brady hauled himself to the top of the stone steps. Archie was waiting impatiently. "You're right," he said. "I need to get fitter. A lot fitter. We're going to do some serious walks in the summer."

He was falling in love with the Moors. He suspected Archie preferred the beach – there weren't any dead fish to roll in up here – but Brady loved the space. The quiet. The time to think. That the Moors had looked like this long before he'd arrived in Whitby and they'd look like this long after he'd gone.

"Good morning," he said as two walkers approached him.

"Morning. Lovely day." Mr and Mrs Perfect Walker. Colour co-ordinated jackets and trousers. Even their walking poles matched.

Brady was wearing a red North Face jacket, a bottle green t-shirt and maroon shorts that had faded to pink. "Tasteful, Dad," Ash had said as he left the house. "Maybe you should let Archie choose your clothes."

"Come on, mate," he said. "Twenty minutes and we'll be back at the car."

What was he going to do about Kara? He'd spent half the night listening to the rain and trying to decide what to do about Kara.

Whatever he'd said, he had to help. He owed it to Patrick. And like Dave said, old habits die hard. He wanted to find the killer. But he didn't want to go back. No wonder he hadn't slept.

Again.

And now Bill was making the decision for him. Find the killer and it was problem solved. Fail to find the killer and Kara was the obvious suspect. The obvious target for the gossip. Arrest Kara and... He kicked a stone across the path and into the heather. "Let's cross that bridge when we come to it, Archie."

...Always assuming Kara *was* innocent. 'We went into the alley because it turned us on.' Yes, he could believe that. She needed the loo? Fair enough. Supposing it had been him? With Grace? Would he have wandered a few paces down the alley? Possibly. If it led to the sea.

Then what? He'd turn. Wait for her to come out. Especially dressed like that. Not that he'd ever gone into an alley with Grace.

Patrick wouldn't have had his back towards her. No man would. If what Kara said was true Patrick would have been expectant. Anticipating. Waiting for her to come out of the bar. Why would he turn round?

Brady couldn't think of a reason.

'Old habits die hard.'

They did.

He needed to check Kara's story. There was only one way to do it.

HE FED ARCHIE. Told Ash there was something he had to do. Checked the tide tables.

And he was back in Church Street.

Sometimes he'd enjoyed it. Sometimes it was just part of the job. Something that had to be done.

It had never made him feel physically sick.

Until now.

It was a simple question. How would he have killed Patrick?

More specifically, how would he have killed Patrick on the Saturday night of the Goth weekend? In the alley, with the long thin blade…

He'd met Patrick and Kara outside the White Horse and Griffin. Standing on the cobbles in Church Street as vampires, Victorian brides and Prussian army officers flowed around them.

"You don't want to come for a drink with us?"

"No. I'm not dressed for it am I? Besides, I told Ash to be in for 9:30."

And as he'd said that the killer was watching. Must have been watching.

Brady walked up Church Street. Stood at the top of the alley.

Saw the street sign. *New Way Ghaut.* Another maroon sign underneath it, a white arrow pointing down the alley to the sea. *Whitby Rowing Club.*

There was only one way it could have happened. But

he had to check. Had to be sure.

How long was Kara inside the Rowing Club? Five minutes? A crowded bar. Maybe a queue for the ladies. Probably not the easiest costume...

Five minutes. At least five minutes.

Brady pulled his phone out. Opened the stop watch.

Pressed start.

And he became the killer.

He'd carried on watching. Waiting patiently for Patrick and Kara to come out.

They're finally out of the pub. Hand in hand? Arm in arm? They're strolling up Church Street.

He walks up the street behind them. On the cobbles. Past the cafés, the jet shops. Sees Patrick in front of him. Distance? It doesn't matter. Five yards, ten yards. Patrick has no reason to be suspicious. What does he see if he turns round? Goths. Nothing but Goths...

Does he have someone with him? Yes. Patrick's a long way from the only Victorian gentleman in Whitby. But he's the only Victorian gentleman with Kara. Even so...

They've reached the alley.

Kara takes Patrick's hand. What's she doing? It doesn't matter. She takes his hand, walks down the alley.

He sees his chance. The alley is narrow. Three, four feet wide. He knows it must go down to the harbour.

'Stay here,' he tells someone. 'Watch this end. Don't move.' He's off.

Walking quickly up Church Street. He needs another alley. Parallel. Running down to the sea. Here. Between two pubs. The Board and the Duke of York.

Down the steps. They're wet and slippery. But he's young,

agile, surefooted.

Twenty-five steps. They open out onto a paved seating area. Old York stone. Balconies of the apartments overlooking the harbour. The twin piers of the harbour curving round to meet each other in the distance, cradling the fishing boats.

Quickly across. Dodging people. Looking for steps. There. Down to the beach.

They're even more slippery. But there's a handrail. He can't risk falling.

And he's on the beach. Low tide. The sea is 20 yards to his right. He jogs across the sand and the seaweed.

There's the window of the Rowing Club. A pint and a perfect view across the harbour. Maybe someone sees him. So what? He's just another Goth...

Eight steps. Two at a time. He's at the bottom of the alley. And there's Patrick. Standing with his back towards him. Looking at the door of the Rowing Club. Waiting expectantly for his wife.

Two, three steps. The blade flashes down. Patrick staggers. He walks past. Doesn't look back. Walks calmly out of the alley. Just another Goth. Maybe he's a Prussian army officer. His outfit wouldn't be complete without a sword...

Brady pressed stop on his phone.

Put a hand on the wall of the alley. Fought down a wave of nausea.

Looked at the stopwatch.

2:35.

It would have been crowded. Goths stopping to talk. Locals standing outside the pubs.

But the killer was young. Fit. Quicker than him.

Two minutes, 35 seconds. Plenty of time.

12

Brady knocked on his daughter's bedroom door.

"Yeah?"

"Can I come in?"

"Sure." Ash was lying on her bed, still in her pyjamas. She was – inevitably – texting.

"Are you OK if I go out for an hour?"

"Again? You're always going out."

"I'm sorry, Ash. I should go and see Kate. See how she's doing."

"Why don't you text her?"

"Because it's not the same. Besides, last time she sent me a text she used those faces. What are they called?"

"Emojis."

"Right. I couldn't understand the message. One face had square teeth. Another one was staring into space. No-one can understand that. And she's the only sister I've got. So I'm going."

"OK. Cool. Bean's coming round anyway."

"Are you going to get dressed?"

Ash shrugged. "Maybe."

BILL'S CAR wasn't in the drive. Good. He could talk to Kate properly.

She looked tired. Not just I-didn't-sleep-well tired but hollowed-out tired. Like there-was-almost-nothing-left tired. Like the face he'd seen in the mirror after days and nights watching a hospital monitor.

"This isn't just Patrick is it?" he said, after the formalities. Yes to coffee, no to cake.

"No, it's not."

"Do you want to tell me? Is it Bill?"

"Is it Bill? No, not really. Bill's the same as he's always been. Or the same as he's been for the last ten years. A complete arse six days a week, turning up with flowers on the seventh and doing God-knows-what behind my back."

"Is it that bad? You're not thinking of – "

"Leaving him? Only three or four times a day. But I'm nothing if not loyal. And we've the girls. They're two years apart. They've spent the last ten years changing schools or doing important exams. They still are. And I'm 45, Mike. And I bloody well look it. You're the one that inherited the eternal youth gene."

"Except for the grey hair."

"It comes to all men, Mike. Grey or bald. Unless you're Donald Trump."

"So what's this week's problem?"

"Maddie. Or the lack of Maddie. She's never in. She's

got her A-levels next year."

"Ash said she had a new boyfriend?"

"Ah, the lovely Tyrone. Ty, as I'm supposed to call him. Three years older than her, unemployed and what isn't pierced is tattooed."

Brady sent a small prayer. *Not just yet, Lord.* "What are you doing about it?"

"As you'll shortly discover, Mike, there is – excuse me swearing – fuck all you can do. Utter the magic words, 'you'll never see him again' and a week later she'll have moved out. You sit and suffer. And then you go to bed, lie awake and suffer some more."

"Sounds familiar..."

"I'm sorry, Mike, I didn't mean to... Well, you know."

He shook his head. "You didn't. Don't worry. What does Bill say?"

"Bill doesn't notice. Bill goes off to work and comes home and as long as the fridge is full and no-one's stolen his golf clubs he doesn't care. He's complaining that Maddie's decided she's a vegetarian. It's the one positive I can cling to. She cares about what she eats."

Brady reached out and took his sister's hand. "No-one's perfect as a teenager..."

"I know. But there's a big difference between one too many Bacardi and Cokes – Christ, I can still remember throwing up on Debbie Clarke's sofa – and what they can get up to these days."

There was the noise of a car in the drive. The front door banged open. "Anyone in?" Bill shouted. "And I see we have a visitor."

He walked through into the kitchen. Grey suit, check

shirt, loosening what looked like a rugby club tie. "Anything to eat? Bloody canteen is still shut."

He opened the fridge door. "Ah, the sun shines on the righteous. Pork pie."

"Gala pie," Kate said.

"What?"

"Pork pie with egg in the middle is called gala pie."

"Is it? So long as it's not bloody vegan I don't care. Has that happened to you yet, Mike?" he asked, finally acknowledging him. "Bloody daughter announces she's vegetarian or vegan and could you buy a new set of pans for her food? No wonder she looks ill all the time."

"No. Ash is eating me out of house and home. She's taller every day. I can't keep up with her."

"Growth spurt," Kate said knowingly.

"Put the kettle on will you, love? Make me a coffee." Kate sighed and got to her feet.

"So how's it going?" Brady asked.

Bill grinned. It wasn't a pleasant sight. "Missing it are you? I knew you wouldn't be able to resist asking."

"He was my best friend. At least when we were growing up."

"Well, remember what Kershaw said. You're a civilian now. You'd do best not to get involved." The last of his pie disappeared. "Cut me another slice of that pie while you're on your feet will you, love?"

"I'm not involved."

Bill raised his eyebrows. "Not what I've heard. Been to visit the merry widow haven't you?"

"She was his wife. I went to see how she was. And she's a long way from merry."

Kate passed Bill his coffee and another slice of pie. He didn't say thank you. "Have we got any brown sauce, love? I was impressed by her," he said, turning his attention back to Brady. "Very calm. In the circumstances."

"Grief affects people in different ways," Brady said. "And at different times. Not being hysterical isn't an admission of guilt."

"We'll see..."

Should Bill even be discussing this with him? No. Of course he shouldn't. But he needed to show off.

"You heard of Occam's Razor?" Bill said. "Some bloody monk back in the 14th Century. The simplest solution is usually the right one."

"It was originally used to explain miracles," Brady said.

"Yeah, well, we won't be needing any divine intervention here. It's all fitting together very nicely. Cherchez la femme, Mikey. And we're not going to have to cherchez very far. Which suits me."

"Why's that?"

"Because I'm due to go into hospital in a couple of weeks. Bloody hernia. But a few weeks off work sitting in the sun'll put me right. Anyway, I've said enough." He paused. He was clearly making one of life's great decisions. "Fuck it," he said. "I might as well finish that pie."

Brady got back into his car. *All OK?* he texted to Ash.

All good. Bean's here

You OK if I'm back in an hour or so? Just need some fresh air.

A thumbs-up. One emoji he could understand.

Moors? Beach? Neither. He wanted to think, not walk.

Besides, going on the Moors or the beach without Archie
was a criminal offence.

13

He parked the car on West Cliff. Sat on a seat – *Susan Mercer 1955 – 2010. Loving mother of four. Grandmother and devoted wife* – and looked out to sea. It was low tide. He watched someone throw a stick into the sea, a Labrador charge after it. Felt guilty at not bringing Archie.

He looked away to his left, to the hill he'd walked up three weeks ago. "This is going to be a mess, Gracie," he said. "A complete mess. But you want to know about Ash. She's doing well. She's settling in, she's making friends."

One day – not that far in the future – he'd be having a different conversation. 'Dropped her off at the weekend. She's fine. She's been ready for uni for the last year. You'd be so proud of her. So just me now. Well, me and Archie...'

He wasn't looking forward to it.

Low tide or not there was a wind off the sea. When was there not a wind off the sea? But plenty of people out for a walk. Everyone still with their coats on. A lot of hats and gloves as well. 'Ne'er cast a clout 'til May be out' as they said in Yorkshire. Everyone looked like they'd taken it to heart.

Kara was pregnant. She'd looked genuinely pleased that Patrick had known. They seemed happy. The story about the alley rang true. There was no way Patrick would have turned his back on her. So she was innocent.

Except that she had the opportunity. And she was strong enough. And stood to gain a lot. How long did Patrick say they'd been married? Six, seven months? And he was a rich man. A lot to inherit for six months of marriage.

But she couldn't have done it. Where had she hidden the weapon?

So not so much 'not guilty' as 'not proven.' Not a verdict the local gossip would accept...

The only way to prove she was innocent was to find the killer. And Bill wouldn't do that if he stopped looking. Yes, of course the simplest solution was often the right one. But it was the easiest one as well. If you were a copper, the one that meant the least work.

Brady stood up and walked over to the railings. Looked down at the beach, the chalets, the RNLI flag blowing in the wind.

If Kara was innocent there was only one person going to prove it. Mistaken identity? It made the headlines when it was a drive-by shooting but in reality there were probably more people killed by cows. Or vending machines. Patrick? Definitely not.

So someone murdered him. Who had a motive? He had no idea.

CCTV? It probably wasn't working. In his experience CCTV was never working when you needed it. And any witnesses would have been drinking. Plus it was dark. And every other bloke in Whitby that night had looked like Patrick.

The Goths weren't important. Kara wasn't important. The answer was in Patrick's life. Not in what happened in Sandside on Saturday night.

But you'll have to find it, Bill.

His mind was made up. He couldn't – wouldn't – go looking for it.

Been there, done that. And seen the broken body of the woman I love lying in the road.

14

'Face to face.' He could hear his dad saying it to him now. *'If you've got bad news for someone, Michael, you tell them face to face. No letters, no phone calls, no letting them find out on the grapevine. Face to face."*

"What about the war, Dad? When they sent all those telegrams?"

"Don't be bloody cheeky."

But his dad had been right. Good news – promotions, awards – in front of the team. Bad news – bollockings, transfers to Blackpool – in your office. And always face to face.

Would he need to have the conversation with Ash at some stage?

'So if you're finishing with a boy, Ash, tell him to his face. Not by text.'

'Yeah, right, Dad. Since when did you know anything about relationships...'

He couldn't wait. But right now he had a more pressing problem.

. . .

"I'M SORRY, I CAN'T," Brady said to Kara.

He was back in her kitchen. Wondering what the hell had come over him. He had what Grace had once pointedly called 'kitchen envy.' About four years too late he realised she'd been dropping a not-very-subtle hint.

"I'm really sorry," he said again. "I just can't do it. I'm here, I'll help you all I can. Patrick's estate. If I can help with that. Whatever help you need – advice, anything – just ask me. But going further. Setting out to find the killer. I can't. I'm sorry."

She nodded. Looked more composed than she had a right to look. "I understand," she said.

Do you? Brady wondered.

"Did Patrick tell you what happened?"

"As much as he knew…"

He wanted to explain himself. Make her *really* understand why he was saying no.

"What happened to my wife. That was my fault. People told me to walk away. I wouldn't. I couldn't let go."

"So someone forced you to let go?"

"Yes. Except they got it wrong. But it still worked."

She asked the question everyone asked. That he'd asked himself a thousand times. "Don't you want revenge?"

Brady took a long time to reply. "Yes. And no. Yes, of course I wanted revenge. Part of me still does. But I have a daughter. She hasn't got a mother and that's my fault. Or the fault of one part of my character. And I won't turn it loose again."

She nodded. "So that's the reason you're saying 'no' to me?"

"Yes. That's the reason I'll be here if you want me. Because I owe that to Patrick. But I won't – I can't – go back to the way I was."

They were both silent for a minute. Then, "What about me?" Kara said quietly. "Am I supposed to walk round Whitby knowing someone murdered Patrick? Wondering if it's the guy behind me at the checkout?"

"The police – " Brady started to say.

Kara cut him off. "They're going to arrest me. You know it. I know it. And I *want* revenge," she added.

Brady looked at her. Couldn't disagree with her.

"This has to be solved," Kara said. "Someone killed Patrick. And I'm frightened of what happens next."

"I know. Anyone would be. But leave it to other people. Revenge won't bring him back. And right now you've got other things to worry about."

"October," she said, suddenly trying to lighten the mood. "The beginning of October. That's when he's due."

"He? How do you know?"

She laughed. "I don't. I don't have a clue. I'm not sure I'd even want to know." She was silent for a moment. Then she stood up. "Just excuse me a minute will you?"

She walked out of the kitchen. She was back in no time. Holding a blue and grey backpack. There was still a bottle of Perrier in one of the side pockets. She held it out to him. "Here. Take it for me."

"That's Patrick's," Brady said. "He had it the other morning. Down on the seafront."

"So you'll know what's in it?"

Brady shook his head. "We were talking about bacon sandwiches."

"His Chromebook."

"So why give it to me?"

"Call it an insurance policy. I don't want to give birth in jail. Everything's on there. Diary, notebook. Spreadsheets."

"I can't do that, Kara. I told you. I'm not going back there. Besides, it's probably evidence."

"There's a desktop in his office. And an iPad. All the evidence anyone could want. Please."

Brady reluctantly reached his hand out and took the backpack. It was from Mountain Warehouse. The sort people take when they're going walking for the day. A bottle of water in one side, a flask in the other. Sandwiches and waterproofs inside. A special pocket for the car keys.

He'd need to go shopping. Buy one that was big enough to take a dog bowl...

He put the backpack down on the floor. "It's tampering with evidence," he said.

"Please," she said again. "For Patrick. And the baby."

Brady sighed and finished his coffee. Kara picked the cups up and moved across to the dishwasher. She said something as she bent down to put the cups in. He didn't catch it. The doorbell was ringing.

"I'll go if you're busy," he said.

15

Brady opened the front door.

"And what the fuck might you be doing here?"

"Bill. Always a pleasure to see you."

And not just Bill. The girl he'd been talking to at the party. Frankie Thomson. And a uniformed WPC. This was a long way from a social call.

"Is the grieving widow at home?"

"That's who I've come to see."

"Then we're coming in."

Brady turned quickly. He didn't want Kara to see Bill marching into her kitchen. Nine, ten steps and he was there. She was standing by the dishwasher. She'd clearly heard the conversation.

But Bill was right behind him, followed by Frankie Thomson and the policewoman. Kara's eyes widened in fright.

Bill didn't waste any time. He was flushed. Scenting victory.

He looked straight at her. "Kara Lauren Smith, I am

arresting you for the murder of Patrick Smith. You do not have to say anything, but it may harm your defence if you do not mention when questioned something which you later rely on in court. Anything you do say may be given in evidence."

Brady took a step forward. "You're making a stupid mistake, Bill."

It was a token protest. Bill had what he wanted. A quick, easy arrest. Confirmation – at least in his own mind – of his first theory. "Just keep out of it," Bill said. "I've already told you. This has nothing to do with you. You're a civilian. Irrelevant." He turned back to Kara. "Do you understand what I've said to you?"

She nodded.

"I'll phone the solicitor," Brady said. "And I'll sort out someone local in the meantime."

Bill nodded to the policewoman. They stepped forward and each took one of Kara's arms. "I didn't do it," she said. "I did not bloody well do it. I love him."

They started to walk Kara out of the kitchen. Brady saw Bill realise they wouldn't be able to walk down the hall three abreast. He let go of Kara's arm with visible reluctance. He turned as he walked out. "DS Thomson. You make sure that Mr Brady leaves the property in the next two minutes. Make sure he doesn't touch anything. Then turn everything off and secure the house. I'll send SOCO over. They'll give you a lift home. And while you're waiting see what you can find."

Brady heard the front door slam. The back door of the police car would be opening now. The policewoman putting her hand over Kara's head as she was ordered into the back seat. Nothing said 'you've been arrested' more than that hand on your head. That and the next door neighbour breaking off from mowing the lawn to look over the hedge.

DS Thomson turned to Brady. "You heard him, Mr Brady."

Brady decided to play for time. "The dishwasher's on," he said. "And Kara's got a friend staying with her. Rebecca."

"Where's she then?"

"Out. Shopping. She seems to do a lot of shopping."

Frankie Thomson raised her eyebrows. "In Whitby? She must have found shops I don't know about. Be that as it may, Mr Brady, I'm going to have to ask you to leave. And try as much small talk as you like. I'm not going to say anything interesting."

She looked coolly back at him.

I could work with you. You're bright. Which may not endear you to your superior officers. But you're bright. And tough.

"Your boss has arrested the wrong person," he said.

She shrugged. "He's still my boss."

And he's still my brother-in-law. But I don't like him. And I know half a dozen people doing time for fraud that I'd rather trust. And while you're bright and tough, Frankie Thomson, you're going to do as you're told. So...

He bent forward to pick the backpack up. One of the straps was trailing on the tiled floor. Frankie took a pace forward and stepped on it. "Yours?" she said.

"Of course."

"What's in it?"

Brady shrugged. "I'm a writer. Notebook. Pens. The usual stuff."

She bent down and hooked a finger through the handle. She pulled upwards, testing the weight. "Laptop?"

Was she taunting him?

"Chromebook," he said.

"So it'll have a passcode?"

"Of course."

"And it is?"

It sure as hell wouldn't be Patrick's birthday. Kara's birthday?

'And why would you use the accused's birthday as a pass-code, Mr Brady?'

He hadn't. Because he didn't have a clue what it was.

He stood up. "2 – 1 – 0 – 3 – 0 – 2," he said. "My daughter's birthday."

"It always is," she smiled. "Even for coppers." And she moved her foot. Brady bent down, picked the backpack up and started to leave.

"Take care, Mr Brady," she said to him. "Brother-in-law or not, my boss is a vindictive sod."

Brady turned. "I've known him since I was a teenager," he said. "He hasn't changed."

It was Christmas Eve. They were all back from their first term at university. Some of them still 18, Patrick's 19th birthday three days earlier.

"Whose bloody idea was it to come to Robin Hood's Bay?"

"Yours, if I remember rightly. 'Let's get out of Whitby. Let's go somewhere different. Let's go to Bay for Christmas Eve.' Can I just say, Michael, as I stand at the bottom of the hill

completely pissed, with a car I am unable to drive at the top of the hill, that it was a fucking genius idea? Not."

"Come on, Patrick, I'll race you."

"Oh fuck off."

"How the bloody hell else are we going to get to the top?"

"What about the girls?"

"Fuck's sake. They're probably fitter than us."

"They're nowhere near as pissed, that's for sure."

The four of them finally made it. From the Bay Hotel at the bottom to the car park at the top. Michael Brady – studying Law, although he had no intention of becoming a lawyer: Patrick Smith – Maths, and intending to make a fortune in the City: Angie Carter – English, and destined for a career on Channel 4: and Lizzie Greenbeck, who'd just finished her first term at Cambridge and was destined for anything she wanted to be destined for.

"We need a taxi," Michael said as they stood in the car park. He tapped furiously on his new mobile. "I can't get a signal. Seriously, what is the point of these mobile phones if you can't get a signal anywhere? Patrick, can you put Angie down for ten seconds and see if your phone works?"

"You guys having trouble?"

Michael looked up. "Hi, John. What are you doing out here?"

"Same as you I guess. Getting pissed in the Bay. Except the lounge not the bar."

John Clayton. Michael knew him vaguely. One of Whitby's rich kids. Educated at a private school in the Dales. He'd played cricket there. A pavilion bigger than most people's houses. Now the rich kid was standing next to a metallic blue Astra. Or leaning on it for support.

"Anyway," he said. "We're going back into Whitby. Got space to give one of you a lift if you want."

"You can't drive. You can barely stand up."

"You're right there, old son. Mr Macdonald is driving. Says he's not pissed at all and he's a better driver after a few pints."

Graham Macdonald. Another one. Son of the local police chief wasn't he? "No thanks," Michael said. "We'll phone for a taxi."

"Mike…" It was Lizzie. "If they've got a spare place, I wouldn't mind a lift."

"Don't be stupid, Lizzie. You can't get in a car with them."

"I need to be back, Mike. You know how strict my dad is."

She started walking towards the car. Michael grabbed her arm. "Lizzie, no. Just no. We won't have to wait long for a taxi."

She shook herself free. "Mike, it's Christmas Eve. Why on earth does a taxi driver need to come out to Robin Hood's Bay when he can make plenty of money driving drunks round Whitby? It's only five miles and there won't be any traffic."

"Lizzie…" It was too late. She climbed into the car. Michael watched Graham Macdonald open the door of the Astra. He put a hand on the roof to steady himself and somehow managed to fall into the driver's seat.

It started. Stalled. Started again and finally lurched out of the car park. Michael watched it disappear. "At least turn the fucking lights on," he shouted after it.

Patrick was now holding his phone above his head. Very clearly, still no signal.

"One of us is going to have to walk back to the pub and use the phone there."

"I can't go," Patrick said. "Angie needs me. She'll get hypothermia without me."

"Piss off," Michael said. "Sticking your tongue down someone's throat isn't a recognised way of keeping them warm. When did you see the St John's Ambulance people do that? We'll toss for it."

"Heads," Patrick said.

It was. Patrick smiled and turned back to Angie. "You should never gamble with a mathematician," he said as Michael started trudging back down the hill.

"Christ, you're lucky buggers," the taxi driver said. "Reckon I'm the only daft sod who's driven out here tonight. Someone staying at the Victoria. Anyway, where to? Back into Whitby, please God."

Michael gave him the address. "And then if you can take the other two home as well," he said.

"Aye. No problem."

The taxi drove through Robin Hood's Bay and up the hill towards the Whitby road. Up the steep, winding hill. "Tell us if any of you are going to puke," the driver said. "Give us fair warning. Don't want you puking in the car."

"Don't worry," Michael said. "It's only ten minutes. We'll make it."

"Good session then?" the driver asked.

"Christmas Eve," Michael said. "You know how it – "

He stopped as a car came hurtling round the corner towards them. Middle of the road, headlights full on. The taxi driver braked sharply, swerved to the left. Michael felt the car run up on the grass bank. And then it was back on the road, *the danger past. "And that," said the driver, "Is why it's treble fare on Christmas Eve. That and my daughter jumping on me after I've had three hours' sleep."*

He turned right onto the Whitby road. "Hey up," he said half a mile later, lifting his hand off the wheel and pointing down the road. "Trouble ahead. Looks like some poor bugger's been pulled over."

The flashing blue lights were clearly visible against the night sky.

The road bent left and then right. "Christ almighty," the taxi driver said.

The car must have hit the tree on the left. Then bounced across the road and slammed into the other tree. It looked like the passenger side had taken the full force of the impact.

And not that long ago. Michael could clearly see the steam coming off the engine. The police must have arrived minutes after the crash.

The taxi driver pulled over. Stopped the car, unfastened his seat belt. Michael did the same. "Patrick," he said. "Come on. We need to help."

He was halfway across the road when he realised. Not many people in Whitby had a GT Astra. Even fewer had a metallic blue one.

The passenger side had taken the full force of the impact...

"Lizzie!" he shouted, running towards the car.

His way was blocked by a policeman in uniform. "I'm sorry, sir. You can't go any further."

He looked up. "Bill? What are you doing here?"

"Mike? Bloody hell, I might ask you the same question."

"Bill, let me past. There's a friend of mine in that car."

Bill Calvert, newly back from training college, PC341 in

North Yorkshire police, refused to move. "Don't be stupid, Mike. I can't let you past."

"What's the problem, Bill?"

His partner was much older. A tough, experienced copper. Pissed off that he was having to spend Christmas Eve with the rookie. Even more pissed off that he'd be here until three in the morning. Or later.

"I'm just explaining that I can't let him look in the car."

"You can't. There's three people badly injured. The Fire Brigade are on their way. Now piss off and let us do our job."

"There's four in the car," Michael said. "We know them. We were with them in Robin Hood's Bay."

The older PC drew himself up to his full height. "There are three casualties in the car, sir. And that's more than I should be telling you. Now leave us to do our job."

Michael felt someone pulling his arm. "Come on, Mike," Patrick said. "There's nothing we can do. Don't get yourself into trouble."

"Know that copper do you?" the taxi driver asked as Michael slumped into the passenger seat.

"You could say. He's just started dating my sister."

The paper came out five days later. It was the lead story.

Local teenager dies in tragic accident

Hero police officers are minutes too late

Despite heroic efforts to save her by two local police officers, Whitby teenager Elizabeth Greenbeck was killed in a Christmas Eve crash on the A171.

Lizzie, as she was known, had been a pupil at Whitby Community College and was in her first term at Selwyn

College, Cambridge. Her former head teacher, Hugh Casey, described her as, 'a model pupil. Someone who was destined for great things. She will be much missed by everyone at the school.'

Paying tribute to his officers, Chief Constable Niall Macdonald said, "PCs Muirhead and Calvert exemplify everything that is best about the police force. We only wish they could have reached the scene of the accident earlier. Everyone in North Yorkshire Police sends their heartfelt condolences to the family and friends of Miss Greenbeck."

The driver of the car, John Clayton, son of local businessman Ernest Clayton, has been charged with causing death by dangerous driving and remanded on bail.

16

Brady sat at his desk and opened his laptop. He tapped his password in and waited. Maybe it was time to add 'new laptop' to his to-do list. But Grace had bought him this one. This was the laptop he'd opened her last e-mail on. So he'd carry on waiting sixty seconds for it to wake up.

His eyes strayed to the corner of the room. Patrick's blue and grey backpack. Containing – officially at least – Michael Brady's Chromebook.

He hadn't looked inside. It was evidence. *Possible* evidence. Possible evidence he could take down to the police station.

'Kara Smith gave me this by mistake. She thought it was mine. I've got one exactly like it. I'm sorry. I wasn't thinking straight. Long term stress. Death of my friend...'

'Thank you for your help, sir. We'll make sure it's passed to Inspector Calvert.'

Or he could open it. And once he'd done that he was

tampering with evidence. The prosecution counsel wouldn't spare the sarcasm.

'Surely, Mr Brady, given your long service in the police force, you must have realised...'

Maybe he should check the current penalties...

And then there was Frankie Thomson. Did she think her boss was making a mistake? Very probably. Did she think the backpack was Patrick's? No, she *knew* the backpack was Patrick's.

...Which raised an interesting question. Why had she let him walk out with it?

Brady was trapped. The one thing the backpack could not do was lean peacefully against his bookcase. He had two choices. Get rid of it. Or hand it in.

Or...

Or curiosity got the better of him and he opened it. Which was not just tampering with evidence, it was the first step. The first step on the journey back.

But if he didn't open it, Bill was in charge. Bill was making the decisions, Bill was in charge of everything. Hand the backpack in and he was giving up any chance of helping Kara. Of doing the right thing for Patrick.

Hand it in and Kershaw was right. 'You're Michael Brady, writer. A civilian. You left DCI Brady in Manchester.'

"Make a decision," he said out loud. Doing nothing was the biggest risk of all. Bill knocking on the door. Bill looking smug, a uniform behind him. 'We've reason to believe you took something from the crime scene...'

No wonder he couldn't get any bloody writing done.

He sighed.

Archie didn't need a second invitation.

17

It was Archie's favourite part of the walk. Dave threw him a sausage and nodded across the street. "There's an unholy fucking alliance if ever I saw one."

Brady followed his gaze. Enzo was coming out of his arcade. He was laughing and joking with someone. "Well, well. Detective Chief Inspector Calvert. My brother-in-law."

"Not the first time either," Dave added.

Bill looked across the narrow road and saw Brady. "I thought you were writing a book?" he called. "Go and do some bloody work."

"Bacon sandwich," Brady called back. "I need some inspiration."

He watched them walk towards the town centre. "Do you know the story, Dave?" he said.

"What story?"

"Bill Calvert. Plus me and Patrick. And a few others."

"Can't say I do."

"You got five minutes?"

"It's May. Ask me when the schools break up and the answer's no. First week of May, it's your story or clean the griddle."

"It's Christmas Eve – 23 years ago – we're all back from university at the end of our first term. Four of us: me, Patrick, Angie Carter – except you'll know her better as Angie Carmichael."

"What, the lass that interviews them politicians on a Sunday morning?"

"The very same. I sat next to her in History. And a girl called Lizzie Greenbeck. We went to the pub in Robin Hood's Bay. Right down the bottom of the hill. One of us had planned to stay sober and drive home. But you know how it is. So about midnight we're in the car park at the top of the hill, phoning for a taxi."

"Must have been bloody freezing."

"Patrick was alright, he was wrapped round the future TV star."

"So the other lass was your girlfriend?"

"No, not really. We'd been out a couple of times. But she had this ferocious work ethic. And her dad was really protective."

He could see her now. Straight black hair parted in the middle. Wearing a Selwyn College rugby shirt. Maroon with yellow hoops. Brown eyes gazing out from behind her glasses.

"I didn't realise it at that time," Brady said. "Her dad had given up on his own life. Like some men do. He was living through his daughter. Anyway, she had to get back. Her dad had told her to be in by midnight. So she got a lift in someone else's car. It belonged to a guy called John

Clayton. His dad was a local businessman. Owned three or four hotels."

"Died last year didn't he?"

"If you say so. Anyway, John Clayton's too pissed to stand up, never mind drive. So the driver is a young man called Graham Macdonald."

"You've lost me."

"His father was Niall Macdonald. At that time Chief Constable of North Yorkshire."

Brady paused again. Finished his tea. It had gone cold. He could see the car, crushed against the tree. The blue lights dancing across it...

"They set off for Whitby. Don't even turn the bloody lights on for about a hundred yards. Anyway, they get to the top of the hill and turn right on to the Whitby road. Half a mile further on and Macdonald bounces the car off one tree and straight into another. The front passenger door takes the full impact of the second tree. Lizzie dies at the scene."

He glanced up at Dave. "You can probably guess where this is going. We're in a taxi. We're the second people to arrive on the scene. The police are already there. A gnarled old veteran called Jim Muirhead and in his brand spanking new uniform, PC Bill Calvert."

"How did they get there so quick?" Dave asked.

"Your guess is as good as mine. Just lucky? Sure as hell no-one in that car phoned for help. Or you want my guess? There were chasing them. They'd seen what they thought – rightly, I suppose – was a drunk driver."

"So you think the police caused the crash?"

"No, you can't say that. What you can say though, is

that when we got there the car had three people in it. When it left Robin Hood's Bay it had four. Macdonald was gone."

Dave turned his attention to someone else. Two fishermen having a late breakfast.

"Any good?" Dave asked.

One of them shrugged. "A few lobsters. Some nice crabs. Trouble with the engine though so we'll have lost money on it." The smell of fish and diesel battled with the smell of frying bacon.

"How the hell did he do that then?" Dave said when they'd gone.

"Macdonald? You tell me. I bumped into him about a week later. Walking round town like nothing had happened. He'd managed to bounce a car off one tree into another and come out of it with a few bumps and bruises. All he had when I saw him was a black eye."

Dave shook his head. "What did you say?"

"What could I say? He knew what had happened, I could guess what happened. But who'd believe a first year law student who'd have to admit he was pissed against two heroic and stone cold sober police officers and the son of the Chief Constable?

"But he was the driver. He'd legged it…"

Brady nodded. "Yeah, you're right. I'm ashamed to say there's a part of me that admires what Muirhead did. He recognised the driver, saw he wasn't that badly injured and told the young master to piss off across the nearest field. Quick thinking, initiative, decisive action. Exactly how you're trained to react. And a shedload of brownie points when the big boss hears the story."

"Except that someone else got blamed - "

"Inevitably."

"- And the other guys were in the back."

"No. One of them was lying on the ground. They probably told the paramedics – ambulance men, they weren't called paramedics in those days – that he must have managed to climb out of the car and then collapsed."

"Christ," Dave said. "There's a bloody morality tale if ever there was one. What happened to them all then?"

Brady paused. A retired couple needed their breakfast. The old man ordered. "Beautiful morning," he said to Brady.

"Beautiful," Brady agreed. "Best time of the day."

"Best time of the year," the old man said. "We're going to walk to Sandsend. No better place than Whitby on a morning like this. God's in his Heaven and everything's right with the world."

Brady smiled. "You'd like to think so."

"Go on," Dave said. "What happened to them all?"

"Well, DCI William Calvert you know about. That night was the story of his police career. Easy options, short cuts. Always just managing to be somewhere else when the shit hits the fan and now five years away from a prosperous retirement."

"What about the others?"

"Muirhead took early retirement. Someone told me he was living in Spain. Bought a pub in Fuerteventura."

"Don't be stupid, Lizzie. You can't get in a car with them."

He could still hear himself saying it.

Brady shook his head. "The saddest one was Lizzie's

dad. Blamed himself for telling her to be in by midnight. Couldn't see any point in living without his daughter. Six months later he went for a walk on the Moors. Sat down on a rock, opened a vein and went to join her."

"The poor bastard. What about the buggers in the car? Did they get away with it then?"

"Yes and no. Remember the one lying on the ground? That's John Clayton. It's his car, it's reasonable to assume he was driving. He's charged with causing death by dangerous driving. But his dad spends a fortune on a top brief. Came up from London and told the judge the boy was some sort of superstar student. And played the patriot card. Said Clayton had set his heart on a career serving his country. Wanted to join the army. So he gets two years suspended, about 100 hours community service and a whopping fine."

"Which his dad paid."

"You'd assume so."

"But no career in the army?"

"No, they took him," Brady said. "That part was true. He joined the Paras. Died in Afghanistan. Took the rap for his friend - "

"Nothing he could do about that though."

"True. Macdonald, Muirhead and Bill Calvert had trapped him. But he died a hero. You can Google him. The Taliban captured him. I can't believe it was quick."

Dave shook his head. "Poor sod. So maybe the old feller was wrong about God. What about Macdonald?"

"Don't you read your papers, Dave? Son of a Chief Constable. Brought up with an unshakeable belief in law and order. A commitment to protect society. What else would he be? He's a bloody MP."

"There's one missing," Dave said.

"Crees. Jon, Jonty. Something like that. God punished him alright. He's an estate agent I think. Somewhere in the West Riding."

Brady stood up. "Time to get back to work," he said. "The book's calling."

"How's it going?"

"Slowly," Brady admitted. "Slowly, badly, weakly."

"Sounds like a film."

"Chance would be a fine thing…"

18

Brady turned to go. "Hang on," Dave said. "I've got a question for you."

"Yeah? What's that?"

"Are you happy?" Dave asked.

"How do you mean am I happy?"

"What I say. Do you sing and dance down the street? Do you fall out of bed every morning with a smile on your face?"

"This is a bit lyrical for you, Dave. I thought men didn't talk about feelings. Have you got a girlfriend or something?"

"No. I've got a bacon sandwich shop on Whitby seafront. 'It is not in the stars to hold our destiny, but in ourselves.'"

"Shakespeare at a rough guess."

"Who else?"

"What did you do before this?"

"I was a forensic accountant. Combed through balance sheets and tax returns. I bet I caught more villains from my desk than you did in 20 years of police work. But I'd had enough. All I saw was the bad side of human nature. So I retired. Like I told you. Came to Whitby for a day's fishing and never left. I'm 62. I go fishing, I ride my bike on the Moors and I shut shop in January and February and me an' the wife go to Spain for two months."

"Where you bump into the ones you didn't catch..."

"Very good, young man. And not so far wrong. But are you happy? No, you're not. So I've another question for you. What are you going to do about it?"

"What am I going to do about what?"

"About what's happened."

A seagull screeched overhead. Brady looked up. Two of them. Squabbling in mid-air over a scrap of fish.

"How long have we known each other?" Dave said. "A month? What've we had? Eight conversations? Nine?"

"About that..."

"So we're friends. I like you. Which means I'm going to be honest with you. And you're not happy. And you won't be happy until you sort this out."

Brady didn't speak.

"Patrick's dead and a bloke you wouldn't cross the road to piss on has arrested the wrong person. You want to sort it out but you won't let yourself sort it out. Your book's going nowhere. And you want to know why?"

"Why?"

"Because your mind is somewhere else."

Brady looked across the harbour to the alley.

"You know I'm right," Dave said.

Brady stood up. "Maybe. But I don't want to talk about

it. And I don't want to fall out with you, Dave. I've got to go and write. My daughter's started demanding my word count every day. I'll see you later."

Dave held his gaze a moment longer. "I don't want to fall out with you either," he said. And then he played his trump card. "I'm only telling you what your wife would have told you."

Brady walked back to his car. If only...

He opened the door. Was nearly knocked over by Archie. "God, Archie, I'm sorry. You must be starving. Come on, let me in."

He needn't have worried. There was a note from Ash. Maria brought me home. Needed clothes. Fed Archie, let him out. Love you. Love Mum x

He went upstairs. Put his tracksuit bottoms on. T-shirt, dressing gown. Went into the bathroom. Realised he was so worried about Grace he'd forgotten why he was there. Walked downstairs to the kitchen. Remembered. Went back to the bathroom, opened the cabinet, took two paracetamol.

Back in the kitchen. Made some tea. Realised he was hungry. Realised he was so sick with worry he couldn't eat.

He should sleep. Back upstairs to the bedroom.

Grace had changed the bed that morning. Brady couldn't bring himself to get into it. Ever since he'd been a child he'd loved clean sheets on the bed. Clean sheets on the bed with Grace. Holding her. Telling her he loved her.

They didn't make love as often as they used to but who did as you got older? Especially with a nearly-teenage daughter in the next bedroom. Their definition of foreplay had become a whispered, 'Is she asleep?' A hurried, 'Yes, I think so.'

Saturday night. The last time. And Ash was definitely

getting older. "Is Dad alright this morning?" she'd coyly asked on Sunday morning. "It's just that he looks tired and I heard him groaning last night..."

He wandered back downstairs. Sat on the sofa. Somehow fell asleep. Woke up two hours later. Ate a slice of toast, took two more paracetamol. Drove to the hospital. Sent a text to work. But they'd know by now. His wife was a crime report. Detective Chief Inspector Brady was a witness. He'd need to give a statement...

19

Another fruitless day's writing. He'd given up at three and finally succumbed to Sainsbury's. Made Ash mac n' cheese and then taken Archie onto the Moors.

Now Brady parked the car outside his sister's house. "Ten minutes, Archie," he said. "Just have a snooze. There's something I have to do."

He wound the window down a fraction, reached across to the passenger seat and got out of the car. "Ten minutes. No more, I promise," he said, tossing a dog biscuit across the seats.

He rang the bell. Kate answered it. "Hi," he said, handing her the flowers. "I've brought you these."

She put her hand on his shoulder and kissed him. "Ah, Michael, you shouldn't have."

"I just wanted to let you know I was thinking of you today."

Kate smiled at him. "Five years today."

Brady nodded. "Yeah. I hope she's giving Dad some

peace though. Not still telling him off for leaving his shoes in the hall."

Kate laughed. "Come into the kitchen. Let me put these in some water."

"Just five minutes, I've left Archie in the car."

He followed her into the kitchen. Kate reached for a vase. "She'd have loved these. Mum always loved lilies."

"It's the cherry blossom for me," Brady said. "Do you remember the road up to the crematorium? All the cherry blossom."

"Do I remember? I was only thinking about it the other day."

Bill crashed into the kitchen. "I thought I heard your voice," he said. "Flowers. What are the bloody flowers for?"

"It's the anniversary of Mum's death," Kate said quietly.

"Is it? Bloody hell. What's that? Three years? Four?"

"It's five, Bill."

He turned his attention to Brady. "I'm glad you're here," he said. "Been meaning to talk to you. Come through to the lounge will you?"

Brady looked at Kate. Her expression very clearly said, 'no idea.'

Bill flopped down into his armchair. Remote control on the arm rest. A small drinks table at the side. No-one else was going to sit there.

"I'm just having a whisky or two to take away the pain. These bloody... This bloody hernia is driving me up the wall." Bill shifted his position in the chair. "Sorry, I just can't get comfortable with it. Anyway, I wanted to talk. Thought we hadn't been seeing eye-to-eye lately."

Brady didn't say anything. His job was clearly to listen to the lecture.

"Look…" Bill held the whisky glass up to make his point. "You're Kate's brother. We've known each other a long time. I don't want any bad blood between us. But you need to let us do our job. You need to let *me* do *my* job."

…Which so far has seen you arrest the wrong person while the real killer enjoys the freedom of Whitby.

Brady opened his mouth to speak. Bill cut him off.

"You think she can't have done it don't you? You bought that crap about giving him a blow job. She told us what she'd told you. And you're thinking, 'Well, if someone was giving me a blow job I'd be waiting for her to come out of the pub. No way would I have my back turned."

"It's a natural train of thought…" Brady said, trying to be as non-committal as possible.

"Only if you've got shit for brains. That's your problem, Michael. All those conferences and speeches and now you think you're a fucking writer. You've forgotten how ordinary people think. You've forgotten the bloody basics of police work."

Brady doubted that. But he didn't reply. 'Never interrupt your enemy when he's making a mistake.' Was that what Bill was now? His enemy? Or did he just stand for everything that was wrong in the police force? Either way, Brady was certain he was going to say something he shouldn't. So don't interrupt.

"What you saw was a pretty girl. So you think, 'she can't have done it.' Maybe she's had a chequered past but she can't have done it. I'm sorry to say this, Michael, but you need to fuck someone. Your wife's dead. She isn't coming back. And when you looked at Kara bloody Smith you let your cock rule your brains. You might not think it, but I know what happened."

Brady didn't like physical violence. For some coppers it was a perk of the job. Not him. He'd rather write a report. How many times had he hit someone in the last 20 years? Three. Maybe four.

But keep talking like this, Bill, and number five isn't far away.

He breathed in. Closed his eyes for a second. Kept his anger under control. "I'm not sure that's true, Bill…"

"Of course it's fucking true." Bill squirmed in his seat again.

Best not to get a hernia. That looks bloody painful.

"It's true because there are two theories that prove you're wrong. Number one, Mikey boy, she wanted a piss. The bar's too crowded. So she says, 'Darling, just stand in front of me and spread your coat out will you…' And he does. The poor bugger turns round, spreads his coat out and Bob's your uncle. But not for much longer."

Something clicked in Brady's brain. His anger disappeared. He was back in the interview room. He'd got a suspect in front of him. And the very best sort. One who was determined to prove how clever he was.

Brady nodded. "I can see that, Bill. There's a simple logic to that theory." There was. If your starting point was Kara murdered her husband.

The trick was to keep Bill focused. And to pour a little more petrol on the flames. "You said there were two theories..."

Bill got to his feet and poured himself another whisky. Brady wondered if he'd be driving into work in the morning.

"You sure you won't have one?"

"No, I'm good. Got an early start tomorrow."

What Brady really wanted to say was, 'Not when I'm working.'

"Where were we? Second theory. Should I be sharing this with you? I suppose I'm alright. You're still a copper, even if you're swinging the fucking lead for another six months."

"Something you found, I'm guessing. You'll have organised a thorough search."

"Course we organised a thorough fucking search. And you're right." Bill paused theatrically. Brady was surprised he didn't call Kate in and order her to play a drumroll. "A blindfold," Bill said.

"A what?"

"A blindfold. A yard of expensive red silk. Know how far it is round someone's head? A bloke's head? Two feet. So case proven. 'Oh baby, I'm going to suck that cock so good. But let me make it *really* hot for you. Just turn round, baby.'"

Brady resisted the urge to vomit at Bill's impersonation of a porn channel. "So where was Kara hiding that?"

"She wasn't. It was in the victim's pocket."

So there was no evidence that Kara had put it there or

that she intended to use it. It's in Patrick's coat, the chances are he put it there. And still no murder weapon. That didn't sound like a case Brady would want to bring to trial. Any decent QC would pick a hundred holes in it.

And – even half a dozen whiskies down the road – Bill must know that. He must know his case was weak.

So there had to be something else.

Brady had a feeling he wasn't going to like it. But he had to find out what it was.

Bill lapsed into silence. He gazed into his whisky glass. Brady was worried he was going to fall asleep. "So she was either having a pee," he prompted, "Or she was going to blindfold him. I can see where you're going with that. Sorry – no joke intended." But he needn't have bothered saying it. Bill was too drunk to notice.

"I'm not sure it adds up to a motive for murder, though. Especially without the weapon..."

Bill took another slug of his whisky. And tipped over the edge. Brady saw the exact moment he passed from boastful drunk to fighting drunk.

He remembered his mother saying it. The morning after he'd staggered home from Tim Shepherd's party. "Alright are you? Not that you deserve to be. But at least you've set my mind at rest. You're a sentimental drunk, Michael. Not a fighting drunk. You sat on that stool in the kitchen and told the dog how much you loved her."

Bill wasn't. Bill was a fighting drunk. "You're not fucking bright enough to work it out, are you? You're still looking at her thinking she couldn't have done it. Pregnant, she's having Patrick's baby. Happy fucking families."

He drank some more whisky and stared at Brady. "It

wouldn't be happy fucking families when she presented Patrick with a black baby."

Brady was stunned. Beyond stunned. Bill might as well have punched him. "What?"

Bill nodded and smiled. "She never told you did she? You thought we were just simple fucking plod in Whitby. All we do is roll up at two in the morning and catch some poor sod pissed on the beach. We've moved on from those days, Mikey boy. We made a few enquiries. Talked to one of the saintly Mrs Smith's best mates. Three of them went to London a couple of months back. Girls' weekend."

Brady knew what was coming. Whether he was drunk or not, Bill was right. He'd been a fool. Six months sitting by his wife's bedside. Trying to be a good dad. He'd forgotten how to think.

"You know what they say, Mikey. What happens in London stays in London. Well this time it hasn't. This time it's come home to roost. In Whitby." He threw the last of the whisky down his throat and banged his glass on the table in triumph.

"So best mate – probably not her best mate now – she tells me that they go out. To a club. Where they bump into someone's ex. And at two in the morning Kara Smith and her footballer ex-boyfriend are seen climbing into a taxi."

Bill twisted the knife one last time. "You'd know him as well, Michael," he said with a smile. "He scored against Middlesbrough."

"You've no - "

"No what?" Bill was laughing at him. "No evidence

they had sex? No, of course we haven't. But let's go with the balance of probabilities, shall we?"

He was right. Of course he was right. What had he said to Kara? 'Tell me the truth. If you tell me the truth I can help.'

She hadn't. And now Bill was tormenting him. Feasting on his pain. His complete bewilderment.

"He knew I was pregnant. He thought, 'I'm going to be a father.'"

Brady could hear Kara saying it. He felt sick.

"Game, set and match," Bill said. "Or should I say full time? And given how many people have scored against Middlesbrough this season I'll give you another clue. He's Nigerian. Might have been a bit of a shock for Patrick in the maternity ward."

Bill winked drunkenly at him. "Not a fucking risk I'd take if I was pregnant. Not a risk I'd take, Mikey boy…"

"You're not fucking bright enough to work it out, are you? You're still looking at her thinking she couldn't have done it."

"She never told you did she? You thought we were just simple fucking plod in Whitby. We've moved on from those days, Mikey boy. We made a few enquiries. Talked to one of her best mates."

It wasn't the best recipe for a good night's sleep. Brady had been awake since three. Turning the conversation with Bill over and over in his mind.

Bill had done what he would have done. What any competent copper would have done. Made enquiries. Talked to Kara's friends. Done what Brady couldn't do now.

Was the 'best mate' Rebecca? Is that who he'd talked to? Was she another one who'd been laughing at him?

Becky put his coffee down. Walked round and sat next to Kara. Took her hand.

Is that what she'd been thinking? While she was

holding Kara's hand? 'I know the truth. Which is a lot more than you're going to do.'

At 4:30 he'd given up the struggle. Written a quick note to Ash. *Taken Archie for an early walk. Back in good time for breakfast x*

Brady walked up to the top of the hill. Grace's hill.

What had Ash said to him? "Are you looking forward to this, Dad?"

Yes. If the pain allowed him to look forward to anything, he *had* been looking forward to it. Writing the book, watching his daughter growing up. Gradually putting his life back together. Making a new start.

Not even a month. How had it all gone so wrong so quickly?

Not just Patrick. Life.

He wasn't in control any more.

Brady took a step closer to the cliff edge and looked out to sea. The same red and white fishing boat was there. A seagull drifted slowly up to him. Lazily tilted its wings and was gone.

What would Grace have told him to do? Well, here he was. He could ask her. But he already knew the answer.

He was hesitating over whether to apply for a promotion. Didn't know whether to put his name forward or wait to be asked. Worried he'd be seen as too young. Too ambitious.

"Do you want it?" she said.

"Yes."

"Are you capable of doing it?"

"Yes."

"So apply. Take action, Michael. It's simple. Either you control your life or someone else does."

That was that then. He couldn't let someone else control his life. Especially when 'someone else' was Bill Calvert.

He owed it to Grace, to Ash. Most of all to himself.

He hadn't asked for this. But he had to deal with it.

Sort it out, find the killer. And *then* start his new life.

"I love you, Grace," he said.

For the second time Brady turned and walked back down the cliff path to his car. This time to a date with a backpack.

Brady took two steps across the room and picked up Patrick's backpack. Sat down, the backpack on his knee. The bottle of Perrier was still in the side pocket. Probably flat by now…

He unzipped the small front pocket. A gel pen. A crumpled packet of paracetamols. Patrick had taken four. Two AAA batteries. Sinex. He vaguely remembered Patrick suffering from hay fever as a teenager.

The second pocket. *Cura-Heat. Continuous warming relief. Back and shoulder pain.*

Blimey, Patrick, you were falling apart, mate.

And a black charger. A three pin plug. Not for a mobile phone. Brady took a guess at a camera. Maybe Patrick took photos of his properties. 'My window's leaking.' 'OK, let me take a photo. I'll send it to the handyman so he knows what I'm talking about.'

The main pocket. More pens. Two notebooks. Both Black n' Red. A4 and A5.

"Jackpot," Brady said out loud. Maybe he wouldn't need the Chromebook after all.

Or maybe he would. The A4 notebook was brand new. Completely empty. The other one had sketches in it. Very clearly plans to convert some of Patrick's flats. Is this what Patrick was doing at the bank? A preliminary meeting? Before he hired an architect? Whatever the reason, it was no use to Brady.

He did what he always did with a notebook. Turned to the back page. *Everyone* made notes at the back. Notes they didn't want to keep in the front. The not-quite-secret notes. The bills-they-couldn't-afford-to-pay notes.

Everyone except Patrick. But the notebook didn't close properly. Brady flipped through the pages.

There was a theatre ticket. Puccini. *Madame Butterfly*. Newcastle Theatre Royal. A date in February. A message was written on it. *My first time at the opera.* Three kisses. Clearly from Kara. Brady liked her handwriting.

He unzipped the back pocket. The one with the Chromebook. It slipped out into his hand. A silver Acer. And certainly not new: the bumps and scratches of several building sites. Brady put the backpack on the floor and sat the Chromebook on his desk. He opened it, pressed the switch to turn it on.

A picture. Whitby pier stretching out into the North Sea, the sun just coming up out of the water. The date and time in the bottom left hand corner.

He right-clicked. *Patrick Smith*, it told him uselessly. Patrick hadn't uploaded a picture of himself. No surprise there. And a box, politely requesting a password. Patrick's Google password.

Brady had thought long and hard about this. He'd come up with one date. 10th May 2006. The day Middlesbrough Football Club finally made it to the UEFA Cup Final. He'd been on a training course in Birmingham. Bored senseless.

But he knew Patrick had gone. The Philips Stadion in Eindhoven. The greatest night in their team's history.

They lost 4-0.

But it was still a significant date. He tapped it into the box. Boro100506.

The password is incorrect. Please try again.

It had always been a longshot. Patrick would have used a random combination of letters, numbers and exclamation marks.

Brady knew he'd get a second chance before the machine closed itself down or self-destructed. Well, seeing as they'd lost, let's try it backwards... Boro605001.

The password is incorrect. Please try again.

He could spend all morning thinking. In films the hero guessed the password on the third attempt. Not with Patrick. He could have 300 guesses and be nowhere near.

He reached for a packet of wipes. Very carefully, very methodically he removed any trace of his fingerprints from the Chromebook.

He could still walk down to the police station and hand it in. It was the right thing to do. The only sensible thing to do.

"You want to sort it out but you won't let yourself sort it out. Your book's going nowhere and you want to know why? Because your mind is somewhere else."

"Take action, Michael. It's simple. Either you control your life or someone else does."

"Let's do this," Brady said out loud.

He reached for his mobile. And stepped back in time.

EIGHTEEN MONTHS since he'd last dialled the number. He could still remember it.

The call went straight to the recorded message. A new one. But the sentiment was the same.

I'm not in. I'm never in. Leave a message. Unless you're a Liverpool fan. In which case fuck off.

Brady smiled to himself. "Give me a ring back," he said. "And rumour has it they're after Klopp. You could be in trouble."

His phone rang ten minutes later. "You're in luck, Detective Chief Inspector." The voice had always intrigued Brady: a Manchester accent with a slight hint of the Welsh valleys. "That number was three phones ago. I only check it once a week. And he's German. Tell me the last successful German manager in English football."

Brady couldn't. "I need some help," he said.

"No shit. What's the name of my cat?"

"What?"

"Security. And sorry, it's Mr Brady now isn't it? So yeah, just like your mother's maiden name. Which is Simpson if you need a reminder. What's the name of my cat?"

He'd been introduced to 'Scholesy' by an accountant. A not-always-on-the-right-side-of-the-law accountant. But this time they'd been on the same team. In both their interests to make sure the torrent of money being laundered through one of Manchester's casinos became a trickle.

"Here," the accountant said, passing him a slip of paper. "The best hacker in the North West. It won't be admissible in court. But he'll save you six months of police work. Just make sure you've read up on United first."

Brady had been to the flat once. He could see it now. A dark basement flat, a couple of streets back from Cheetham Hill Road.

He guessed Scholesy hadn't seen daylight for two years. Why bother? The pizza shop delivered, *World of Warcraft* was always online and multiple TV stations across the world supplied illegal streams of Manchester United games. And somewhere amid the chaos, a black and white cat called Giggsy.

"Giggsy," Brady said.

"No. You're wrong. Some prick ran him over. Almost certainly a City fan. Ahmed from the corner shop carried him back to me. I've got a new one. Nicky Butt."

"So that's the security question now?"

"It'll do. What do you want, Mr Brady? Some more evidence the judge won't allow?"

"I need a name, Scholesy. Someone like you. But in this part of the world. I've moved. I'm living - "

"Fuck sake, Brady, I know where you live. Nice kitchen by the way. Fifty quid for old time's sake. Pay the new guy. He'll send it on. And forget about pounds, Brady. Get yourself a Bitcoin account. That's the future."

The line went dead.

22

Brady was doing his best to dry a very wet dog – "Every rock pool on the beach, Archie. How do you do it?" – when his phone buzzed.

A message. Number unknown. Well it would be. Just an e-mail address. And a name.

Mozart.

Scholesy had taught him the rules. "You've got to tell the truth. But we'll tell you what we want to tell you. And it won't be the truth."

Brady sent the e-mail as soon as he was back at his desk.

My name is Michael Brady. I live in Whitby. Scholesy has given me your e-mail. Hopefully he's also given me a reference. I need some help. Thank you. Look forward to hearing from you.

He assumed it was bouncing round half the world's servers, but the reply was there in less than five minutes. *Drive to Saltburn. Park your car. Stand across the road from the Zetland Hotel. Face the sea. Monday 11am.*

Saltburn? He was in luck. Not much more than half an hour up the coast. He'd expected Middlesbrough. Or Leeds.

And here he was. He'd dropped Ash at school, apologised to Archie for cutting his walk short and driven up the coast road. Past Runswick Bay, through Hinderwell, up to the top of the hill at Boulby and then down through Loftus. Conscious all the way that he ought to know more about the history of the area. The ironstone mining, Whitby's whaling fleet, the landslide that destroyed Runswick Bay. When you're growing up it doesn't matter. When you were back for good it did.

He stood opposite the Zetland Hotel. Built in the 19th Century he guessed, as the railways opened up the English seaside.

But he couldn't look at the building for too long. Brady did as he was told. Turned round and gazed out to sea. Presumably while someone had a good long look at him.

A longer look than he'd expected. It was ten minutes before his phone buzzed.

Come into the Zetland. 22.

He'd read about the Zetland Hotel being converted into flats. He looked up at the windows. Not that he could tell which was no. 22. But he'd been given a number: presumably he'd passed the interview.

He pressed the buzzer. "Good morning. Come on up," a cultured voice said.

He was softly spoken, mid-thirties. Maybe 40. Wearing an olive green jumper with leather elbow patches. He looked like someone who'd become a Maths professor at 26. Someone spoken about in hushed tones. A man who could prove Fermat's Last Theorem but was hopelessly confused by the checkout at Aldi. He held out his hand. "Mozart," he said simply.

"Michael Brady."

He'd expected a carbon copy of Scholesy. He'd expected a desk surrounded by cans of Monster and the remains of last night's takeaway. He'd expected a black t-shirt, black jeans. Signs of an addiction to heavy metal. Another grimy staircase. The smell of stale beer.

Instead he was being shown into a lounge. Pale green wallpaper. An eclectic mix of paintings. Two sculptures, one so abstract Brady had no idea what it was. The other was a weightlifter. Who managed to look as though he had the weight of the world on his shoulders but was still smiling.

The room was dominated by screens. A beautiful L-shaped desk, very clearly handmade from reclaimed wood. A chair a professional games player would cheerfully have died for. And a bank of six elegant, state-of-the-art computer screens.

Six? Brady had no idea how anyone could work on two screens at once.

Classical music played faintly in the background.

"I owe you an apology," Mozart said.

"For making me stand outside? It's a sunny day."

"Partly. You can tell a lot from watching someone stand still, Mr Brady. I don't trust impatient people. Patience is a skill few of us master."

Brady smiled to himself. Best not to put him in touch with Bill, then...

"But..." Mozart shrugged, gestured at the room with his hands. "You're disappointed. I can tell. You wanted a real nerd. Iron Maiden t-shirt, discarded pizza boxes, thick glasses, any excuse to open a window as he clearly hasn't washed for a month."

Brady laughed. "Is it that obvious?"

"It's the standard expectation. Hollywood doesn't have any imagination when it comes to people like me. And, of course, our mutual friend reinforces the stereotype. I'm sorry," Mozart added. "I'm forgetting my manners. Would you like coffee? Tea? I've Earl Grey. Fruit teas, obviously."

Brady liked Earl Grey. And Dave was 20 miles down the road. It seemed safe to admit it.

"So what can I do for you, Mr Brady?" Mozart asked when he came back from the kitchen. The tea set was art deco. Frosted pale blue cups, pale yellow on the inside.

"Michael. Or Mike. Please." He unfastened the backpack. Pulled the Chromebook out and passed it across.

"You want access to it? You could have watched a YouTube video."

"And wiped all the data."

"Not necessarily. Gone in as a guest. Reset the password."

Brady shook his head. "I daren't take the risk of losing the data. It's all I have."

"So you need Patrick Smith's password? I'm guessing it's Patrick's?"

Brady nodded. "You've clearly read the papers. And I suspect that's not much of a challenge?"

Mozart smiled. "No, it's not quite going mano a mano

with the Chinese Red Army." He gave him a quizzical look. "But it's clearly important to you."

"Yes."

"...And you had to scratch the itch."

It was a statement, not a question. "You know my history then?" Brady said.

"Of course. Not that I've had time to read the whole file. But my deepest sympathy, Michael. Your wife and your friend."

"Thank you. I appreciate it."

"What are you looking for? On the machine?"

It was like Scholesy had told him. His only option was to tell the truth. "It's the only lead I've got. Whatever reason someone had for killing Patrick – it's in there. At the very least there's a clue."

"OK, let me explain a little. My apologies if I tell you what you already know." Brady looked again at the imposing bank of screens. He doubted that was going to happen.

"This is a Chromebook," Mozart said. "So we're almost certainly going to find what Google call Docs, Sheets, Calendar, Gmail, obviously. Google's version of Office."

Brady nodded. "That's what I guessed."

"But you've a problem," Mozart said. "Because this will have been linked to Patrick's phone. Whatever was on the Chromebook was on his phone as well. And I think we both know where his phone is..."

Brady did. Very clearly. In a sealed evidence bag at the police station. "So what you're saying is if I can – if you can – access the information, so can the police."

Mozart nodded. "But there are two stages. First things first, the police need to access the phone. You know, passcode. 1-2-3-4 or whatever highly secure PIN people usually go for. When they've done that, then they can go into Google Docs, Sheets and so on."

"Without Patrick's password?"

"That depends on how security conscious he was. Did he sign in every time he opened the app? Most people don't."

Like my Gmail. I'm permanently logged in.

"Your big problem is the date," Mozart said. "You open, say, a document, and it will display the last date it was opened."

"So if the police are looking at it as well, they'll realise someone has been looking at it? After Patrick's death."

Mozart nodded. "And they're not going to believe in miracles."

They weren't. And with Kara in custody there was only one place Bill was going to look for an explanation. Brady gazed past Mozart and out of the window. He could still walk down to the police station with it.

"What it comes down to," Mozart said, "Is how thorough you think the police have been. Will be. Let's assume they've access to the phone. Did they just check Patrick's messages? The last numbers he called? Or did they dig deeper?"

What it really comes down to is simple. It comes down to my assessment of my brother-in-law. How much work has he done? Or has he arrested Kara and put all his effort into proving a case against her? Is Patrick's phone sitting quietly in an evidence bag? Or is it on Bill's desk?

"You could tell when someone last looked at a file?" Brady said.

Mozart nodded. "Yes. Once I have access. And obviously if it's before Patrick died, then the police haven't looked at it."

"And I'm in the clear?"

"Not necessarily. Once you look at a file you create a new date."

"So I'm gambling on the police not looking at the phone after that date?"

"They can look at the phone. That doesn't cause you a problem. It's when – if – they look at Docs. And wonder why Patrick has risen from the dead. Simply put, Michael, once you start looking at this – " he gestured at the Chromebook – "Once you start looking you've crossed the Rubicon. There's no going back."

Brady stood up and stared out of the window. Cars going past. People walking down to the beach. Normal life. The life he'd been planning.

The life that would have to wait.

"How long will it take you?"

"Give me two days. I could send you out for coffee and do it now but I've a deadline for some gentlemen – I use the word loosely – in the Netherlands. So two days. A DHL package will arrive. I'll let you know the password."

"Patrick's password?"

"Yes, that's what you want isn't it? The Chromebook to think you're Patrick. I could change the password for you – say, Ashley123 – but I think that might be a bit of a clue if anyone else has a look."

The mention of his daughter's name unsettled him.

Like Scholesy discussing his kitchen. But it was the price you paid.

Brady stood up. It was time to leave. *Part* of the price you paid. "How much do I owe you?"

"Do you have a Bitcoin account?"

Brady shook his head. "No, but it looks like I'll need one."

"The future. At least for people like me. Five hundred pounds. I'll send you the details."

"Can I ask you a question?" Brady said.

"Of course."

"How do you work on six screens at a time?"

Mozart smiled at him. "I don't. It's marketing. It's expected. People have seen nerds – God, I hate that word – in films. Very few people ever come here. But they *expect* to see six computer screens. Between you and me, I only ever use three of them."

"So it's just business?"

"Of course. Like the name. Supposing I was called Roger Johnson? Well, that's not very impressive is it? He can't be very good. And you've read *Girl with the Dragon Tattoo*. Who does she go to? Lars Bjorklund? Ingmar Svenson? No, she goes to Wasp. So it's expected. I thought I'd go to the top end of the scale. And Einstein's pretentious. So, Mozart."

"So poor old Roger's at the bottom, Wasp's in the middle and Mozart's at the top?"

"Exactly. *Reassuringly expensive* as the Jaguar ads used to say. But I think you're going to be a long-term client. We may even become friends. So Mozart service, Wasp prices."

23

Mozart was as good as his word. Wednesday morning and DHL sent him a text. *Your DHL shipment CQ919051975DE is estimated for delivery by DHL Parcel UK between 13:28 – 17:28.*

So it was. A few minutes past three and there was the yellow and red van outside the house. "Thank you," he said, signing for it.

He carried it up to his office. Ash was going to Bean's after school: she'd promised to be back for seven.

So nearly four hours with Patrick's Chromebook. Three hours. He'd forgotten Archie. But even that must be enough to find everything he needed.

He opened the package, eased the Chromebook out and sat it on his desk. Lifted the lid. There was a small white card lying on the keyboard. At least 20 numbers, letters and characters. Just as Mozart had promised.

56!U_x_-gsq8DfH*kWfSr

No, he probably wouldn't have guessed it.

He turned the machine on. And carefully typed in the password.

A dialogue box popped up. *Do you want Google to remember this password?*

No, that wasn't a risk worth taking. He copied the password into his notebook. At the back, obviously. And put the card in his desk drawer.

And there was Patrick's life, laid out in front of him. Gmail. Docs. Sheets. Calendar. Keep.

Opening the Chromebook was fine in theory. But now he was face-to-face with it.

Decision time.

And the same feeling he'd had when Kara had been sitting in his kitchen. When she'd asked for his help.

He'd felt clean.

He didn't want to feel dirty again.

Twenty years in the police force and feeling that way had crept up on him. Feeling dirty was simply the clothes he wore every day.

Detective Chief Inspector Brady hadn't had a choice. Michael Brady, writer, did have a choice.

Now he was taking a conscious decision.

But here he was. Rifling through his wardrobe, looking for the old, familiar clothes.

He sighed. There was no other way.

Gmail was the obvious place to start. Brady clicked. Opened it.

Slightly over 250 e-mails. If the line of neatly ordered folders was any guide, all in the last ten days.

The first one was from Kara.

Brady hesitated. He didn't want to read e-mails

between Patrick and his wife. Would he want someone else reading the last e-mail Grace had sent him?

No. Definitely not.

But the old clothes still fitted him. He closed Gmail and opened *Sheets.*

"You're not fucking bright enough to work it out, are you?"

You shouldn't have said it, Bill. You shouldn't have tried to warn me off...

There were only three spreadsheets. *2015 Cash Flow Forecast. Weekly stock market figures. Trading 14/15.*

Five minutes and Brady knew that Patrick's property business was far bigger than he'd guessed. And that he made a significant income trading currencies and stock market futures – doing what he'd intended to do before his father's death brought him back to Whitby.

Just doing it for himself, instead of doing it for a merchant bank.

Docs next. Targets, draft e-mails, a proposal for the bank...

Another 20 minutes and Brady understood the extent of Patrick's ambition. The property business was going to grow. He was planning to sell all the properties he'd inherited from his father as he moved into upmarket student and corporate lets. There were proposals for developments in York, Middlesbrough and Newcastle. Barclays were going to lend him £5m. And if Barclays wouldn't do it there were plenty of banks that would.

Brady was also beginning to suspect that Patrick had kept a significant amount of information in his head.

Google Keep. Brady wasn't entirely sure what Keep was.

Ah... A notebook. A series of notes. Colour coded notes. Personal, business and what looked like ideas. Some notes on Kara's birthday. A link to a booking site. Another night at the opera? Clipped illustrations of other properties.

And one note headed simply *15C*. With three entries. *Missed November. Missed December. £350 deposit.* What was that? A tenant struggling with his rent? That must go with the territory. Whitby was hardly awash with summer jobs in November and December.

Just *Calendar* then.

Brady wasn't expecting much from the diary. If Patrick could keep stock market figures in his head he could certainly keep *11:00 Dentist* there as well. But no – here he was: *Breakfast – Mike*

What else for that day? *11:00 Conference call*, exactly as he'd said. *3:30 PT*. Personal trainer?

He scrolled forward. A meeting with an architect. The local council – presumably the planning department. More PT. No wonder he'd had those heat pads in the backpack.

Dinner with Kara. When would she have told him? Clearly she had to tell him at some point.

Whatever he thought about Bill he was right on that one. Not a risk anyone would want to take if they were pregnant. She must have been frantic with worry. Working out her dates four or five times a day. Brady felt a moment of sympathy for her.

He went back through the diary. The same mix of personal and professional. Except one. *Wednesday 21ˢᵗ 15C/EB.*

What was that? Something to do with Patrick's stock market trading?

No. 15C was a flat. The one where the tenant hadn't paid. Brady went back to the note he'd found.

Missed November. Missed December. £350 deposit.

So was EB the tenant who hadn't paid his rent? And where the hell was 15C? Was he going to have to walk along every street in Whitby looking for a 15C?

Quite probably. It was the only lead he had.

It was a job for a team of eager, young detectives. Not one man and his dog.

24

When he was 16 he'd thought Patrick's mother was old. But when you're 16 you think everyone over 30 is old. She must have been in her late-40s then, which meant she'd be 73 or 74 now.

But needing full-time care, Kate had told him. "Dementia. She can't be on her own any more."

It was a surprisingly modest house. A three-bed semi. Brady rang the bell. A woman in her 40s answered the door. The carer: Brady guessed there were three or four of them working in shifts.

"I've come to see, Mrs Smith."

"And who might you be then, love?"

Brady smiled at her. "I'm an old friend of Patrick's. We were at school together. I was passing. I thought I should – "

Her face clouded. "Blimey. That's a bad business. They've arrested the wife. Obvious she did it. Bad business," she said again.

"Does she know?" Brady asked.

The carer shook her head. "We told her. But she didn't take it in. You're best not mentioning it, love. Only upset her again."

He was still standing on the doorstep. "Can I come in?"

"Oh, sorry, love. I was distracted. I'm supposed to ask for some ID though if I don't know you. She's vulnerable, you know."

More security to get past...

"That's fine," Brady said. "No problem." He showed her his driving licence. Much as any competent burglar would show her a driving licence...

He was allowed into the hall. Cream walls, one of those pictures of the house taken from the air. A chair lift winding its way upstairs. A telephone on a telephone table. Yellow Pages on the shelf underneath it.

"Do you mind, love? If I pop out for five minutes? She's set her mind on some custard. Ginger pudding and custard she wants. Well, if you're alright with her – and with you being an old friend – I'll pop to the corner shop."

Brady didn't mind at all. Was five minutes long enough? That depended on Patrick's mother. And the state of her dementia.

"She's in the lounge," the carer said, "Just here. Joyce, love," she called, "You've got a visitor. A good-looking man come to see you. Don't set the neighbours gossiping, mind. He's going to take care of you for five minutes."

Brady tapped lightly on the lounge door. "Mrs Smith? Joyce?"

"Come in, love. Just come in. It takes an age to struggle to me feet."

The first thing that hit him was the photographs. Patrick. Patrick playing football, Patrick in cricket whites. And his sister. Brady rummaged around in his memory. Victoria? Vicky. And what were very evidently Vicky's children. The last he'd heard she was in New Zealand. Was she on her way back? Or was she waiting to find out when the funeral was? Not for a while, probably...

Patrick's mother was sitting on the sofa, the *Daily Express* on the table in front of her. Brady held his hand out. "You might remember me, Mrs Smith. I was a friend of Patrick's when we were growing up. Michael Brady."

She stared up at him. "You're the policeman aren't you? Patrick said you were a policeman. Are policemen allowed to have beards these days?"

"I was. I'm not now. But I am living in Whitby again. With my daughter."

"That's nice, dear. And are you and Patrick playing football this weekend? That was a nasty gash he got last week. But he said you won, so that's good."

It had been the one lesson he'd learned from his father's final months. You had to go into their world.

"Aye," he said. "We've had a grand day, your mother an' me. Out on t'bikes all day."

The nurse tried to stop him. Tell him he hadn't been out on his bike. "No," Brady said. "Leave him. He's fine. He's happy."

"Did mum keep up with you then, Dad?" he asked. "You can fair fly up them hills..."

The old man smiled. "She's a good 'un is yer mum. Never

*once complained. Even when I ate the last ham sandwich. Aye,
it were a grand day."*

*They'd talked for ten minutes. They'd been as far as Blakey
Ridge. "You should take that lass of yours up there. What's her
name?"*

"Grace, Dad."

"Aye, Grace, she's a good 'un n' all. Like your mum."

And now it was the same with Patrick's mother. There
was no point trying to drag her back into his world. She'd
only be more confused. He had to go into hers.

"Played this morning, Mrs Smith. Against Redcar. We
won 3-1. Patrick scored a cracker."

She beamed. "Did he? Mind he'll have left me a pile
of dirty kit no doubt. He's a bugger for dirty kit is that
one. When are you playing again?"

"We've a game on Wednesday. Middlesbrough."

"Well, I do the washing on Monday, so that'll be fine.
But why you play in white shorts is beyond me."

He heard the door open. Any minute now the carer
would stick her head round the door and ask if she
wanted a cup of tea. The spell would be broken.

"Mrs Smith, I hope you don't mind. I've come to ask
for some help."

"Well you're a good lad, Michael, ask away."

"My cousin's coming over for the summer. She's going
to work in Whitby. Get a summer job. But she'll need
somewhere to stay. Patrick said you might have a place.
Number 15, he mentioned. 15C he said. But he forgot to
tell me the street."

She looked puzzled. "It rings a bell, Michael. But
Patrick's dad hardly talks to me about the business."

"Maybe one of the blocks of flats he owns?" He could hear cupboard doors opening and closing in the kitchen. Whatever she'd bought, she was rapidly putting it away. A cup of tea couldn't be far away...

"Joyce?" The carer didn't put her head round the door, she just shouted from the kitchen. "Do you want a cup of tea, love? And I bought some digestives for you. And I got your custard powder."

The old lady looked at him. "What did she say?"

First his daughter, then Frankie Thomson. Now Patrick's mother.

Brady was lying to everyone he talked to.

But it was now or never.

"It's one of your tenants, Mrs Smith. Said she's come to pay her rent. 15C..."

Patrick's mother looked surprised. "That's odd, they don't come to the house to pay their rent. But I'd best take it, I suppose. 15C you said? That'll be Elmet. Patrick's dad bought it last year."

She pulled herself painfully to her feet.

Brady closed the wardrobe door. The old clothes still fitted him. Perfectly.

He reached out a hand to help her.

"Middlesbrough did you say? Smoggies, Patrick's dad calls 'em. You mind you beat them buggers."

25

Elmet Road? Avenue? Crescent? Google maps offered him three options. Street View quickly dispensed with two of them.

Brady walked along Elmet Road. Run down terraced houses, the bins kept in the front yards. A few of them chained up. A ginger cat eyed him suspiciously from a first floor window.

No. 15 had a 'for sale' sign outside it. And he was in luck, the front door was open. Brady stepped over the pile of junk mail and walked along the hall. Pale lilac wall-paper peeling away. Not a house Patrick had spent a lot of money on.

Up two flights of stairs and he was standing outside 15C. A maroon carpet with a pattern straight from a low budget hotel. Marks on the door. Two cigarette burns, a thin brown stain running from the handle to the floor.

He knocked. But even as he was knocking he knew there'd be no reply. Brady could hear the sound echoing round an empty flat. The tenant had moved out. Or been evicted. And Patrick had been keeping it that way.

He walked back down the steps. Stopped. There was music coming from 15B. He knocked on the door.

Ten seconds. Twenty seconds. It opened. But on a chain.

"Who is it?"

Brady briefly considered lying: his new default option. From the landlord? From the council? Neither of them were likely to get him what he wanted.

"My name's Michael Brady."

"Congratulations. So who sent you?"

"No-one sent me. I'm looking for the guy who was upstairs."

"He's gone."

"Yeah, I can see that. Any chance you can open the door and we can talk?"

"What's in it for me? And who the fuck are you anyway?"

Two entirely reasonable questions. Brady didn't feel like handing over a £20 note. Besides, there was no guarantee it would get the door opened.

"There's nothing in it for you. You might even have to make me a coffee. And like I said, my name's Brady. I'm a writer."

There was no reply.

15B was clearly making a decision.

The door closed. Brady heard the chain slide out of the lock rail. The door slowly, grudgingly opened.

He was 18 or 19. Hair combed forward, cut straight across the middle of his forehead. An attempt at a beard outlining a round face. Brown eyes. A grey round-necked sweatshirt. Brady thought he looked like a medieval squire.

"I figured that if you wanted to beat me up you'd have kicked the door down."

Brady nodded. "Seems like a reasonable deduction. Michael Brady," he said again, putting his hand out.

The squire tentatively shook it. "Carl," he said.

"Like I said, I'm looking for the guy who was upstairs. 15C."

"He's gone."

"You said. Any idea where?"

Carl shook his head. "Who cares?"

"You know anything about him? His name? What he did? Where I could find him?"

Carl shrugged. "His girlfriend made a lot of noise if that helps."

So it was going to take some time. No problem. Brady looked around him. He was standing in a hall. There were three doors, all half-open. Lounge/kitchen, bedroom and bathroom. Even from the hall he could understand why Patrick wanted to sell it.

"Can we talk?" Brady asked, gesturing towards the lounge.

"So who the fuck are you?" Carl said again. Brady glanced across at the kitchen area. He lost interest in coffee.

"I'm a writer. And I was Patrick's friend. Your landlord's friend."

"My dead landlord." Carl was smiling.

...And if he was smiling there was a story to tell.

Brady told himself to slow down. He'd heard musicians say it. 'If I don't practice every day I lose it.' He had to re-learn the skill. How to get the information he wanted. And the first step was to slow down.

"I was driving up to see him," Brady said. "Driving up to the hospital when I got the call."

"Yeah? I heard he was stabbed. With one of those swords the Goths carry round with them."

Brady nodded. "That's what I heard."

"Then someone told me they arrested his wife."

"Yeah, that's right."

"So why do you want the guy upstairs?"

Brady shrugged. "Patrick was my friend. We went to school together."

"So what's that got to do with the guy upstairs?"

A good question. "You going to make me a coffee?" Brady said. Risking the kitchen was the price he'd have to pay for time to think.

"Maybe. Is this going to be worth it?"

"That depends on you. Make us both a coffee. Black for me." He doubted that Carl's milk was on first name terms with its sell-by date.

So what had happened? Something that made Patrick put 15C in his diary. Something that needed sorting out. The rent not being paid. But that was in November and December. This was April.

Brady looked around him. Two chairs, the stuffing coming out of one of them. A table pushed up against the wall. Damp patch on the ceiling.

There were two pictures on the wall. Drawings done in pencil on the sort of paper that comes in a Ryman's sketch pad. Fastened onto the wall with four strips of adhesive tape. They were in pencil, the sea merging into the sky. Shades of grey on a stormy day. You could see the rain on the horizon.

Brady stood up. Looked closer. You couldn't see where the sky became the sea. Take a step back and you could.

Grace had always dragged him into art galleries. He'd seen far worse pictures next to a small card with a large price tag.

Carl was back with the coffee. "Did you do those?" Brady asked.

"Yeah. That one." He pointed at the sea merging into the sky. "Sat up on West Cliff all day. Just me and Captain Cook. And even the statue was freezing its bollocks off."

"Is that how you support yourself?"

Carl shook his head. "Not really. Getting started. It's hard. Every third person in Whitby thinks he's a fucking artist."

"So what do you do?"

"A bit of work down on the seafront. You know, summer jobs. And then..."

He didn't finish the sentence. He didn't need to. Brady had met enough part-time drug dealers. It was the trainers. Always the ridiculously expensive trainers that gave them away. Carl's were black and grey, half way between trainers and basketball boots, intricately patterned, dark blue studs coming out of the toecaps.

Brady sipped his coffee.

"That's really good," he said.

"The coffee? It's Nescafé. Fuck me, you've led a sheltered life."

Brady laughed. "The drawing. You should take it seriously. Go to art school or something."

Carl shook his head. "I don't do that crap. Lessons. Someone telling you what to do. Home, school, I've never been able to do it."

"So you get by..."

"What else is there in Whitby? Gutting fish for a living? Zero hours contract at Sports Direct?"

"I need you to help me," Brady said. If he wasn't going to get the story now he was never going to get it.

"Why?" Carl was back on the defensive.

"Because we can do this in one of two ways – "

"I thought you were a writer?"

"I am," Brady said. "But..."

It was time for good cop/bad cop. The first time he'd played both parts.

"I used to be a detective. It's obvious how you earn your money."

He'd expected some reaction from Carl. The standard response – 'Prove it' – at least. Instead Carl sipped his coffee and said nothing.

"So I can phone the police..."

Carl raised his eyebrows. He still didn't say anything. Didn't look remotely concerned. Brady would have left him sweating in the interview room for ten minutes. But if he left the flat now he'd never get back in.

"...Or I can be a customer." Brady nodded at the wall. "For that one."

"How much?" Carl said. "Factor in a day freezing to death on West Cliff."

"Thirty quid," Brady said. "The drawing and the story."

Carl laughed. "You see? That's why I don't take it seriously. There's six hours' work in that."

Brady nodded. "Yeah, you're right. But you're not David bloody Hockney. Not yet anyway. So tell me what happened. Sign the drawing and I'll give you a hundred quid."

"Hundred and fifty."

"Twenty."

Carl walked across to the wall and carefully unfastened the adhesive tape. "Your mate came round," he said, still with his back to Brady. "Two or three weeks ago. There's a lot of shouting. You know. You're-moving-out type of shouting."

Brady counted out six £20 notes. "Anything else?"

"Yeah. He banged on my door. Told me the house was for sale. Said he wouldn't be renewing the lease."

"What did you say?"

"I said there was three months to go." Carl turned with the picture in his hand. He smiled. "But doesn't look like I need to worry now, does it?"

"Don't forget to sign it," Brady said.

Carl walked over to the table, picked a pencil out of a pot that held half a dozen and signed the picture.

Brady watched him twist the paper round to an angle. "Left-handed," he said. "My daughter's left-handed."

"Yeah," Carl said. "Durer, Escher, Paul Klee. Even Michelangelo. She's in good company."

"Here," Brady said, handing the money over. "And sort yourself out. You've got one life. Don't waste it."

"Writer. Detective. What are you now? Bloody life coach?"

"Friend," Brady said.

He lightly rolled the drawing into a tube. Held it carefully in his left hand. "And thanks," he added.

"Kilby," Carl said. "Kirby. The guy upstairs. Something like that. Like I said, his girlfriend made a lot of noise. And he stank of fish."

26

Kilby? Kirby? Could it be Bilby? Burby?

Brady couldn't think that he'd ever come across anyone called Bilby or Burby. Was Burby even a surname? Yes, according to Google. Someone who 'lived at the brook or the valley of the burg.'

Wherever they lived, it wasn't 15C Elmet Road.

He drop-kicked the ball and watched Archie make a complete hash of the catch. "Come on, Archie. You're supposed to catch it, not head it," Brady shouted across the beach.

He clipped Archie's lead on and walked up the slipway. No chatting to Dave this morning. Time to get back to the book. Besides, Dave was busy, serving breakfast to a scrum of elderly walkers. "Morning," Brady shouted, more out of politeness than any expectation he'd be heard.

He glanced across the road.

'You're supposed to catch it, not head it.'

And you're supposed to be a detective. Or at least someone who might once have passed for a detective.

15C/EB. He'd found 15C. He hadn't even needed to look for EB. He stared at the amusement arcade.

'A bit of work down on the seafront. You know, summer jobs.'

Enzo Barella.

THERE WAS no point wasting time. Phone and Enzo would be busy for the next fortnight. Then his horse would be running. Then it would be his children's Sports Day. The middle of the summer season...

But he'd have to wait. For a few hours at least. Give himself the best chance.

There'd always been a quiet time. When the holiday-makers booked in for 'Bed & Breakfast & Evening Meal' were eating meat pie, chips and peas. When the day-trippers were heading home. Luca had always been in the office. Sorting out the change. Checking the staff. Making sure everything was ready for the evening.

Let's hope Enzo's the same.

Brady parked the car, walked down to the sea front, passed the filleting sheds on the pier and reached the arcade.

Just gone 6:00. A few people playing on the machines. A cleaner idly dusting and polishing something called a Sega Storm Rider. A bank of ridiculously complicated fruit machines along the back wall. The bingo – where he'd spent two summers giving out change, calling the numbers and chatting up girls from the West Riding – long gone.

There was a girl sitting in the change booth. A mechanic – the inevitable chain of keys round his neck – was talking to her. Even from ten yards away it was obvious she'd rather be reading her book.

"Evening," Brady said. He wasn't sure which one he should be speaking to. "I've come to see Enzo." He compromised and spoke into the gap between them.

The girl answered. "Is he expecting you?"

Brady shook his head. "I'm an old friend of his dad's. Michael Brady."

"Hang on." She picked a phone up.

Brady had – again – considered lying. Enzo would be in the office. They'd phone up to him. 'I've got a horse with the same trainer. I was just passing' would get him up the stairs. But that would be the end of it.

He needed to talk to Enzo. The only way to do that was to tell the truth.

The girl put the phone down. "He says you can have five minutes. Out of the arcade, turn right. There's an alley at the end of the building. Go up the steps."

"I know," Brady said. "I used to work here."

He'd been sent up to see Enzo's dad. They'd run out of change on the bingo. Like every 16 year old in Whitby he was convinced Luca Barella was a Mafia godfather. Nervous didn't begin to describe it.

The top half of a stable door swung open. He had a glimpse of a table, one half of it covered in bundles of notes. Then he was being handed two bags of cash. 'Barclays £5' was stencilled on one of them.

"Michael, isn't it?" Luca had said.

"Yes, that's right."

"Good lad. Busy down there?"

He'd nodded. "Yeah. Really busy."

"Better run then. And Michael..."

"Yes?"

"They know how much is in the bags. Don't get any ideas." Then the Mafia godfather winked at him. *"But you're too clever for that."*

Twenty-five years had passed. He'd seen Luca a few times when he'd been back from university. Been invited up to the office for a Christmas glass of wine. Shared his plans, his ambitions with him.

Now he was knocking on the stable door again. A girl answered it. About Carl's age. She could have been his sister. Long, brown hair that hadn't been washed for a few days. A black top, low cut with thin straps. Rings on three of her fingers.

"I've come to see Enzo."

"Yeah, he's in the back. Two minutes he says." She made no move to open the door. Brady stood and waited. Looked back down the alley and across the harbour. Wondered what the hell he was doing. 'Leave it. Go home and write the book,' a small voice said.

He heard a door open and close. Enzo's voice. "OK, Chloe," he said. "You can run along now, love."

Chloe opened the door. Brady stood aside to let her pass. Pale blue jeans, ripped at the knees. Flat black shoes.

"What can I do for you?" Enzo said as Brady walked into the office. His hair was wet. He needed a shave. His perfect designer stubble wasn't perfect any more. Brady caught a glimpse of himself in a mirror. Not that he could talk.

He looked around. A bank of screens showing different parts of the arcade. One of them showing the alley outside. Two of them turned off. Maybe the same table his father had used. A bottle of whisky, Glenkinchie. Two glasses, a machine for counting banknotes.

A blown-up photograph of a racehorse dominated one wall. A beaming Enzo was leading the horse in. The jockey was wearing green and white diamonds, a red cap.

"You took your colours from the Italian flag then?" Brady had decided to ignore Enzo's question.

"Yeah. Haydock last year. The bookies are still squealing."

"Your first winner?"

"Fifth. But you're not here to talk about horse racing. And like Sharon said, five minutes."

No, 'I've given my dad your regards' then. Fair enough. There was no need for subtlety.

"Patrick's dead," Brady said. "You know his wife's been arrested. I don't think she did it."

"You're a fool then. Everyone could see she was only after his money. Won't be much use to her in Low Grange."

Brady raised his eyebrows. "Is that where she is then?"

"Fuck sake, I thought you were a shit-hot detective?"

I was. And I know about Her Majesty's Prison Low Grange as well. But I didn't know Kara was there. And it can't be common knowledge...

"So what do you want from me?" Enzo said.

Enzo clearly thought he was an idiot. There was no need to change that view. "I just want to understand," Brady said. "Patrick was my friend."

"Yeah well, you know what they say. We don't know the people we think we know best. Your friend was a complete shit. Wrecked my sister's life. Drove her to drink. God knows what else. Then fucks off to Spain and comes back with that slut on his arm."

"Did you ever do any business with him?" Brady asked. "When – you know, when you were his brother-in-law?"

"It's no business of yours, but 'no' is the answer. I put a couple of property deals to him. He was too stupid to see the potential."

Brady doubted that, but he didn't reply. "When was the last time you saw him? To speak to?"

"When I saw him that morning with you."

"Before that?"

Enzo stared at him. "You're an irritating prick, I'll grant you that. Months ago. I haven't got a clue. And your five minutes is up. I've got a meeting. With someone who knows what the fuck he's talking about."

Brady held his hand out. "Thanks. Maybe we'll talk again."

Enzo shook it reluctantly without making eye contact. "I doubt it," he said.

Brady lifted the latch on the door and stepped out. He'd taken two steps when someone turned into the alley at the bottom.

A casual brown jacket, cream shirt. He took the steps up to the office two at a time.

"Good evening," Brady said, moving to the side to let him past.

The man looked up. A square, Slavic face. Close-cropped blonde hair. His nose clearly broken and reset. If your football club smashed its transfer record to sign a defender, that was the face you wanted to see on the back page. One that didn't take any prisoners. One that didn't even consider taking prisoners.

He flicked his eyes up and down Brady. Dismissed him. "If you say so." A broad Scottish accent.

He was past. Brady started down the steps. He heard the knock on the stable door. Just one.

The door opened instantly.

27

"Come on, mate," Brady said as they walked up the slipway and off the beach the next morning. "We owe someone an apology."

"Morning, Mr Brady," Dave said. "And good to see you. We've not fallen out then?"

Brady grinned. "No. And I'm sorry. You were right. You said I had to do something. I am doing something. At least I hope I am."

"So we'll celebrate with the usual then? And one for the boss?"

"Yes for me. And yes please if you've got a spare one. Archie's hooked. You've trained him. Like one of Pavlov's dogs. He comes off the beach, he starts salivating for a leftover sausage."

Dave turned his attention to the griddle. "So how's it going?" he asked over his shoulder.

"What? Life in general? The book?"

"You know what I'm talking about."

"OK, then. I've annoyed Enzo. And I've got one clue. The smell of fish."

Dave laughed. "It's not quite Agatha Christie is it? *Murder on the Orient Express. Death on the Nile. Fish on the Seafront.* I don't see Poirot being too excited by the smell of fish."

"It's all I've got."

"Fair enough. And here you go." Dave handed him his bacon sandwich. Then he leaned over the counter and tossed a sausage to Archie. It never came close to touching the ground. "Sorry," he said. "Thought I'd cut out the middleman."

"It's a bloody mess," Brady said between mouthfuls.

"What is?"

"The case. Patrick's wife being arrested."

He realised that he needed to talk. That if he was going to make any progress he had to go back to how he'd always done it. Stand in front of a roomful of coppers and talk to them.

But in reality, talk to himself. Work through his ideas as he was speaking.

He didn't have a roomful of coppers.

But he did have Dave.

"It's still May isn't it?" Brady said.

Dave look confused. "Of course it's May, you daft bugger."

"So I can talk to you for five minutes?"

Dave nodded. He seemed to understand what Brady needed to do.

"So it's a mess. Patrick's wife is arrested. She's got motive, she's got opportunity. But you know the main reason she's been arrested? Bill Calvert's decided she's done it. And of course she's covered in blood. Patrick's just been stabbed. It'd be more suspicious if she *wasn't* covered in blood."

"So she's innocent?" Dave said.

"Yes, despite what she's - " Despite nothing, Brady said to himself. What Kara had done in London could stay in London. He wasn't going to stain Patrick's memory with it. Time enough for the rumour mill to do that.

"Whatever Bill thinks, she didn't do it. I'm not even sure it would come to trial. There's no murder weapon. No witnesses."

"No witnesses you *know* about."

Brady nodded. He could still see Bill laughing at him. That wouldn't happen again.

Were there any witnesses? No. Because Bill was a boasting drunk. Because he would have told him. Hinted at it. Rubbed more salt in the wounds.

"Even if it did come to trial," Brady said. "Any half-competent QC would drive a coach and horses through Bill's case. So she's found not guilty."

"Except in the local gossip..."

Exactly. Wherever Kara's future was, it wasn't in Whitby.

"You're right," Brady said. "But even if she is found guilty she appeals."

And maybe she wins and maybe she loses. And what do you do then? Patrick's dead, the wrong person's convicted. And she's giving birth in jail.

"Are you alright with this?" he said.

Dave nodded. "Aye. Catch a murderer or do the cross-word? Same choice I make every morning."

Brady laughed. "One across," he said. "Person you think did it. Seven letters."

"Easy," Dave said. "Not Kara."

"Very good. But that's three, four. You can't cheat."

Brady looked out across the harbour. The swing bridge to his right. St Hilda's Church and the Abbey up on the hill. The pier, then the open sea, the early morning sun bouncing and sparkling across the water.

And somewhere inside himself he recognised a feeling. Not happiness. That was a long way off. Years, maybe.

But a familiar feeling. A good feeling.

Work.

The right sort of work. Not goading a whisky-soaked Bill Calvert. But slow, painstaking, methodical work. Work that made him feel secure again. That he recognised – and wrapped around himself. A comfort blanket.

Back in his old clothes. And now they felt good.

"Alright," Dave said. "If Kara didn't do it, who did do it?"

"Not 'who,'" Brady said. "How? We work out how, then who is going to be a lot easier."

"I don't follow you..."

"OK. We rule out Kara. We rule out mistaken identity. So someone wanted to kill Patrick."

"Why?"

"Good question, Hercule. I'm coming to that. But put yourself in the killer's shoes. It's Saturday night. If you want to murder someone Saturday night of the Goth weekend is Christmas and your birthday rolled into one. He's dressed like a Victorian gentleman. Maybe you are as well. But *whatever* you're wearing, so are a hundred other people. But you're the only one following Patrick round Whitby, waiting for your chance."

"Morning. What'll it be?" Dave broke off to serve two fishermen.

The same two as last week? Brady wasn't sure. He was out of practice. Had stopped looking in that way. Asking questions, looking, *really* looking.

He'd seen the aprons, the water still dripping off them. Seen what was easiest to see.

And that's what Bill had done. Seen Kara. Seen an obvious suspect. Seen 'case closed' stamped on the file.

"So he's following them round Whitby," Dave said. "Supposing his chance doesn't come?"

"He waits. But it does come. And I've walked up Church Street. Down the steps, across the beach. The route he took. He had plenty of time. And he sees Patrick and Kara go into the alley. Thinks one of them isn't feeling well."

"Or needs a pee."

"Come on, Dave. When was the last time you had a piss behind a tree? You didn't invite your wife to watch."

Dave laughed out loud. "How do you know what my wife's into? She's from Sunderland. You've no idea…"

"Ugh. There's an image I won't be able to get out of my head. Stop distracting me. You're the killer. This is your chance. What happens if someone's throwing up?"

"They bend over."

"Right. And the person with them puts his hand on

their back and says, 'Are you OK?' They're both distracted."

"So the killer walks down the alley after them?"

Brady shook his head. "No. Too many possible witnesses. Maybe there's CCTV. He's done his homework. He knows Whitby's full of alleys. If there's one going down to the harbour there'll be another one. That's what I did. Walked up Church Street. Found an alley. Steps going down. More steps down to the beach. He runs across the beach. And he comes up the steps behind them."

"Supposing he misses them? Supposing they've gone?"

"He's not on his own. He has someone watching the front of the alley while he runs round the back."

"And you reckon that's what he did?"

Brady nodded. "It took me two-and-a-half minutes. Like I said, plenty of time."

"Bloody hell," Dave said.

'Bloody hell' was right. 'Bloody hell' meant that whoever murdered Patrick had done his homework. Been prepared to wait. Been cold, calculating and ruthless. That he'd found Patrick alone. Defenceless. His back turned. And he hadn't hesitated.

"Hang on," Dave said. "If he goes on the beach he'll have left footprints."

"Yeah, you're right," Brady said. "And do you think Bill Calvert thought of that in all the excitement of Saturday night? The killer knew he could take the risk. And now they're long gone."

Brady could see it. The tide coming in, the footprints

disappearing. Like lovers' names in the sand: washed away by the first wave.

"So where do you go from here?" Dave said.

Brady shrugged. "The only place I can go. Following the smell of fish."

28

Or maybe not. There was a letter waiting for him at home. And five minutes later Brady was on the phone.

"HMP Low Grange..."

"Good morning. I've just had a visitor request – sorry, visitor order – in the post. One of your - " Brady didn't want to use the word 'prisoner.' Or 'inmate.'

"Someone wants to see me," he said.

"Name?"

"Kara Smith. She's on remand."

"So that'll be tomorrow. Can you get here tomorrow?"

If Ash will go to Bean's after school... "Yes, I can."

"Visits are at 1:45. Until 3:45. And your name is?"

"Brady. Michael Brady."

"We'll see you tomorrow then, Mr Brady. Do you know where we are?"

"Don't worry," Brady said. "I'll find you."

HE HATED PRISONS.

He hated heights, he hated deep water and he hated prisons.

He hated the clanging gates. The sense of finality when you heard a door lock behind you. He hated being searched, the forced smiles of welcome.

But they'd been a part of his life. A necessary evil. And one he thought he'd left behind.

He sat in his car outside Her Majesty's Prison and Young Offenders Institution Low Grange. It was a depressing, red brick building. Kara had drawn the short straw. He'd once been to interview a woman in Foston Hall, a former stately home nestling in the Derbyshire countryside.

Kara was on remand in the County Durham drizzle.

The next village along the road was called Pity Me.

This was his last chance. What had he achieved so far? Nothing. Bill had laughed at him, Enzo had insulted him. But there was still time to go back.

And there was high tide.

Go home, take a hammer to the Chromebook, put the pieces in a sack, add a couple of stones for luck and wait for high tide. Safely into the harbour, never to be seen again.

But then he'd have to live with the memory of Bill laughing at him. Of Enzo insulting him. Of both of them thinking he was a fool. Of Dave saying, "What are you going to do about it?"

Kara had stabbed Patrick in the back. Metaphorically in London. Maybe literally in Whitby. Let her deal with the consequences.

He could see the sack hitting the water.

It won't wait. It won't linger on the surface for a few

seconds before it decides to sink. The stones will take it straight down. Straight to the bottom of the harbour. Gone for good. Like the Chromebook never existed. Go home, make a coffee, finally – finally – get serious about the book.

Brady opened the car door and stepped out. The drizzle had turned to rain. He skirted the puddles in the car park, walked across to the visitor centre. Booked himself in, proved his ID with his driving licence.

Just a normal member of the public.

Submitted himself to the search. Stood still while a golden Labrador sniffed him suspiciously. "I've got a Springer," he explained. "He can probably smell dog biscuits."

Brady was shown into the visit hall. The packed visit hall. Maybe a dozen other prisoners, most of them with their mothers and children. Husbands and boyfriends were in short supply.

He looked around. Red, blue and green chairs. Art on the walls. Prisoners' art. Their children's art. A lot of hopeful rainbows.

And motivational posters. Was there a special category of motivational posters for prisons?

Hardships often prepare ordinary people for extraordinary destinies

What I learn today doesn't make yesterday wrong. It makes tomorrow better

But it was the smell. The smell hit him like something solid. He'd thought Dave's bacon sandwiches scrapping it out with the fish and diesel had been spectacular. This was in a different league.

Twelve different perfumes fighting each other. Overlaid with chips. And more chips, straight from the canteen.

Chemical warfare? Here's your winner, ladies and gentlemen.

The tables were widely spaced, a prison officer weaving her way between them. Three others stationed around the room. Brady guessed there was another one watching on video.

Kara was at a table on her own. She looked surprisingly well.

Or maybe she didn't. He hadn't known what to expect. She was wearing faded jeans, a navy blue hoodie. Her hair was tied back in a ponytail. Was she wearing make up? Some. But no jewellery.

"Thank you for coming," she said.

"No problem. Are you alright?"

"Well, I'm in prison. I've been charged with a crime I didn't commit. Patrick is dead. I've been accused of the murder. But if you mean has the prison dyke trapped me in the showers yet, then I'm alright. And no-one's made me wear an orange jumpsuit."

"How are you coping? Mentally?"

She shrugged. "I'm OK. My dad was in the army. We moved around a lot. I was at a girls' boarding school for two years. It's not that different. We don't play hockey every day. Otherwise..."

"Your room's OK?"

"I'm in the remand wing. The expensive rooms. And thank you again for coming."

She moved her hands forward. Brady thought for a moment she was going to take his hand in hers. "I wanted to see a friendly face. Someone who's on my side. Tell me you're making some progress, Michael."

Yes, plenty. I've tampered with evidence, I've tricked an old lady with dementia, I've bought a picture off a drug dealer and I've managed to convince most of Whitby that I'm an interfering idiot.

He nodded. "Some progress," he said. "It takes time. And it's hard without... Without the back-up I used to have." He didn't want to get her hopes up. "Have you seen the solicitor?"

She nodded. "But he's talking about the trial. About my defence. About witnesses. About what I should wear in court. About how being pregnant will win me some sympathy."

Brady sighed. He was getting less patient as he got older. This wasn't going anywhere. There was no point wasting time.

"So you still want me to help you?"

She looked confused. "Yes. Of course. Why would I change my mind?"

He took a deep breath. "Look, Kara, you sat in my kitchen. 'Tell the truth,' I said to you. I can help, but if you lie to me we're both screwed. Words to that effect."

She nodded. Looked straight into his eyes. "I know. I have told you the truth."

He resisted the urge to stand up. To say very loudly and very clearly that it was tell the truth or go to trial. Tell the truth or face the possibility of not being in the remand wing.

"Who's the father?" he said quietly.

For a minute Brady thought she was going to cry. But

she was tougher than that. Quick to compose herself. He reluctantly found he had a grudging admiration for her.

"What do you mean 'who's the father?' What are you talking about?"

"I know what happened in London."

"Right."

She sat back in her chair. "So Calvert told you. So much for police confidentiality. Yes, that's what happened."

"So you had sex with him? Whoever it was."

"Sam - "

Brady held his hand up. "Don't. I don't want to know. Don't need to know. Is he the father?"

Kara shook her head. "No. I'm almost certain."

"*Almost* certain?"

"The time of the month."

Was there a test they could do? They'd had one child. Grace had found the first two months difficult, sailed through the next five and been completely fed up from 7½ months onwards. In the last month she'd slept sitting up and Brady had slept in the spare room. But the delivery was mercifully uncomplicated, Ash was perfect and that was the last he'd thought about pregnancy.

Was there a test you could do? And even if there was, what the hell did you say to your husband?

'Can I just swab the inside of your cheek, darling? Oh, no reason. There's nothing on TV, I thought it would be something to do.'

Bill Calvert didn't get many things right but he was right about that. It was a hell of a risk to take.

"What were you planning to do?'

"I was certain," she said.

She didn't say it with 100% conviction. Brady trans-lated it as 'hope for the best.'

"Look," he said. "From now on you have to tell me the truth. I don't like what you did – and that's putting it mildly – but right now it's irrelevant. I want to know who killed Patrick. But I'm not going to be in a position where my brother-in-law is laughing at me again."

"I understand."

"Good. Because I'm all that stands between you and the Crown Court. So let's start again. Can you think of anyone who wanted to kill Patrick?"

It was the most basic of basic police questions. And in Brady's view, pointless. He'd learned it from bitter experi-ence. One man's mild irritation was another man's motive for murder.

She shook her head. "Patrick didn't talk to me about the business. I told you that. And he didn't mix work and home. When he shut his office door that was that. But - " she said.

"But what?"

"We got some packages pushed through the letterbox."

"What was in them?" Brady could guess, but Kara may as well confirm it.

"Shit in the first one," Kara said.

"So we can rule out Amazon."

She smiled. The first time she'd smiled that afternoon.

Brady didn't attach much importance to it. People

who planned cold blooded murders were not people who pushed a jiffy bag of shit through your letterbox.

"What about the others?"

"There was only one more. Rotting fish. We were both out. It was on the doormat all day. Took us about a week to get rid of the smell."

"Did Patrick go to the police?"

She shook her head. "He said he didn't want the paperwork. And the hassle. And what would they do? Tell him to put a camera up. So that's what he did."

A bell rang. Time was up. The end of the perfume wars.

There was a lot of hurried hugging and kissing. 'Mummy loves you.' 'You be good for Nana.'

Brady stood up. "OK," he said. "I'll do my best."

"Thank you," she said, holding her hand out. They shook hands. Formally, awkwardly.

"Hey, Kara!"

Brady looked across. A prisoner at another table. Older, harder. Bleached blonde hair. "Nice one, sweetheart. Send him down the corridor when you're done with him."

She blew Brady a kiss. "And keep the beard, handsome..."

29

He had a name. Half a name. He had the smell of fish. Nothing else.

Brady was back at 15C. He needed more. More information about Kirby. Or Kilby. Or whatever the last occupant of 15C was called. He'd been a tenant, Patrick had thrown him out, he'd smelled of fish, a jiffy bag full of fish had come through the letterbox. It was probably no more than a coincidence. But it was all he had.

He walked up the stairs. Nothing had changed. The door of no. 15 was still open. There was still a pile of junk mail on the mat. The lilac wallpaper was still peeling.

Brady was surprised to see Carl's front door open. Music again. Louder this time. It was Pink Floyd. *Comfortably Numb*. A flatmate at university had persuaded Brady to listen to them. Grace hadn't been a fan.

He walked up the extra flight to 15C. Might as well check. But it was the same carpet, the same stains on the door, the same knocks still echoing round an empty flat.

"Carl?" Brady knocked lightly on his door. There was

no reply. Now Pink Floyd were insisting that *The Show Must Go On.*

"Carl? Are you in there? It's Brady. The art collector."

Still no reply. Brady pushed the door open. "Carl! Answer me. It's Brady."

He walked into the lounge. Pink Floyd were significantly louder. Just as well upstairs was empty. They'd have been running down to complain.

Carl's phone was on the table. Resting on a cradle between two circular, grey speakers. Brady took three steps and turned it off. David Gilmour fell silent.

He heard the moans.

Carl was in the bedroom.

A pile of dirty clothes in the corner. Double bed. Pale blue quilt. Bloodstains.

And Carl. On the floor. Slumped against the bed. His back towards Brady. Even from this angle holding his right arm awkwardly.

Brady bent down. Knew better than to move him. "Carl? It's Brady."

Carl moaned again. Brady could see the side of his head. More blood. An ominous cut over his left eye.

"Who did this to you?"

Carl shook his head. Or did his best to shake his head.

Brady's choice was simple. Phone for an ambulance. Which gave him five, maybe ten minutes to find out what had happened.

Or take care of Carl himself. Which gave him plenty of time. Unless he had to take him to hospital.

Carl was shivering. Almost certainly from shock. And

panting. So he was in a lot of pain. And Brady had no choice at all. He stood up. Pulled the phone out of his pocket. Dialled 9 9 9.

He bent down again. "Carl. I'm not going to move you. The paramedics will be here soon. Just tell me what happened."

Carl finally spoke. "Nothing," he whispered. "Nothing happened. Fuck off."

"Come on, Carl. Tell me." But it was the answer he'd expected. Brady stood up. Looked around for a blanket. Didn't see one. Went into the bathroom and came back with two paper-thin towels. Draped them over Carl's shoulders. Went into the kitchen, found a glass, filled it with water.

"Here, Carl. Try and take a sip of this."

Carl did his best. Turned his head slightly. Gave Brady a better view of the cut over his eye. The blood dripping steadily down onto the floor.

There was a noise on the stairs. A knock on the door. "Hello?" a voice called.

"In here," Brady replied.

A woman in a green uniform walked in. Straight off the set of *Holby City*. One of those faces that was severe and kind at the same time. The auntie that came twice a year and tutted at the state of your bedroom but loved you really. Grey eyes, dark hair just betraying the first signs of grey. She looked vaguely familiar.

And she had enough equipment to fit out a small hospital.

"Hi, I'm Louise." She gestured at someone following

her in. "This is Jamie." Fresh faced, early 20s, a slightly chubby face, eager to please.

"So what's happened here?" Louise said.

"He's had a visitor."

Louise raised her eyebrows. "Clearly not his best friend. What's his name?"

"Carl."

"And you are?"

"Brady. Michael Brady."

"OK, give me some space, Mr Brady." He moved out of the way. Louise bent down. "Carl, can you hear me? My name's Louise. I'm going to sort you out. Let's have a look here..."

She pulled the towels off and threw them on the bed. Pulled gently on Carl's shoulder. Carl moaned as she moved him. "Hurts ... hurts ... leave me alone."

"I'm sorry, love. I just need to see what the damage is." She pulled again. "Come on, Carl, let's see your face..."

She turned. Spoke over her shoulder. "Jamie, get down here. Try and support his weight as I turn him round."

There was barely room. Brady watched Jamie come to terms with kneeling on Carl's discarded boxers. "Come on, love, let's just turn you round..."

"Oh. Oh... fuck. Fuck. Stop it..."

But between them they finally had Carl propped against the bed. Brady looked at his face. An ugly gash over his left eye. A huge swelling on the right side of his face. And his nose: definitely, decisively, broken.

Carl was still shivering. Still panting quickly. Shock and pain. Partners in crime. Or in the aftermath of crime.

"Carl," Louise said. "Tell me what happened. Who did this to you?"

What did they call it? ABC? Airways, breathing, circulation. Carl could talk, so his airways were clear. He was breathing – erratically, but he was breathing. Blood was still dripping onto the carpet: his circulation was working.

"Who did this to you?" Louise said again.

Was he concussed? Had he suffered any brain damage? And in the circumstances, 'who did this?' was a lot more relevant than, 'Who's the Prime Minister?'

Carl didn't reply.

"Carl? Who did this to you?"

"No-one," Carl whispered. "I fell over."

Louise turned to Brady, a look of resignation on her face. "I don't suppose you know anything?"

Yes. I know this wasn't an argument about drugs. It's punishment. And it's a warning. And not just to Carl...

"I don't," he said. "He draws..." Brady gestured round the apartment. "I bought one of them. Came back for another one to go with it."

Resignation gave way to scepticism. A senior paramedic has seen a lot of policemen. It wasn't hard to recognise another one.

"Jamie," she said. "Get some details from Mr Brady, will you? And pass me the oxygen."

Jamie handed her an oxygen mask. Turned his eager-to-please face to Brady. "What's his name?"

"Carl ... Robinson, I think." The signature on the drawing hadn't been clear. 'Robinson' had been Brady's best guess.

"Do you know his date of birth? His GP?"

Brady shook his head. "I'm sorry."

"So you won't know if he had any allergies?"

He glanced down at Carl's face. The cut over his eye, Louise trying to stem the bleeding.

Yes. Men who wear rings on their right hand. Or come with knuckle dusters...

"No, I don't," he said.

"Ohhh... Oh. Fuck." Carl had moved. Fallen over to his left. For the first time his right hand was visible. It was swollen to twice its normal size. Blood seeped out of a deep cut on the back of it. But it was the fingers. The middle finger. Crushed. Bent at an obscene angle.

Louise didn't even touch it. "Ouch," she said. "Go and get the stair chair, Jamie. And be quick."

She turned back to Carl. "Carl, this is serious. We'll have to inform the police."

Carl managed to shake his head. "No," he said. "No police. I tripped over. I fell."

Brady looked down at him. The bruises. The bleeding, the broken hand. But the real damage was inside. Carl was several steps beyond terrified.

LOUISE AND JAMIE managed to get Carl into the chair. He'd offered to help. "No," Louise had said. "One, we know what we're doing. Two, we're professionals. We get paid to have bad backs."

Now Carl was in the ambulance. Jamie was driving.

"Are you going to come with us?" Louise said.

"No, I'll drive down tonight. You're taking him to Scarborough?"

She nodded.

"I'll lock his flat," Brady said. "And see if I can find any details. Any family. And thank you," he added.

Louise nodded at him. Then she climbed into the ambulance. Jamie had already started the blue light.

Brady walked back into the house.

'I don't do that crap. Lessons. Someone telling you what to do. Home, school, I've never been able to do it.'

He knew he wouldn't find anything. Carl had left home as soon as he could.

Brady looked at Carl's front door. No marks. No-one had broken the lock.

For the second time Brady could see what happened.

A knock on the door. Carl opens it. Cautiously, like he always does. But it's someone he knows. He takes the chain off.

The man steps inside.

Carl would have had his back to him. Walking into the lounge.

He says his name. 'Carl, see this...' Carl half turns. One punch to the head – the gash above his eye – and Carl is on the floor. There's no damage to the flat. This isn't a tables-turned-over-lampshade-smashed fight.

It's not even a fight.

Two more punches. The last one breaks his nose. Then he kneels over Carl. Takes hold of the front of his hoodie. Pulls his face up. Gives some short, simple instructions.

Then he stands up. Almost certainly kicks him. Matching broken ribs. Bends down again. Maybe one knee on Carl's chest. As if the pain needs increasing. Repeats the instructions. Describes what will happen if they're not followed.

Time to go. He stands up. Looks around the room. Sees the drawings. Maybe he works out that Carl sells them. Maybe he already knows. Maybe he thinks Carl just likes drawing.

So there's one final act. Vindictive. Not part of his instructions. For his own pleasure.

He stamps down hard on Carl's right hand. The heel of his shoe.

Brady can hear the bones crack.

He leaves the door open. He wants Carl found. Maybe Carl can crawl onto the landing. Maybe he can lie there until 15A comes home.

He doesn't. Somehow, Carl crawls to the bedroom. Feels the pain. Feels the blood running down his face.

Knows the damage to his hand is serious. And knows he got lucky.

He draws with his left hand.

BRADY DROPPED the latch and closed the door. He'd found a key in the kitchen. He'd give it to one of the nurses. He glanced at his watch. Just time to get to school and collect Ash. Then he'd drive to the hospital.

He walked down the stairs and into the hall. What was it with flats? It was the same every time. The unopened pile of post in the hall.

He stopped. Shook his head sadly.

How in God's name did I ever manage to arrest anyone?

A dozen letters. He bent down and picked them up.

Leaflets for the town council elections. Three from a

particularly enthusiastic Green candidate. A bank statement for Miss Theresa Sawyer. A charity letter for Ms T Sawyer. Another one. Teresa Sawyer this time...

Mr C Robinson. So it had been Robinson. At least he'd know who to ask for at the hospital. Two to go. Now it was Mrs T Sawyer. Congratulations on your marriage, Theresa. Or Teresa.

Brady looked at the last letter. And finally had what he wanted.

Mr D Kidby.

Kirby, Kilby, Kidby. It was more than close enough.

Mr D Kidby, 15C Elmet Road. And he smelt of fish. Brady smiled. He was almost there.

What was it Sherlock Holmes had said? 'You're a doctor. And a military man. So you're an army doctor. And you've just been injured. Where could you get injured? Afghanistan. So you're just back from Afghanistan, Dr Watson.'

A Study in Scarlet. Brady had been given a Sherlock Holmes book as a school prize when he was 12 or 13. Maybe that's what planted the seed. By the time he was 15 his mind was made up. He was going to be a detective.

And Holmes was right. Sometimes it *was* elementary. And straightforward. Just like Bill Calvert had said. Occam's Razor, 'some bloody monk.'

Who smelled of fish? Someone who worked with fish all day. Where did you find fish? On the fish pier. In fish and chip shops. On fishing boats. Despite Dave's analysis – 'half the buggers in Whitby smell of fish' – there couldn't be that many. And there'd only be one called Kidby.

It was the ideal job for a keen, eager new recruit. One of the young lads in Manchester would have been perfect. 'I want you to walk along the sea front – start with the fish pier – see if you can find someone called Kidby.'

How old would he be? Not much more than 30. So he was born in 1985. What were parents calling their baby boys then? David, Daniel, Darren. Surely Derek and Donald had gone out of fashion? Dustin? Too American.

'You got a first name, Guv?'

'Probably called Dave. Maybe Dan or Danny. Daz if he's called Darren.'

But the young lads in Manchester were 120 miles away. There was only one candidate for 'keen, eager new recruit.'

And he'd be starting work in the morning.

30

He drove home and fed Archie. "I'm sorry, pal. Got to go out again. I'll make it up to you, I promise."

He climbed into the car. Out of town, past Sainsbury's – Ash had said they needed something. He'd forgotten what – and he was on the Scarborough road.

And five minutes later he was there.

How many times had he driven past the scene? No more than three or four in the last 20 years.

He glanced to his left. The tree was gone now. But the bend in the road would never change. He could still see the blue lights dancing across the car. Lizzie slumped in the passenger seat. Clayton on the ground. Bill Calvert and Muirhead stopping him getting any closer. And a hundred yards away, Macdonald was staggering across a field...

"This won't be the last time you drive to Scarborough," he said out loud. "Get used to it."

Or the last time he'd drive to a hospital...

Four days later. Four days after what DC Simpson had dryly described as 'the incident' as he took Brady's statement.

Back at the hospital. Dr Sharma again. Looking rested. Like a man who'd finally had a good night's sleep. Less dishevelled, less beaten down. He held out his hand. Brady shook it. Saw the expression on his face.

'It's over between us.'

'You haven't got the job.'

People have a way of looking at you when they're going to deliver bad news.

Sharma hesitated. Brady waited. He was used to waiting for people to speak.

But not like this.

"We put your wife into an induced coma."

Brady nodded. "So the swelling could go down. So you could assess the damage."

All credit to him. He had the courage to look into Brady's eyes. "It's far worse than we thought, Mr Brady. Your wife is still in a coma. Except now... Well, now it's not induced."

Brady felt the world shift under him. "So... She'll come out of it on her own? When she's recovered."

"Possibly, Mr Brady. But your wife has suffered very serious brain damage. The angle - "

He's going to paint me a picture, Brady thought. A picture I'll never stop seeing.

"The angle her head hit the kerb. The skull fracture. The brain hitting the inside of the skull. As I explained..."

He carried on talking. About lobes and cortexes and impact. About the damage to Grace's brain. About her chances of recovery. Her almost non-existent chances of recovery.

Brady turned. He saw Grace walking up the aisle towards

him. Not walking. Floating. Shining, shimmering. He'd never seen anything more beautiful. He never would.

"I'm sorry, Mr Brady. Grace may never recover. And if she does..." Sharma took a deep breath. Suddenly looked weary again. "Even if she does she won't be the woman you remember. The wife you had... I'm truly sorry, Mr Brady."

The doctor was in his 50s. The face of a life well-lived. A man who looked like he still enjoyed a rock band, a guilty cigarette and a pint of Guinness. He put his hand out. "Pieter van der Bijl. A&E Consultant."

He was South African. Brady liked that in doctors. It had been a South African doctor who'd first levelled with him about his mother. 'Take her home. Let her enjoy her grandchildren. It won't be long. And she knows it.'

"Michael Brady."

"And you're..." Van der Bijl hesitated, clearly trying to guess the relationship.

"I'm his friend," Brady said. It was almost true. He'd bought a drawing. "I'm the closest he has to next of kin. At least I think I am. And I'm the one who found him."

"So would you like good news or bad news, Mr Brady?"

"I'm – I used to be – a detective. I've had my share of both."

"OK. Let's start with the glass half full. I suspect your friend didn't suffer for long. Whoever did this to him did it quickly. His ribs will heal, so will the cuts and bruises. He'll have a scar, but scars fade in time. His nose? A regulation broken nose. That's the good news..."

"And the bad?"

"His right hand. The middle finger and fourth finger

are badly broken. In more than one place. Did you play rugby, Mr Brady?"

Where was this going?

"A little. I was more of a football man."

"When a rugby player was taking a kick at goal – in the old days – he dug his heel into the pitch. Then he ground his heel from side to side. So the ball would hold still. That's what someone has done to your friend's hand. Stamped down hard. And ground his heel from side to side."

"Can I see him?" Brady said, trying to push the image out of his head.

Van der Bijl shook his head. "No, he's sleeping. We've given him fairly strong painkillers. And my colleague will operate on his hand in the morning. He's excellent. But saving that finger will be a challenge. And give your friend a couple of days. Ring the ward."

They shook hands again. "Thank you," Brady said.

"You're welcome. It's what we do. But one more thing..."

Whatever 'one more thing' was, it was going to be bad news.

"...You can obviously tell where I'm from. I've seen far worse than this. I did some of my training in the townships. But take care of yourself. Whoever did this to your friend knew what he was doing. And I suspect he enjoyed it. You look like you've seen some of life's dark corners, Mr Brady. This is one you'd do well to avoid."

31

It was back to basics. Back to the days when he *was* the keen, eager – desperately eager, he now realised – new recruit.

But it was good. It felt right. He'd spent his last year in Manchester working on one case. *The* case. The rest of his time disappeared into management meetings and policy initiatives. Talking to men in suits about policing instead of doing any policing himself.

Maybe he could be a private investigator? Free to take his own cases. A little office with a frosted glass window. *Brady PI* stencilled on it. Whitby's equivalent of Della Street in the outer office. He'd need to invest in some clothes though. A raincoat with a belt. A snap brim fedora.

Or maybe not. Sitting outside a Travelodge fiddling with a telephoto lens while he waited for an unfaithful husband. Crouching behind a bush on the golf course, trying to catch someone who claimed he'd been disabled in an accident at work.

Back to basics. And this was as basic as it got. Door to door. Or fisherman to fisherman.

Brady walked across onto the fish pier. He looked across the harbour. He could see New Way Ghaut. Just another of Whitby's alleys now. Church Street to the harbour. Eight steps up from the beach, washed clean twice a day by the high tide.

He turned round. And looked at the empty sheds.

He'd loved the fish pier. The boats unloading their catch, the filleting sheds working flat out. He'd watch them in the mornings before he went to work. Ten minutes before he started another day on Luca Barella's bingo.

It was the speed that impressed him. Always the speed.

Not the smell, or the blood dripping off the benches, or the severed fish heads in the wooden crates, gazing lifelessly up to Heaven.

The speed. A huge cod – as long as his arm – sliced into fish and chip shop fillets in under two minutes.

And how casual it was. The filleter slicing through the flesh. Bare arms, hardly ever wearing gloves, carelessly discussing the football as he sliced the 30lb cod into 'fresh caught Whitby fish.'

They wore white aprons. Teams of filleters in white rubber aprons. Water swilling across the floor, fish guts tossed into a bucket, the filleting knives glinting wet in the early morning sun.

He'd timed it one day. Used the stop watch on his new Casio.

The filleter sliced through the fish's gills. Tossed something – too quick to catch what it was – into a slop tray and exposed

a huge gash where the head joined the body. He sliced along
the fish's back, pulling the first fillet away, exposing the bones.
Lay the fillet on the workbench, trimmed it, threw it into a
tray packed with ice.

Picked the grey/brown fish up by the head and turned it
over, its dead eyes staring helplessly upwards. Another cut
down the length of the body, another fillet. He pulled the head
off the body and tossed it into a crate.

He'd pressed stop. A minute and twenty-five.

Not now. The filleting sheds were empty, the tradi-
tional fishing industry was long gone. "Crabs, lobsters,
maybe a bit of scalloping," Dave had said. "There's still
the odd one goes out line fishing. Hardly worth the diesel
though."

Most of Whitby's 'fresh caught local fish' came in a
lorry from Peterhead.

THERE WERE two men sitting in an office. Very clearly
eating Dave's bacon sandwiches.

The younger one took a bite and looked up. "Morning, mate," he said through a mouthful of bacon and
tomato. "What can I do for you?"

"I'm looking for a guy called Dave Kidby."

There were only three possible replies. 'Never heard
of him.' 'Don't know any Dave Kidby. There's a Darren
Kidby though.' Or a brief nod and, 'That guy down there.
Just coming ashore.' Or words to that effect.

It was the first one.

It was always the first one. The guy sweeping out the
sheds. The one stacking the lobster pots.

Taking a break from welding a new section onto one of the pier gates.

Shouting down to the deck of the *Pride & Joy*...

It was the first one every time.

Brady walked back to the tea hut. "Morning," he smiled. "Cup of tea if I may?"

"Milk and sugar?"

"No sugar. Just a dash of milk."

He took his tea and stood on the side of the harbour next to the stack of lobster pots. Looked at the filleting sheds again. Did they have a preservation order? Otherwise he'd come down one morning and they'd be the Harbour View Apartments. And another slice of the town's soul would have been carved off.

THE SWING BRIDGE WAS OPEN, a bright yellow barge – *Sandsend* – coming through it. Six rubber tyres on the bow, a token nod at damage limitation if it hit a fishing boat. There was an orange digger – a JCB's big brother – on it. Two men, one in bright orange overalls, leaning nonchalantly against a guard rail with ominous gaps in it. Going to dredge the harbour, Brady guessed.

"Hey, mate!"

Brady turned. The man was in his late 20s, wearing jeans, a black hoodie, a pencil behind his right ear. Squinting against the sun.

"You the guy that was looking for Dave Kidby?"

Brady nodded.

"Heard you asking. I was upstairs in the office. What do you want with him?"

There was no point lying. "His landlord was my best friend. I'm trying to find out what happened."

"The guy that was killed?"

Brady nodded again.

He rubbed his hands on his jeans. Squinted at Brady a second time. Made a decision.

"Darren Kidby," he said. "He's my cousin. Everyone calls him Daz."

"So where can I find him?"

"Right now? About 20 miles out in the North Sea. But he'll be back in a couple of days. Friday. Early afternoon, maybe. The boat's called *Sea Shanty*."

"Thanks," Brady said. He held out his hand.

Daz Kidby's cousin shook it. "You're welcome."

"So most of the people I just asked knew him?"

He laughed. "Course they bloody did. This is Whitby. Everyone knows everyone. But no bugger knows you."

32

It had been a long two days. He'd walked Archie. Thought about what he was going to ask Kidby.

Always assuming he'd talk to him.

"Hi," he'd said to the first one off the boat. "I'm looking for Daz Kidby."

"Blue jumper," he replied, gesturing behind him. "Baseball cap."

Brady had introduced himself. Said he'd like to talk. Kidby had said he'd like to go home. Needed a shower. A sandwich would be nice. "If she's got anything in. Probably forgotten I'm due back."

They'd arranged to meet in the Ship.

The Ship, the Bell, the Pier. There was none of your Ferret and Lettuce nonsense in Whitby.

"Four o'clock then," Brady had said.

Kidby had nodded. And Brady had reckoned the chances were no more than fifty-fifty.

But there he was, sitting at a table. Waiting. Drumming the middle finger of his right hand on the table.

"Thank you for this. I appreciate it. Let me get you a drink."

"Thanks, pint of Guinness."

"You want anything to eat?"

Another lesson he'd learned from Jim Fitzpatrick. *"Moment of maximum danger, Mike. Informers, people you want to talk to – they don't want to be seen having a drink with you. So you go to the bar, they fuck off. But if there's steak pie and chips on the way it's a different story..."*

"Wouldn't mind a sandwich. She'd forgotten."

"No problem." Brady ordered a side of chips as well. A nod to Fitzpatrick's memory.

They sat down. Kidby wasn't 30. He was nearer to 40. Long hair escaping from under a black baseball cap, the light brown fighting a losing battle against the grey. A goatee beard that had already surrendered. A face lined by sun and salt. Sharp blue eyes that flicked constantly round the room. The middle finger of his right hand still drumming on the table.

Two pints, then he's off.

"Patrick Smith was my friend. My best friend when we were growing up. I'm trying to find out what happened."

Kidby leaned forward across the table. Not threatening, intense. Not nervous, brittle. "He threw me out. Said I was in breach of my lease. Gave me two days."

"Why did he do that?"

Kidby drank half his pint of Guinness and sat back. Suddenly relaxed. "Can't hurt to tell you now. He's dead. Besides, the police don't give a shit about it."

"About what?"

"I was growing grass."

"Cannabis?"

"What else? Weed, pot, dope. Call it what you like."

"In the flat?"

"Well, I'm not growing it at the bottom of the garden am I? Besides, I've got a south facing window. Shame to waste it. Grow Bag on the table. Gardeners' fucking World."

Brady laughed. "What were you growing?"

"Dope, I told you."

"No, specifically."

"Green Gelato."

"Is that good? I'm not an expert."

"Fucking lovely." Kidby gazed up to the roof. Possibly to Heaven. Rubbed his thumb against the fingers of his hand. Brought them to his nose. Inhaled deeply. "The best. Blending sweet and citrus notes with earthy tones."

"You sure you're not describing a bottle of wine?"

"Way better than wine, mate. Way better. Way, way better."

"Why?" Brady said.

"Why what?"

"Why grow it yourself? Why risk your landlord finding out? Why not buy it locally?"

Because your landlord did find out. He came round to fix a window. No, Patrick sent someone round to fix a window. His odd job man. But maybe Patrick wanted a word with him. Knew where he'd be. And he was putting the house up for sale. So he went round to check what state the top flat was in. And

there it was, sitting in a Grow Bag in a south facing window,
this summer's crop.

"Can I have another beer?"

Brady nodded. "Sure. Guinness again?"

"If that's alright."

"Why?" Brady said again as he sat down. The second pint. He needed to make some progress.

"Quality," Kidby said. "Fed up of the shit they sell in Whitby. Just like growing your own veg."

"And then Patrick came round?"

"Yeah. While I was at sea. Gone for three days. My girlfriend was watering them for me. But he turns up with the fucking joiner when she's at work. Come to fix the window."

And then comes back two days later, Brady thought. When Carl heard the shouting. He could see Patrick's point of view. Can't use my property as a pot factory. But he found he had some sympathy for Kidby.

"Why do you smoke it?"

"Why not? Citrus notes and earthy tones."

A waitress brought the sandwich. "Chips?" Kidby said. "You're serious about finding the answer, aren't you? Help yourself if you want one, mate."

"No other reason?"

Kidby turned on his seat. Stretched his right leg out so Brady could see it. Pulled the leg of his jeans up. "There's this," he said.

His right leg was missing below the knee. A prosthetic lower leg went into his trainer.

"What happened?" Brady said.

"I was in the Army. IED. Didn't go off properly. Must

have been one they made on a Friday. Or whatever passes for Friday in Afghanistan. So I only lost half a leg."

Kidby ate one of the sandwiches. Drank half his beer again, his eyes still flickering round the room. His middle finger only still when he was holding the glass.

"I was lucky," he said. "Two weeks before one of the lads stepped on a proper one. One that a grown-up had made. Fucking slo-mo. You ever had that? Something fucking dreadful happens? Life suddenly goes into slo-mo?"

Brady shook his head. "No, nothing. I've been lucky."

"Make sure you stay lucky. I was 40, maybe 50 yards back. Watched Davey Catlow's leg float past me. Like a film. Like someone had slowed it down. Army boot on one end of Davey's leg. Fuck all on the other."

"So that and..." Brady hesitated. The diagnosis was easy. But saying 'getting your own leg blown off' seemed a touch insensitive. "That and your own injury added up to PTSD?"

"Yeah. That and being in the fucking desert for two days before they rescued us. Lucky again. One of the lads was a medic. But fucking scary. Who's going to find us first? The cavalry or the fucking Taliban? So, yeah, the Gelato helps. Keeps the demons under lock and key."

Brady nodded. "I can see that."

Kidby finished his second pint. Put the glass down on the table. The finger started drumming again. "Only option," he said. "That shit you buy on the street just makes it worse. Nearly fucking killed me one time."

He gestured towards the sea. "Especially that crap the prick down the road sells."

And Brady knew he'd made a breakthrough.

"The prick down the road?"

Kidby took a last bite of the sandwich. "Enzo fucking Barella. Like I said. Nearly killed me."

"Enzo Barella? The amusement arcade guy?"

And when you've got what you want, just sit there, Michael. Otherwise they'll realise it's important. Then they get cold feet. Then they run off and tell someone what they've told you. And you've wasted a steak pie.

"How do you manage on the boat?" Brady said. "The North Sea gets pretty rough."

"How do I manage? How do you think I manage? Fucking carefully. And I tie myself onto something."

"You don't fillet any fish on the boat do you?"

"Don't be stupid. Rough sea and a sharp knife? Don't really go together do they?"

"You want another?"

"No, mate." Kidby's finger had finally stopped. He levered himself to his feet. "I'm going to watch football. My lad's playing. Under-11s cup final. Proper player he is. Scouts watching him already."

"Hope they win for you. Does he live with your girlfriend?"

"Ex-girlfriend," Kidby said. "Ex, ex, ex. He doesn't even know I'm his dad. That's the way she wants it. Didn't see a druggie with one leg as a good role model. She was pregnant when I went inside. Living with someone else when I came out."

"That must be tough. More than tough."

Kidby shrugged. "She's probably right. Can't stop me

standing on the touchline though. That boy's the only good thing I've done in my life."

He held his hand out. Brady shook it. Daz Kidby limped out of the bar and went to watch his son play football.

33

"I've got some news for you," Frankie Thomson said.

Two days after he'd talked to Kidby. Brady had been buying his breakfast from Dave. And there she was. Grey shirt, brown leather jacket and clearly just on her way into work. Even more clearly a woman who hadn't slept much.

"Morning," Brady said. "I didn't know you were a regular customer of Dave's."

She raised an eyebrow. "Is that some sort of sexual harassment, Mr Brady? Are women not allowed to eat bacon sandwiches? Should we be at home eating Special K so we can slip seductively into a tight pair of jeans?"

But she was smiling as she said it.

Dave handed him his sandwich. "Regular customer? You've a way to go to beat this one, Mike. Plenty of stamps on her loyalty card. Like I could be bothered wi' that bollocks."

"You want to eat breakfast with me, Mr Brady?"

"So long as you don't mind my plus one."

"I was brought up on a farm," she said. "I shared all my teenage secrets with a Springer."

And here they were, sitting exactly where he'd sat with Patrick. The same view, probably the same seagulls circling overhead.

"So..." Brady said.

Frankie took a bite of her sandwich. "What do you think?"

"I don't think Kara did it."

She shook her head. "Not the murder. The bacon. I think it must be the griddle, don't you? I can buy the same bacon, same butcher. Grill it, fry it. It still doesn't taste like this. So, Watson, it must be the griddle."

"Sherlock Holmes," Brady said.

"Yep. When you've ruled out everything else, what's left is the truth. And," she said, "The truth is that Patrick's wife didn't do it."

Brady was surprised to find that he didn't feel pleased. He didn't feel vindicated. He didn't even feel happy for Kara.

He felt suspicious.

The investigation had stopped. Bill had stamped 'Case closed, job done' on the file.

So what had happened?

"Who did do it then? You clearly know."

"A local guy. Used to be a tenant of Patrick's."

"Darren Kidby," Brady said.

Frankie looked at him shrewdly. "That's an inspired guess."

Brady could feel himself getting angry. "Let me make another one. He walked into the station and confessed."

"OK. It'll be in the papers soon enough. Midnight last night."

And you were hauled in to take the confession. Back home, three hours' sleep and back on duty this morning. No wonder it was a bacon sandwich and a black coffee.

"So he just walked into the station? And confessed? To Patrick's murder?"

She nodded. "Around midnight. My boyfriend wasn't impressed."

"So you were called in to take his confession?"

Brady had known it before. Jack Trueman. Happily married for 30 years – or so everyone assumed. Mrs Trueman fell asleep in front of the TV, Jack smothered her. Made a cup of tea, tidied the kitchen and then phoned the police. Sat there patiently until Brady turned up. "I'm sorry," he said. "I just needed some peace."

But not Kidby. It wasn't logical. He suffered from PTSD. He was irrational. Yes, he'd pushed shit through Patrick's letterbox.

No, he hadn't disguised himself as a Goth and patiently stalked his victim – limped after his victim – and killed him with a single stab wound.

Kidby didn't work with other people. And he didn't walk calmly into a police station at midnight and confess. Not willingly...

"You know he's a fisherman?"

"We've checked. The boat was in the harbour that weekend."

"And you know he's a drug user? You know he smokes pot to cope with PTSD? You know he's almost certainly unstable?"

"He seemed stable enough when I talked to him last night. And..." She paused. "He's done it before."

"You're telling me he's killed someone before? He was in Afghanistan. That doesn't mean he brings it back to Whitby. Especially on one leg."

Frankie shook her head. "Stabbed someone. Drunk on Boxing Day."

She was pregnant when I went inside. Living with someone else when I came out.

"I assume you've found the murder weapon in his cutlery drawer?"

"No. He says he threw it in the harbour - "

Where I should have thrown Patrick's laptop and spared myself all this crap.

"What was it?"

"A fish filleting knife."

That figured. Even if Kidby didn't cut fish up on the boat he'd hardly have a problem getting hold of one.

"Is it always like this in Whitby?" Brady said.

"Like what?"

"Ready-made solutions. Patrick dies, his wife's arrested. Then it occurs to someone that there might be a few holes in the case. So a fish filleter conveniently confesses. Kidby's a good suspect, I'll grant you. Military training. Access to a weapon. A reason to dislike the victim." Brady shook his head again. "But it doesn't make him Patrick's killer."

"He signed a confession."

Brady stood up. "It's fucking nonsense. The world is full of ex-vets with PTSD who've signed false confessions. It's bollocks, Frankie. You know it and I know it."

She didn't reply. Instead she pulled a pen out of her pocket and started stirring her coffee.

"Sugar?" Brady asked. Maybe he should lighten the mood a bit. She'd let him take the backpack.

She nodded. "Yeah. There's always that bit at the bottom that doesn't dissolve properly." She met his eyes. "I'm a woman with all life's vices, Brady."

"And what about your boss?" She'd dropped the 'mister.' Did he mind? No. "There's a man with all life's vices. What does he say about this?"

"Case closed. And by the time he comes out of hospital he'll be claiming that he knew it was Kidby all along. That arresting Kara was part of his masterplan."

Brady was surprised. "I didn't know he was going into hospital."

"He's your brother-in-law. So much for close-knit families."

"I knew he was going," Brady protested. "I just didn't know it was now."

Frankie nodded. "Monday."

"How long will he be off for? A hernia's about three weeks isn't it?"

You don't often do it, Brady thought afterwards. Maybe two or three times in your whole life. Time a joke so perfectly that someone actually snorts coffee down their nose.

"Hernia," Frankie spluttered. "Hernia? Is that what he told you? Sorry," she added, "That wasn't very ladylike."

"Yes, hernia. That's what Bill told me. That's even what my sister told me."

Frankie took some time over replying. Whatever she

was going to say, it was clearly giving her a lot of pleasure. Brady could see her rolling the reply round her mouth, savouring the words like a fine wine.

She looked up to St Hilda's Church on the headland, possibly seeking divine guidance.

"Piles," she said.

"Piles?" Brady said. "Piles? Haemorrhoids?"

"I believe the two words are synonymous. Yes."

It was impossible not to laugh. "He told me a hernia. No wonder he couldn't sit still. Poor bastard."

"There are no secrets in a police station. You should know that. Detective Chief Inspector William Calvert has a bad case of haemorrhoids and will, I am afraid, require surgery. Current estimates are that he'll be off for three weeks. Although PC Keillor says his uncle had the same operation and... Anyway, you're having breakfast. You don't want to know what PC Keillor said."

"Is the station sending flowers?"

"Obviously. And a rubber ring. Maybe two rubber rings if Keillor's uncle is a reliable guide."

"So who's in charge while he's in hospital?"

"I am. So if it's alright with you, Brady, I'd appreciate a quiet three weeks when nothing happens. So could I respectfully ask that you write your book? This case is closed. Let's leave it that way. We wouldn't want Bill to worry while he's recovering. DI Calvert will have enough on his mind. Difficult decisions to make. The red ring or the blue ring..."

34

His phone rang as he was walking through the front door. Brady pulled it out of his pocket and glanced at the display.

Kara. Presumably, the newly-released Kara.

So where did getting out of prison rank? Especially when you'd been falsely accused of murdering your husband?

Going in was right up there on the stress scale. Ahead of a major illness. Ahead of getting fired. So coming out must be equivalent to... Maybe not the birth of your child. Getting married? Definitely higher than getting engaged.

"Congratulations."

"Thanks," Kara said. "Yeah, it feels good."

"Where are you?"

"I'm at home. Becky's here. She collected me."

"How are you doing? You sound good."

"Yeah. I'm OK. I'd rather have spent a week in Spain

but you know what they say. What doesn't kill you makes you stronger."

"Nietzsche," Brady said.

"Who?"

"Friedrich Nietzsche. The German philosopher. He said it."

"Right. Well, whatever. What are you doing tomorrow? Come round for coffee. There's something I want to ask you."

A DAY later and here he was. Back in her kitchen. Back in the kitchen where she'd been arrested by Bill. Back in the kitchen where she'd promised to tell him the truth.

He looked at her. All trace of prison seemingly gone. Two years at a girls' boarding school? Whatever else she'd learned, she'd learned resilience.

"What are you going to do?" Brady said. Whatever she wanted – and his money was on suing Bill for wrongful arrest – she'd ask soon enough.

"Not make any rash decisions," Kara replied. "I'm going home. Back to my parents for a week. Wrap myself up in my dressing gown, watch a box set and talk to my mum. Eat chocolate. Get my hair done. Be good to myself."

And then she'd come back and put the 'For Sale' sign up, Brady thought. She must realise that her future wasn't in Whitby. And there was nothing to keep her here. Not once they'd had the...

"Do you have a date for the funeral yet?"

She shook her head. "The solicitor is sorting it out for me. He's doing everything. The properties, all of it. But I guess – now everything is... sorted out... Not long, I guess. And it's only going to be small. Just family. And you, if you'll come."

Brady nodded. "Of course. Of course I will."

So when was she going to ask him about Bill? He'd rehearsed the argument already. 'No. Just don't. The police can show they did everything according to the book. Reasonable grounds. Reasonable suspicion. Don't put yourself through it. Bad things happen. But let it go. Learn from it if you can.'

She reached her hand out. Placed it on Brady's arm. Smiled at him. "There was one decision I made in prison," she said.

Here it was. Brady suddenly felt nervous.

"The baby is due in five months," she said. "And... whatever happened, Patrick is the father."

Brady stayed silent.

"I've got friends," Kara said. "I've got a brother. But the baby's going to need a Godfather. I'd – well, on Patrick's behalf – I'd like that to be you, Michael."

Life in Whitby. It never failed to surprise him.

Brady nodded. Smiled. "Thank you," he said. "I'd like that. I'd really like that. I'd be honoured." He paused. "But I've a condition. Something I want in return."

"I promise you. Patrick is the - "

Brady held his hand up. Shook his head. "No, not that. I want you to tell your solicitor to do something. And that's tell, not ask."

"What's that?"

"He needs to find a flat for someone. A good one. The guy can pay the rent. And if he can't pay, I'll pay."

Kara looked surprised, but nodded. "What's his name?"

"Carl Robinson. And you should buy one of his drawings."

35

He was back in Kate's kitchen. Another worried phone call.

"I don't know what to do, Michael. She's still seeing this boy. The one I told you about."

"Ty?"

"Yes. And man, I suppose, not boy. All she does is go out, her schoolwork's suffering. It has to be. She's 17. She's reached that age – you'll find it with Ash – you have to trust them. You can't stand over them all the time."

"What does Bill say?"

"Oh, Mike. What the fuck does Bill ever say?"

Kate never swore. It must be bad.

"He sticks his oar in, starts to lay down the law. Mr bloody Fix-It. Do this. Do that. Then his phone rings and he's off to the station or off to the golf course. Not that he'll be doing that for a while…"

"How long is he in for?"

"Overnight, they said. Depending on how the operation goes." She looked at her watch. "They're doing it about now. I'm going up tonight. And then I'm collecting him tomorrow. And then he'll be recovering. 'Can you get me a coffee, love, while I watch the golf?' Maddie will be the last thing on his mind."

"So you're left with trusting her and hoping for the best?"

"And worrying. It's just grinding me down, Mike. A long way down."

"You're not doing anything..." Was there a tactful way to ask your sister if she was drinking the cooking sherry and hiding bottles of Gordon's?

Kate laughed. "What, Mike, doing anything rash? With running the house and looking after the girls and working two days a week and being there for Bill when he wanders in at two in the morning, I haven't got bloody time to do anything rash."

"I'm going to worry about you."

Kate reached up and touched his cheek. "You've got enough on your plate, Mike. I'll cope. Even if it's by going grey. This is my life, Mike. I've just got to accept it. I married him. I'll go to the hairdresser's once a month instead of once every two months. After I've taken care of Bill, obviously."

He stood up and held his arms out. "Come here," he said. "Let me give you a hug." She lay her head on his chest. Brady held his sister tightly for a few seconds. "I don't know what to say," he said. "But I'm here. Whatever happens, whatever you need."

Kate broke away and stepped back. Brought her right hand up and brushed away the tears. "You're a good guy, Mike. Don't shut yourself away too much.

You'll find someone else one day. Don't build those walls too high."

ANOTHER DAY OF PERSISTENT RAIN. Brady was beginning to wonder if Spain wasn't a better place to write a book.

There was a knock on the door. "I'll get it," he shouted upstairs.

"If it's Bean send her up," Ash shouted back. "She's coming over to hang out."

It wasn't Bean. It was Kate. Standing in the rain. Looking distraught and disbelieving in equal measure. The expression people have as they walk away from a car crash.

"Kate? What's the matter? I thought you'd gone to collect Bill?"

"Pour me a drink will you, Michael?"

"Are you sure? You're driving aren't you?"

"Yes. And yes."

He poured some brandy into a glass. Remembered that Kate liked an ice cube, started walking towards the kitchen.

"Don't bother," she said. "Just give it to me."

He passed her the glass. "What is it?"

"It's Bill. It's bloody well Bill."

"Is he in the car?"

"They're keeping him in."

Brady nearly made a joke. The expression on her face stopped him just in time. "What's wrong, Kate?"

"They're doing some tests. Bloody hell, Michael, they

think he might... They think he might have cancer, Mike."

"You're not fucking bright enough to work it out, are you? You're still looking at her thinking she couldn't have done it. Pregnant, she's having Patrick's baby. Happy fucking families. It wouldn't be happy fucking families when she presented Patrick with a black baby."

Brady saw Bill slam the whisky glass down in triumph. Remembered him savouring the taste of his pain, his bewilderment.

But he wouldn't wish cancer on anyone...

"Ah, shit. I'm so sorry, Kate."

What was the right question to ask. Where? How badly? Are they sure?

He chose the first one. "Where? He's too young for prostate, surely?"

"Close. You're in the right ball park. Sorry, Michael. I'm going to need a sense of humour. They think my husband might have bladder cancer."

"What - "

The doorbell rang again. "Sorry, Kate. It's Ash's friend." He walked quickly into the hall. Opened the door to a very wet Bean. Told her to go up to Ash's room. "And grab a towel from the bathroom, Bean."

"What happened?" he said, walking back into the lounge.

Kate took a deep breath. Drank half her brandy. "They did some blood tests when he was having the operation. Didn't like what they saw. So he had an MRI scan. They found a – fuck, Michael, I don't need this, not with Maddie – they found a shadow. They said it wasn't necessarily... You know how it is." She finished her drink. Took another deep breath. "I'm sorry, all that sounds selfish."

Brady walked over and put his arms round her. "No," he said. "It's not. I can't tell you. Some of the emotions I had with Grace. No, it's not selfish."

"They're doing some more tests," Kate said. "More scans tomorrow."

"So you've got to go home and try and sleep?"

She nodded. He knew how she felt.

"I've got to go back in the morning. Take him some things. He was only supposed to be in overnight."

"Have you been there all day?" Brady said. "Have you eaten?"

"No. I've been waiting mostly. Drinking Costa coffee. Wondering how to tell the girls."

"Let me make you a sandwich."

She shook her head. "No, I'll get something at home. You're OK. I just wanted... I don't know. I just wanted to get my head together before I told the girls. See someone I can be myself with. Let it all out."

Brady nodded. *Been there, done that, worked out what to say to my daughter. Tried to work out what to say to my daughter...*

"They're doing more tests," Kate said again. "But I know. Now I think about it. He's been tired. More tired than he normally is. Falling asleep after he's eaten. I think he's known as well. Deep down. Known it was more than... I'm sorry about lying to you. Bill didn't want anyone to know. He wouldn't even let me tell the girls. 'Tell everyone it's a hernia.' He insisted."

Brady decided not to share what Frankie Thomson had told him. And PC Keillor's expert medical opinion...

"You need to go home, Kate. See your girls. Give them the news." *Make a better job of it than I did with Ash.* "Tomorrow's another day."

She nodded. Reached for her coat. Hugged him. Thanked him. Hugged him again.

"Kate, hang on. Do you want me to drive you? I can get a taxi back. Bring your car over in the morning."

She shook her head. "I'll be fine."

She hugged him a third time. "Thank you again," she said.

And left him alone with the memories.

He'd somehow mentioned the song on their first date. By the second date it was 'their song.' And the first dance when they married.

'You are so Beautiful,' by Joe Cocker.

He pressed play on his phone and for the hundredth time Joe's raw, raspy voice echoed round the hospital room. The monitor beeped, the machine breathed. And Grace didn't respond.

"What would you like first, darling?" Brady said. "Ash's school play? Or do you want to save that for later? Let me read to you..."

And Detective Chief Inspector Michael Brady sat on the side of his wife's bed and read the Famous Five. 'Five go to Billycock Hill.'

'It was her favourite when she was a little girl,' her mother had told him. 'Oh, she was so determined to have her hair cut short like George. Maybe, Michael. Maybe a memory of her childhood...'

Three chapters of Famous Five and he was done. They'd rescue the pilots in the end. Good would triumph. Not over evil but over Mr Janes, who wasn't really a bad person. According to Enid Blyton, he'd 'fallen in with the wrong folk.'

If only real life were so simple. If only he could have taken Kenny on one side. Explained it to him. 'Look, Kenny, you've fallen in with the wrong folk. Turn over a new leaf and put it behind you. Before it's too late.'

But Kenny didn't. And Brady was drawn deeper and deeper into the investigation. Until someone decided he was far too close to the truth.

None of this would have happened. He wouldn't be sitting on her bed. He wouldn't be pressing 'play' so Grace could listen to Ash sing 'I Dreamed a Dream' one more time...

There was a knock on the door. Brady turned to see Lisa. He knew all the nurses by name now. They'd shared some long nights. He knew about their families. How their children were doing in school.

"How is she?"

"Just the same. I've done Famous Five. We're on Dreamed a Dream now..."

"Your daughter's got a beautiful voice." Lisa looked down. "Doctor Sharma is here. He had an emergency. He wonders – while it's quiet – he wonders if he could have a word..."

He'd been expecting it. Surprised in some ways it had taken this long. "Two minutes, Lis. Tell him I'll be right there."

Brady put Ash on a loop. Bent forward and kissed his wife on the forehead. "I love you, Grace," he whispered.

And then he went to talk to Dilip Sharma, knowing exactly the conversation they would have...

36

"Morning," Dave said. "You're late."

"Sorry," Brady replied. "Had to call in at school. See Ash's form teacher."

"No bother?"

"No, I don't think so. Teenage girl stuff. Not that I know anything about teenage girl stuff." Brady pulled the collar of his coat up and turned his back to the wind. "Hell's bells. Anyone with any brains would have stayed in bed. This is right back to winter."

Dave shrugged. "It's Whitby. It's May. What can I say?"

The wind had been whipping across the beach, flecks of foam blowing off the sea and scudding along in front of them. Archie had chased a couple of them and then realised they weren't as predictable as his ball.

"You might have to get planning permission for a shelter."

Dave laughed. "You wait until winter. The boss will still need his morning walk on the beach."

"I grew up here remember? I lived through a few winters."

"Different now though." Dave flipped the bacon over. Pressed it down to make sure it was crispy. "Now you're past 40. Feel the cold more. Only a matter of time before that daughter of yours is buying you a woolly cardigan for Christmas."

Dave passed Brady his bacon sandwich. And turned serious. "You've not heard then. If you had you'd have said something by now."

"Heard what? The weather forecast says it's going to get even colder?"

"Aye well, it is for some poor bugger. In a manner of speaking. That bloke that turned himself in for Patrick. He's dead."

Brady's first reaction was surprise. Surprise that – for the second time – he wasn't surprised.

"How?"

"How did he die or how do I know?"

"Both, I guess."

"How do I know? Because I make bacon sandwiches. So I'm invisible. Half an hour ago two young coppers bought their breakfast. And assumed the guy that made it was deaf. From what they were saying, suicide."

So Kidby had hung himself.

"That's that then," Brady said. "Signs a confession, then has the good manners to kill himself."

There was no point taking his anger out on Dave. "Give me another napkin will you, Dave? I'll eat this in the car. There's a phone call I need to make."

She answered on the fourth ring. "Frankie Thomson."

Not on duty then. Brady realised he should apologise. "Look, I don't know if this is a bad time - "

"I'm at my mother's."

"I'm sorry. But you must have heard this. Darren Kidby is dead."

"Yes."

Was that it? 'Yes?'

"I heard it was suicide."

"Yes," she said again. Then, "He hanged himself. The suspicion is that someone gave him some drugs."

Brady didn't bother with the ritual protests. Suicide watch. How did they get the drugs in?

Drugs and prisons. They were like bacon and eggs. Inseparable.

"So someone gave him crap drugs and it triggered his PTSD."

"You're guessing now. There'll be an autopsy. Obviously."

He might have been guessing but he knew he was right. Spice probably. Way stronger than cannabis. And about as far as you could get from the mellow citrus of Kidby's grow bag in a south facing window.

"Spice," Brady said. "Last I heard they were impregnating paper with it. One guy we locked up made a good living inside selling his birthday and Christmas cards. They only became suspicious when he got about 20 cards for Father's Day."

"Like I said, there'll be an autopsy."

"Darren Kidby was a father, Frankie. He wasn't perfect but he was a decent guy. Doing the best he could."

Brady saw him limping out of the bar. Going to watch

his son play football. The son who wasn't allowed to know his father. Who'd never know his father.

It was the final straw.

"Just fuck your autopsy, Frankie. Fuck it. But you just sit in your office and accept it. Settle for a quiet life while one innocent person after another dies."

"Don't you talk to me about innocent people, you sanctimonious prick - "

He switched the phone off. He didn't hear any more.

37

Their next door neighbour-but-one had been an ex-professional footballer. Played in the First Division before it became the Premier League, before Sky arrived with their wheelbarrow full of money.

Col had gradually worked his way down the leagues as he got older. 'Because nothing beats playing, Mike,' he'd said at a barbecue. 'Nothing even comes close. Coaching, managing, freezing your bollocks off on a gantry giving your expert opinion. Nothing comes anywhere close.'

"Is that what I am?" Brady said. "A footballer who wants to go on playing as long as he can? A bald rock star who can't stop touring?"

"You're 42, Mike," Kate replied. "Stop feeling sorry for yourself. How's your book going?"

"Yeah, quite well."

If being at 2,624 words when you're supposed to be at 20,000 is your definition of 'quite well.'

"So get it finished. You know that's what Grace would tell you to do."

Brady knew his sister was right.

That was exactly what Grace would have said. It's done. Over. Case closed. You might not like the way it's turned out but it's over and done with. Write your book, go to Sports Day, think about where you're taking Ash on holiday. And if you've decided you're staying in Whitby, maybe think about where you want to live as well.

"I'm sorry," he said. "I came round to see how you were doing. How Bill was doing. And I talk about myself. Bring me up to date."

"He's coming home. The tests are done. We're waiting. He says he feels like a pin cushion. He wants to be on the golf course. He's bad tempered. That's about it."

"And you? And the girls?"

"The girls are... They're OK. I think it'll hit them when he comes home. He's already lost weight. He looks five years older. He looks deflated. Like someone has let the air out of him."

"What about you?"

Kate shook her head. Looked down. "How do you think I feel? One day I say he's ruining my life. The next he's got cancer."

"Not yet. Not officially."

Kate shook her head. "I'm resigned to it. So I feel guilty. That's how I feel. Bloody guilty."

Two of us then...

Not for the first time Brady thought his sister could read his mind. "I'm trapped, Mike. You're not. You can do something. And you have to scratch the itch don't you?"

Brady looked at her. Nodded. "I thought – all those nights sitting by her bed, talking to her, reading to her – I thought I was done with it. But... yes, I can. I can feel it under my skin. I thought it was over, but - "

"But it's not over, Mike. You need to decide what you want. The case is closed. There's only you going to re-open it. But if you do... There can't be any half-measures. You've got be all in."

38

"All set?"

Carl took one last look round what had been his hospital bed. "Yeah, good to go."

Brady picked up the two Sainsbury's carrier bags that had Carl's clothes in them. "Sorry," he said. "I'd have brought a bag if I'd known."

"It's my Nan. She puts everything in carrier bags. At least she went shopping for me. Didn't even think she'd come to visit. She hates hospitals."

"Sorry. I didn't know about her. I told them I was the closest thing you had to a relative. She alright with you staying?"

"Are you joking? I'm her only grandchild. She can't wait."

They walked out of the ward, down the stairs and out of the hospital. Brady unlocked the car, put Carl's matching luggage on the back seat.

"Well," he said, climbing into the car. "For a guy who

can't count up to ten any more you look remarkably well."

Carl started to smile, then suddenly stopped. "Ow. Fuck. Don't make me laugh, you bastard. The broken rib hurts more than the finger. Well, the finger I used to have."

"What did they say?"

"About my finger? Said it was too late. NHS cuts. They were out of superglue."

Brady looked across at him. "So paracetamol, Ibuprofen and black humour?"

Carl shrugged. "Pretty much."

"You want to talk about it?"

Carl didn't reply. He stayed silent, staring straight ahead as Brady drove out of Scarborough, through the villages and up on to the Moors.

Carl still didn't speak. Brady went past the Flask, up and down the dips and turned left to Ruswarp.

"He's not going to make the same mistake a second time," Carl said quietly.

"There isn't going to be a second time."

Carl wrapped his arms round himself, drew his knees up slightly. Got as much into the foetal position as someone with broken ribs and wearing a seatbelt can get. "He's mad," he said. "Just fucking mad."

"Who is?"

Tell me his name and I'll finally know what we're up against. Once Mozart or Scholesy find out for me.

"If I tell you his name I'm fucked."

The road bent round to the right. Brady glanced across.

Work had started on the potash mine. "My Nan's dead against it," Carl said. "Says however many jobs they promise it'll fuck the Moors. Says you'll see it from everywhere."

"Yeah, she's probably right. But you're wrong, Carl. You're not fucked if you tell me his name."

"I am. You don't know him."

"No. But I know the type. And I'm sorry to say this but you're fucked either way. If he's as mad as you say he is then he won't believe you. Sadly, mate, there's a small percentage of the human population that are turned on by the sound of breaking bones."

"So the only way I'll be safe is if he's stopped?"

"Yes."

"By you?"

"It's looking that way."

Brady drove down the hill, past the garage, over the bridge and into Ruswarp. Turned left 50 yards later. Drove along by the side of the River Esk towards Sleights. Carl still had his arms wrapped round himself.

"You going to be OK?" Brady asked.

"She used to be a nurse. Besides all I'm going to do is sit in the garden and eat toast. Until you tell me it's safe to come out."

"And get back to your drawing..."

This time Carl did laugh. "No choice. Nan'll have put a towel on the bed, a new toothbrush in the bathroom and a sketch pad downstairs. She's my biggest fan. Well... after you."

Brady pulled up outside a cottage with a green door. "This one?"

"Yeah. This one. Thanks for the lift." He reached out for the door handle. Then he turned to Brady.

"I would have been fucked," he said. "Properly fucked if he'd done his job properly. Try it. Go home and try writing your name without your middle finger. I tried drawing that way. I could do it, but no-one was going to pay me for it."

He opened the door. "Thanks again," he said.

Don't force it. Don't ask for the name again.

"You're welcome," Brady said.

Carl opened the back door. Leant in and took hold of the two carrier bags.

"Gorse," he said from behind the shelter of the passenger seat. "Jimmy fucking Gorse. And it'll be you or him, Brady."

Jimmy Gorse. Finally he had a name.

"Jimmy fucking Gorse. And it'll be you or him, Brady."

Carl was wrong. It wouldn't be 'you or him.' Because if Gorse wasn't stopped there'd be another Patrick. Another Carl. A lot more innocent people in 'life's dark corners.'

"The case is closed, Mike. There's only you going to re-open it. But if you do... There can't be any half-measures. You've got be all in."

Brady picked his phone up. Left the message.

Waited to be called back.

It was an hour. The slight pause as Mozart's call bounced halfway round the world to travel 20 miles down the coast.

"Mr Brady. I didn't expect to hear from you again so soon. Maybe we should work out a monthly retainer. What can I do for you?"

"I've got a name," Brady said. "I need the person.

Police records. Anything you can find. Who he is. Where he lives. I'm sure you've done this a few times."

"Mmm... Possibly. A name would be a helpful starting point."

"Gorse. Jimmy Gorse. James, I guess."

"Well, it's not John Smith, I'll grant you that. There won't be many. Give me a rough age? Just in case. Although I'm sure you wouldn't be asking me if Mr Gorse was secretary of the bowls club."

"Mid-twenties? Up to mid-thirties, I'd say. No older." Whatever the books say, by the time they're 40 people like Gorse have come up against someone bigger, stronger and significantly younger. In real life Jack Reacher would have been forcibly retired a long time ago...

"Tomorrow morning?"

"Tomorrow morning will be perfect. Thank you."

HE HADN'T EVEN HAD time to make a cup of tea. In from the walk, rub Archie with an old towel, boil the kettle, turn his laptop on. And the notification flashed up almost immediately.

Brady forced himself to wait. Made his tea, gave Archie a biscuit. Settled into his chair and opened the e-mail.

James Falkland Gorse
June 14th 1982 (the day the Falklands were liberated if you're wondering about the name)

Brady smiled. He had been.

An address in Harrogate. Brady tapped it into Google maps. Looked at street view. Was suitably impressed.

```
Blonde hair, blue eyes. 5 ft 9 inches.
11st 7lbs (73kg)
```

```
No   police   record.   Unmarried.   No
regular girlfriend.
```

```
James  Gorse  snr  was  a  sergeant  in  the
Scots  Guards.  Served  in  Germany  and  Hong
Kong.  Married  a  Czech  girl  he  met  in
Germany.  Fought  in  the  Falklands.  Deco-
rated  for  bravery.  Came  home  and  chris-
tened  his  son.  Jimmy  was  largely  educated
at  schools  in  Scotland.  Also  in  Germany
and  Hong  Kong.  An  intelligent  boy  but…
```

Brady knew what was coming. A succession of schools who all seemed to breathe a sigh of relief when Jimmy left. A boy who excelled on the sports field but was a constant problem off it. Who – almost inevitably – joined the army when he was 16. Who'd served in Northern Ireland and Afghanistan.

Joined the Paras. Dropped behind enemy lines. At which point Mozart had offered an opinion.

```
I  ran  up  against  a  brick  wall  here.  Or
a   cyber   brick   wall.   The   details   of
several   of   the   operations   are   very
heavily  protected.  I  could  have  found
them  but  I  was  mindful  of  your  time
constraints.  You  should  assume  that  Gorse
did  the  work  that  needs  doing  in  war  but
is  never  admitted  to.
```

But the same problems in the army. And the same

sigh of relief when he was discharged. Thanks for everything but we've moved on. Jimmy Gorse had been a necessary evil.

Had he killed people? Without question. Was he still killing people?

Mozart had attached a picture.

A square, Slavic face. Close-cropped blonde hair. Nose clearly broken and reset. A face that didn't take prisoners. That didn't even consider taking prisoners.

The man he'd seen going into Enzo's.

Brady put two and two together.

Felt the hair on the back of his neck stand up. Knew he was looking at the man who'd murdered Patrick.

40

But Jimmy Gorse would have to wait.

Kate was on the phone. And now she was hysterical.

"Calm down, Kate. What do you mean 'she's gone?'"

"Maddie has disappeared, Michael. She isn't here. I came home from work. And I found a note. She's left me a note."

"Take a deep breath, Kate. What's it say? Read it out to me."

"Wait. Let me get it." Brady heard his sister walk across the kitchen. Then, "Ty's in trouble," she said. "He needs me. Ty this, Ty that. Always bloody Ty. *I* need her, Michael. Her bloody schoolwork needs her."

"Does it say anything else, Kate?"

"Yes. We've gone away for a few days."

So Ty was frightened. Running away from something.

"Have you called the police?"

"No. I haven't. What's the point? How long has she been gone? As far as anyone else cares she could be in town having a coffee."

Kate was right. Maddie was a long way from being a missing person. For now, at least. But clearly he had to do something.

"First things first, Kate. Has she really gone away? I mean, she must have taken something? Can you go upstairs and check?"

Not one of his better suggestions. Kate put the phone down. He heard her going upstairs. Then she was back. Her voice had gone up another octave.

"Yes," she said.

"What's she taken?"

"Her bag. The one she takes when she goes on a school trip. Her jeans. A couple of tops that were in the washing."

"What does Lucy say?"

"Nothing. She doesn't know anything. She says she came in from school and the note was there."

"Have you rung her?"

"Of course I have. But she's not answering. Or her phone's out of charge. She was going to get a new phone. You've got to help me, Michael. I have to find her."

He had no option. Bill was out of action, the police wouldn't be interested for another 24 hours. There was no-one else.

"OK. Look, I'll come round. Give me ten minutes. Maybe more. Ash isn't in from school yet. But she'll be here any minute. So just try to relax."

Ash wasn't. Ten minutes, 15 minutes. Half an hour after Brady had promised his sister he'd be there in ten minutes his daughter came through the door. Looking flushed.

"Are you feeling alright, Ash? You look a bit red."

"Yeah. Sorry I'm late, Dad. I realised I was going to be late so ... I ran up the hill."

"OK. You need to have your trainers on for that, not your school shoes. Look, sweetheart, I have to go out. Kate's got a problem with Maddie and - "

"And you're going to have to find her."

Brady stared at his daughter. "How did you know?"

"Because Lucy is my cousin. Because girls talk to each other. Because Ty's on the run and she's with him. It's cool. Exciting."

"No, Ash it's anything but cool. Or exciting. And Kate's worried sick. So I've got to go and see her. I'll maybe be an hour. Can you feed Archie for me?"

"Sure. I need a shower first though."

Brady walked over and kissed her. "See you soon. Love you." He walked towards the door. Then he turned back to his daughter. "This network of spies in year 9 that puts MI5 to shame. They don't happen to know where they've gone do they?"

"Someone said Ty had a friend in Scarborough."

...Which sounded a lot easier – and closer – than London.

"They didn't happen to say where in Scarborough?"

Ash shrugged – "The beach? You know, like in the film? Leonardo DiCaprio? That would be *way* cool" – and went upstairs for a shower.

41

"I'm really sorry, Kate. Ash was late home from school. God knows what she was doing."

"Tell me about it."

Kate looked beside herself with worry. A combination of worry, anger and I-should-have-seen-this-coming.

"She's gone," she said.

"Right. So what we have to do is get her back. She's definitely with Ty?"

Kate visibly shuddered. "You'll have this one day, Mike. Ash will come in with someone and you'll think, 'he's touching my daughter.'" She shook her head. "Ugh. Jesus. I'm sorry. You need me to be rational."

Brady nodded. "I do. Just tell me a few details. How long has she known him?"

"Four months. They met on Boxing Day, I think. Maddie went to someone's 18th. Down–bloody–hill ever since."

He needed Kate to be dispassionate. Just give him the facts. But like she'd said, supposing it was Ash...

"Do you know where he lives?"

Kate shook her head. "Somewhere near the football ground? Some bloody flat? We always say, 'tell us where you're going' when she goes out but she just says, 'I've got my phone.'"

"What else has she taken with her, Kate? Debit card? Passport?"

Brady watched Kate's face fall as he said the last word. She reached out for his hand. "Christ, Michael, they could have gone to Newcastle. Caught the ferry. She could be on her way to Amsterdam."

Brady thought the school rumour mill was probably more reliable than his sister's worst fears. But he needed to know.

"You know where she keeps her passport?"

Kate nodded.

"Then go and check."

"It's there," she said a minute later.

So this was a spur-of-the-moment decision. Which means that Ash is probably right. They're not far away and Ty is frightened. Very frightened.

"What's Ty look like?" Brady asked. Hopefully Kate had seen past the tattoos and the piercings. "He's dark. Hairy. You know, one of those men who'll be bald when he's 30. He wears rings."

"How tall is he?"

"Your height? Maybe a bit taller. Much taller than Maddie. They just... Damn it, Mike, they just look so wrong together."

"If he's dark he'll have brown eyes." Kate nodded. "How long's his hair?"

"Longer than yours. Not much though, now you've let it grow."

"Don't compare me to him too much, Kate. I'll have to get a tattoo. Accent? Yorkshire? Whitby? Preferably something distinctive..."

"Whitby. Through and through." She looked up. The anguish, the need for help, for some reassurance, plain on her face. "What are you going to do, Michael? How are you going to find her?"

Brady smiled at his sister. "What do you think I'm going to do? What any logical person would do. I'm going to break the law. Give me her phone number will you?"

42

Something told him this one was more Scholesy than Mozart. Which meant he'd probably need to do some research first. Brady switched his laptop on.

I'm not in. I'm never in. Leave a message. Unless you're a Liverpool fan. In which case fuck off. And there's a security question. What is God's middle name?

Brady quickly checked his laptop. "On the assumption you're not talking about your current manager, Alexander Chapman Ferguson. So Chapman," he said. "And it's Brady in case you don't recognise the voice. And sorry about you only finishing fourth. Give me a ring when you're free will you, Scholesy? It's urgent."

He had to wait. An hour. Two hours. His phone rang.

"I'm in love," Scholesy said. "I was having sex. What can I do for you, Brady?"

He was too shocked to reply.

"What is it, Brady? You think I only exist in the dark? Coke cans, pizza and Pornhub?"

"No, no. Not at all. Where did you meet her?"

"The Young Conservatives, obviously. Or online. Make a guess. She has interesting tastes. I'll send you some links..."

"Thanks, Scholesy. Maybe next time. Right now I need your help."

"What's up?"

Brady explained. "So I need to find her. Quickly."

"How quickly?"

"Tomorrow. At the latest."

"You got her phone number?"

Brady gave it to him. "But it's dead," he said.

"Since when did that matter? You think the Chinese security services give a shit about a triviality like that? You heard of Huawei, Brady? They're coming for us..."

"I'm thinking tomorrow morning," Brady said.

"Careful. You're a bit old for dawn raids. Don't want to go abseiling down a building at your age, mate."

"I need an address first..."

"Ten minutes' work," Scholesy said dismissively. "The number she most texts. That's her boyfriend right? He texts someone – what? Two days ago? 'Can I come?' Then the next day. 'I'm on my way.' Another one. 'I'll be there in ten minutes.' That's the number you want. Track that one. Track the boyfriend. Job done. Go and make a cup of tea, Brady. You could be there this afternoon."

No. He was going tomorrow morning. Because he knew they'd be in. They'd stay up late. They'd sleep in. They'd be there first thing in the morning. When he knocked on the door.

There was just one question. Brady couldn't get it out of his head.

Would I have been so dispassionate, so patient, so ready to wait for the right time if it had been Ash?

He knew the answer.

Scholesy was as good as his word. Ten minutes and he was back on the phone. "Scarborough," he said. Brady sent a small nod of congratulation to the school spy network. "Right now, he's just behind the cricket ground. You know it?"

"Yeah, sure. Used to go to the cricket festival."

"Seriously?" It was Scholesy's turn to be amazed. "You spent like – a whole day? Watching cricket? Wow. I've never met anyone who's actually done that. Awesome endurance."

"So tomorrow morning..."

"Yeah. Park behind the cricket ground. Trafalgar Square. Then ring me. What time?"

"Eight-thirty."

"Eight-thirty? What the fuck, Brady? That's the middle of the night."

"I'll pay you extra," Brady said. "Overtime. After all, it takes a long time to abseil down a building at my age."

He put his phone down. Tried not to imagine Ash in a flat in Scarborough. Tried not to imagine Ash with a 20 year old boyfriend. Rang Kate and gave her the good news. "But there's bad news as well," he said. "You'll need to be patient. At least until tomorrow."

43

Brady parked the car outside Bean's. "Sorry again," he said. "I'll pick you up after school, OK?"

"OK," Ash said. "I just hope there's someone awake."

"Ash, it's quarter to eight. It's a school day. Her mum – what's she called? – will have been up for ages."

"Fiona. And make sure you come back with Maddie."

"I'll do my best. But remember what I said."

"Yeah, yeah. Top secret."

"Not. Even. Bean."

"Dad, she's my best friend."

"Not even Bean," Brady repeated.

"Spoilsport." Ash opened the car door.

"Have a good day, love."

Ash nodded. Suddenly looked worried. "Take care, Dad. You're all I've got."

BRADY DROVE INTO SCARBOROUGH. Right at Peasholm Park roundabout, then left up on to North Marine Road. Past the Hollywood Plaza – did any cinema ever look less like a Hollywood Plaza? – and there was the cricket ground on the right. No play today: it had been raining all the way from Whitby.

He eased the car into a parking space. Switched the engine off, glanced at his watch. 8:20. He was early. As if he could have been late...

He locked the car and walked the 50 yards to Trafalgar Square. Passed a sign. *Disc zone 9am to 5pm.* Realised he'd forgotten to put a disc in the car. No problem. This would be over well before 9:00.

Trafalgar Square wasn't a square. Two roads running parallel to each other separated by a surprisingly neat communal garden. Terraced houses, three and four storeys high. Houses for big families, then B&Bs in the boom years after the War. Now – if the number of dustbins was any guide – flats and bedsits.

There was a café on the corner. The Toast Box. *Open 7 days a week. 8am to 4:30pm. 10oz Gammon Steaks*

Maybe another time...

He crossed the road and walked down the side with the even numbers. *No parking* scrawled on a wall. Half a dozen green bins outside the first house, carrier bags full of rubbish spilling out on to the pavement. Two palm trees in the front garden. What passed for palm trees in North Yorkshire. Brady didn't know what they were called.

The next house was dark blue. Four storeys. A *For Sale* sign planted firmly by the front gate.

Supposing I was looking for Ash...

Only the ninth or tenth time he'd thought that.

What time was it now? 8:25. Close enough. He phoned Scholesy.

I'm not in. I'm never in. Leave a message. Unless you're a Liverpool fan. In which case –

The message clicked off. "Fuck, Brady. Is that you?"

"Yep. And I'm here. What've you got?"

Scholesy yawned loudly.

He ran his hand through his hair. Scratched his balls. Sat down at his laptop. T-shirt and boxers. Brady couldn't have seen it any more clearly if he'd been in the room.

"Three phones in the same place. Your niece. Her boyfriend. Boyfriend's mate. Will that do you?"

"Whereabouts?"

"What number are you outside?"

Brady turned round. "Six," he said.

"Cross over. Odd numbers. Maybe eight, ten houses down."

"This guy Ty's with. Does he have a name?"

"Mason. Joseph Henry. And his phone bill's overdue."

Brady did as he was told. Crossed over, walked slowly down the street. "There," Scholesy said. "And now I've got four phones lined up."

"Are you tracking me as well, you bastard?"

"Course I am. How else am I going to do it?"

And that was the trouble. You worked with people like Scholesy. You got what you needed.

But you paid a price.

You paid with more than money. Because you knew that what they did *for* you they could do *to* you. You paid, and the guy in the t-shirt and boxers stopped scratching his balls for a minute and helped himself to a small slice of your life.

Scholesy couldn't help it. It was what he did.

THE HOUSE HAD ONCE BEEN cream. Now it was just a dirty white, the paint peeling round the window frames, a damp patch spreading behind a rusty drain pipe.

All Brady had to do was get inside.

A joiner? Sent by the landlord? The lack of tools might be a giveaway. Police? Where's your warrant, pal?

And Ty was frightened. Running away. So they weren't going to be in a hurry to open the door.

But Ty wasn't his problem. Maddie was.

There were four bells. A neatly written label with 'Mason' on it would have been nice. None of them had names.

Start at the top then.

A girl's voice crackled through the speaker. Asian and still half asleep. "What you wan'?"

"Sorry," Brady said. "Pressed the wrong bell. Go back to bed."

Next one down. He pressed the bell three times. Either it didn't work or the flat was empty.

Third bell. *Don't let me down, Scholesy.* The rain was getting harder. *Don't make me walk up and down this depressing road trying a hundred doorbells.*

"Yeah, what is it?"

A man's voice. Local accent. Mid-20s maybe.

When you can't think of anything else, tell the truth.

"I need to talk to Maddie. It's an emergency."

"What sort of an emergency?"

"A family emergency. I'm her uncle."

"How do I know you're not the police?"

"Because I'm not threatening you with a warrant, I'm not knocking your door down and there's only one of me. And if you want me to step out into the road so you can look out of the window and check I will do. But it's pissing down. So I'd rather not."

"Just wait."

Silence. Clearly a discussion inside the flat. Brady made a futile effort to shelter in the doorway. Then the voice was back.

"We don't trust you. But Maddie says she's got an uncle. So stand back from the doorway so she can see you. Stand on the pavement."

Brady sighed, accepted his fate and took three steps back down the path. Stood on the pavement. Looked up to the second floor window and saw Maddie. She was wearing a long yellow t-shirt. Nothing else. He saw her say something.

'Yeah, it's him. He's okay.' Or words to that effect. The door buzzed, clicked open. Brady was inside. He stood still for a few seconds, dripping on to a dirty maroon carpet.

44

Up two flights of stairs. The walls bearing the scars of someone who didn't make it to the bathroom in time. The smell of last night's pot still hanging in the air. Then a surprisingly pristine chrome '2' on a white door.

Brady knocked. Two beats of two. Carried on dripping.

The door opened. He wasn't dark, so it wasn't Ty. Blonde hair, grey eyes, bad complexion, a wispy goatee.

Joe Mason. But let's not give Scholesy's trade secrets away.

"Brady. The one who's been standing in the rain."

"You'd better come in."

He turned, led the way into a lounge. There was a table, one of the old ones your grandmother had where the extra leaf slid out for Sunday dinner. A TV in the corner with an Xbox connected. A faded two seater settee against the far wall. A grey bed settee on his right. Half pushed back into a settee. Ty perched nervously on it, Maddie next to him. Wearing jeans with the t-shirt now.

Brady looked at her and saw Ash. Had another glimpse into what the words 'single parent' really meant.

"I need to talk to you," he said.

"You can talk here." Ty had a square, pugnacious face. Almost black eyes, full lips. The backs of his hands tattooed. Kate had been right. He ticked every box that Bill wanted unticked.

"No," Brady said. "I can't."

Ty reached his hand out. Put it on Maddie's thigh. Possessive. Said, "She's staying with me."

Brady nodded. "Just let me talk to her. But it's really important. And it's between us."

Maddie moved Ty's hand away. "It's alright. He's one of the good guys."

She stood up and walked out of the lounge. Two steps across the hall and into the kitchen. "You want coffee or anything?" she said.

For a second Brady didn't reply. He was looking out of the window. A clear, uninterrupted view across the cricket ground. He looked to his right.

There, just below the beer tents. That's where they used to sit. Scarborough Cricket Festival. Cheese and tomato sandwiches, a hard-boiled egg, maybe a cold sausage. His autograph book in his backpack. Cricket bat and tennis ball for a game in the lunch interval. And if he'd looked up to his right as he was bowling to Patrick he'd have seen the kitchen window.

Where 27, 28 years later he was trying to persuade his niece to leave her drug-dealer boyfriend and come home with him...

"No, I'm good thanks, Maddie. And you need to come back with me."

She hesitated. Long enough to make Brady think she was already having second thoughts about the trip. "Why? Has Mum sent you?"

"In a manner of speaking. But not for the reason you think."

Maddie reached her left hand up. Twirled her hair. Ash did it, usually when she was nervous. "Why then?"

Kate should be the one telling her this. But it was his job to bring her home.

Brady put his hand on her shoulder. "Sweetheart, I'm really sorry to tell you this. Your dad is ill."

"A hernia? A hernia's not ill. A hernia's just getting old."

Brady shook his head. "I wouldn't be here for that. I'm sorry, Maddie. They've done some tests. They think your dad might have cancer. And – "

"Ty needs me. He's frightened."

"Yeah. I understand that. But right now your mum's frightened as well."

She didn't reply. She was 17. Swamped by the yellow t-shirt. No make-up, bare feet. She didn't look any older than Ash. Brady stepped forward. Wrapped his arms round her.

"How?" she said into his chest. "I mean, where? How bad?"

He let go. Stepped back. Gave her the details. "They think he has bladder cancer. They're doing some more tests."

"Is that bad? Bladder? Is that a good one or a bad one?"

"I don't know, Mads. I'm not an expert. I can't believe there are any good ones."

She was silent again, staring at her feet. Brady looked out of the window a second time. Those games in the lunch interval were the best part of the day. Scholesy was right. By the middle of the afternoon they'd been bored with the real cricket.

"Ty's not going to be very happy," she said.

Is this what it would come to one day? His daughter worrying about the feelings of some boy he desperately hoped she never saw again?

"Yeah, I can understand that," Brady said, impressed by how dispassionate, how logical he was. Even more struck by how wide the gap between 'niece' and 'daughter' was. "Do you want me to talk to him?"

She shook her head. "No, that's only going to make it worse."

Brady followed her into the lounge. "I'm going back," she said.

Ty stood up. "What do you mean you're going back?"

"I mean I'm going back to Whitby. My dad's ill. I've got to."

Ty reached forward and grabbed her arm. "You can't. We have to stay here." He tried to keep the fear out of his voice. Failed. "You can't. We leave here and that mad Scottish bastard is going to find us."

"Jimmy Gorse," Brady said quietly.

"How the fuck do you know that?"

"Because I'm a Good Samaritan. Because I gave Carl a lift. And because I used to be a copper."

"I fucking knew it," Joe said. "I fucking knew we shouldn't have let him in. Should have left him standing on the fucking pavement."

"*Used* to be," Brady said.

And here it was. Laid out in front of him. In a fading bedsit overlooking a cricket ground. The story. What was happening in Whitby. Maybe even the answer to why Patrick was killed.

All he had to do was ask.

And be prepared to deal with the answers.

45

"*Used* to be," Brady said again. "I'm not now. So I don't care about the drugs. And if I'm honest, Ty, I don't really care about you being terrified. But I do care about Maddie. And I care about people I like having their fingers amputated. So why don't you tell me the story?"

"What's in it for us?" Ty said.

Brady sighed. The same question. Always the same question. 'What's in it for me?' And you always had to explain. They could never see it for themselves.

"You know what, Ty? You know what's in it for you? Ten fucking fingers, that's what's in it for you. The chance to go back to Whitby without looking behind you every 30 seconds. The chance to make something of your life." Brady realised he was sounding like his old headmaster. "Or you can carry on smoking pot in a bedsit. Like I said, I don't care."

Ty fished a tin out of his pocket. Started to roll a cigarette. "You want one?" he said to Maddie. She shook her head.

"What are you gonna do, then?" Joe had been silent up to now. "Be a hero? Ride into Whitby on a white horse? Best chance Ty's got is to say nothing and stay here."

Brady sighed. "How do you think I found you?" he said.

Ty shrugged. "Fuck knows. Magic. Like in Harry Potter. *Accio Maddie*, maybe."

"I got someone to track your phones," Brady said. "You think if I can do it, someone else can't do it? How do you get your instructions for the drug deals, Ty?"

Ty didn't say anything. The expression on his face was enough.

"So tell me what happened. And maybe I can do something about it."

Ty looked at Joe. Neither of them seemed capable of making a decision.

"They all know each other," Maddie said. "They were at school together."

"Is that how it started?" Brady was getting impatient. Time to apply some pressure. "Just have a look out of the window will you, Maddie? See if there's a mad Scottish bastard waiting outside. Probably with someone else."

"Alright," Ty said. "Alright. Yeah, like she said. We're at school together. And we're all dabbling a bit. And then word goes out that Enzo's involved. Starting to buy in bulk. There's a chance to make some real money."

"Why do you think he's doing that?" Brady asked. He knew the answer. Trying to plug a hole in the cash flow. It's a long winter. Racehorses still need feeding: school fees still need paying.

"Who knows?" Joe said. "All we knew was that he had enough cash to buy in bulk. And better stuff than we were buying."

"So gradually a network emerges," Brady said. "Enzo's buying in bulk, you're buying off Enzo."

Ty nodded. "Sometimes just selling it for him. But Enzo had no fucking idea. He didn't even know the street value. Couple of the lads were fiddling him right, left and centre. One of them fiddled so much he bought a car."

"And then?" Brady knew what was coming,

"And then Enzo says he's got a partner. Partner my arse." Yep, a partner who'd seen the size of the market. Who'd decided that what worked in Leeds would work in Whitby. Who'd made Enzo the proverbial offer he couldn't refuse.

'We're taking over. You can agree and have a small slice of it or they can find you floating in the harbour.'

"So you've got a new boss? Welcome to the new world."

Ty shook his head. "And then some. We're all told to meet up at Enzo's. Two o'clock. Don't be late. And there's this Scottish prick. And Jonno turns up at quarter past. He says, 'You're late.' Jonno says, 'So fucking what?' And he decks him. No warning. Right there outside Enzo's. Fucking tourists walking past and everything. Bang. One in the stomach, one in the head. And Jonno's lying there on the pavement and he leans over him. Sticks his face right up close to Jonno's. Almost touching. 'Now get in the fucking bus,' he says.

"What bus?"

"There's a minibus. We're all told to get in the minibus."

"So where did you go?"

"Fuck knows."

"What do you mean 'fuck knows?' You must know where you went."

Joe shook his head. "Blindfolds," he said. "Five minutes out of Whitby, the driver pulls into a lay-by and this Scottish twat - "

"Gorse," Brady said.

"Yeah. But we don't know that then. Anyway, he tells us all to put blindfolds on. Fucking Jonno's shaking like a leaf. Says he needs a piss. Gorse makes him have a piss with the blindfold on. Poor bastard's shaking so much he can barely find his dick."

It was straight out of the army's interrogation manual. Humiliate, strip, threaten. Use sensory deprivation. Pick on one of the prisoners. Make an example. Standard practice for TQs.

'Tactical Questioners.'

What had Mozart written? *You should assume that Gorse did the work that needs doing in war but is never admitted to.*

"Then what?" Brady said.

"We're at a house. Or a farm. But we're herded into a barn."

No point asking how long they were in the minibus. The driver probably drove round in circles.

"And now it gets completely fucking surreal," Ty said.

Brady laughed in spite of himself. "What happened?"

"We're in this barn. You know, not a cow shit barn. A

tidy barn. And there's chairs. And this woman. Like something out of a fucking bank advert. And she starts lecturing us."

"What did she say?"

"She says we're a team. Fuck's sake it's like something out of *The Office*. Says we're building a business. What we're doing is a business. Just like any other."

Which it was. £10bn. £15bn. £20bn. It depended who you talked to. The annual turnover of the UK drugs trade. More than Marks and Spencer's. Twenty times Manchester United.

County lines with military precision. County lines meets Dale Carnegie.

"She says we have to recruit. Especially girls. 'Cos the police never suspect girls. Says there's incentives if we do well."

Brady laughed again. "Drug Dealer of the Month? That'll look good on your CV. Then what happens?"

"I told you it was like *The Office*. We all have to get up and talk about ourselves. She says they want to get to know us better."

Brady could see it perfectly. Carl stands up and says he draws. He's sold a few pictures. Thinks he might be able to do it for a living one day. And Jimmy Gorse sits quietly at the back and takes notes. Smiles to himself.

And then Carl steps out of line – buys a flash pair of trainers, draws attention to himself – and it costs him a finger. Make an example. Straight out of the manual.

"So you found out what happened to Carl and you ran away? Were you one of the ones fiddling Enzo?"

Ty nodded.

"And you thought it was alright to drag Maddie into

it? Knowing that Gorse might come after you? Or did that not cross your mind?"

Ty didn't answer. Brady stood up. "Come on," he said to Maddie. "Grab your things. We're going. I'll wait outside if you want to say goodbye."

"No," Maddie said. "I'm good. I'm ready."

Brady took her bag. They walked downstairs and out of the front door. Turned left and walked towards North Marine Road. "You alright?" he said. "You want anything to eat? Breakfast? There's a café over - "

He glanced across to the café. A dark blue BMW was turning into Trafalgar Square. One man driving, another with short blonde hair in the passenger seat.

He lifted the latch on the door and stepped out. He'd taken two steps when someone turned into the alley at the bottom. A casual brown jacket, cream shirt. A square, Slavic face. Close-cropped blonde hair.

There'd been a dark blue BMW parked outside Enzo's arcade.

The car slowed. The driver was looking for somewhere to park.

"Give me your phone, Maddie. Now!"

"What?"

"Give me your phone. Just do it."

Brady went straight to contacts. Ty. With three red hearts. Came within a split second of hitting the number.

Almost made a dreadful mistake.

Handed the phone back to Maddie. Reached for his own phone. "Tell me Ty's number," he said.

Third ring. "Yeah? Who's this?"

"It's Brady. Gorse is here. Get out. There's an alley at the back. Runs down the side of the cricket ground."

Brady pressed the red button. Ended the call. Watched the dark blue BMW ease into a parking space. Took Maddie's arm and steered her back to his car.

46

Brady opened the car door. "Stay there," he said. "Whatever you do, promise me you'll stay there."

She nodded. "What are you going to do? You can't just leave them."

"I'm not. But my first job is to make sure you're safe. So stay in the car. And... if I'm not back in ten minutes phone the police. You can remember the door number?"

She nodded again.

Maybe the ambulance as well while you're on the phone...

"Here." Brady tossed her the car keys. "Lock yourself in. If I do it and take the keys the alarm will go off."

He turned round. Walked back up North Marine Road. Into Trafalgar Square. Past the line of green bins. Down towards the house. Fifty yards away. No idea what he was going to do.

The decision was made for him.

Brady looked up. Saw Gorse and another man coming out of the house.

Realised he was shaking. He wasn't a copper any more. Just a civilian on a deserted street.

Walking towards the man who'd murdered Patrick.

He couldn't turn round. Couldn't look suspicious. Had to keep walking. A man with a Fitbit doing his 10,000 steps.

Thirty yards. Twenty. Brady kept his head down. Ten. Five.

He felt a cold chill as Gorse's eyes swept over him.

Brady caught a snatch of the conversation. "Fucking kettle was still warm..."

They weren't out of breath. Didn't look dishevelled. Not that doing serious damage to Ty would cause Jimmy Gorse to look dishevelled. But his tone of voice had been frustrated. Thwarted. Angry.

So Joe and Ty had got away. But that meant two things. One, Gorse would still be looking for them. They'd have to sort that one out themselves. Cornwall was nice at this time of year.

And two, Gorse would work out that someone had warned them. So he'd go back to whoever had tracked Ty for him.

'Who phoned him? Just after nine. Find the number. Then find out who it belongs to.'

He'd protected Maddie by a split second. And put himself in the firing line instead.

'That phone? Belongs to someone called Brady.'

'Give me his address.'

Brady carried on walking. Turned right at the bottom. Trafalgar Street was even more depressing than Trafalgar

Square. Someone had dumped a car's front bumper in the middle of the pavement.

He walked down towards the bottom of the hill, turned right again. Up the neat terrace of Woodall Avenue.

Turned right at the top. Back on North Marine Road. And there was his car. And the back of Maddie's head. Safe. No sign of the BMW.

He breathed a sigh of relief. Climbed in. Pointed his car back towards Whitby.

'Sometimes you don't want to ask the questions, Mike.' He could still hear Jim Fitzpatrick saying it. 'One day it'll be someone close to you. Maybe even in your family. But you've got to do it. Because if you don't, there'll be another victim.'

"Did Ty try and recruit you?" They'd gone through Burniston and Cloughton, were starting to climb up onto the Moors. "Did he try and get you involved?"

Maddie shook her head. "I told him I wouldn't. I couldn't. Not with my dad."

"So you were just..." Dating? Seeing each other? Brady had no idea how to finish the sentence.

"Yeah," Maddie said, not helping him out.

Up the hill and he was onto the Moors road. Fifteen miles and they'd be home.

"Had you heard that story before?" Brady asked. "The barn? All the rest of it."

"Parts of it. Ty said they were serious. They were going to create a demand. Give it away. Then put the price up."

Brady nodded. "Yeah," he said. "That's what they do. Give the drugs away. Outside the school gates sometimes."

Just good business. Give it away, get people hooked, put the price up. Expand your salesforce. Incentivise them. Salesman of the Month keeps his fingers.

"So how do you stop it?" Maddie asked.

"Stop it in Whitby? Or more generally? I tell you what I'd do. This isn't a very popular opinion in the police – not officially, not when I was there – I'd legalise them."

"Drugs?"

"Yeah, I would."

"Why?"

"Why? Three reasons. One, it's a massive business and it's not paying any tax at all. Two, it'd free up an enormous amount of police time. And three, legalise it and you control the quality. You don't get kids dying because someone's cut their heroin with rat poison."

"But doesn't that make the state a drug dealer?"

"But in that case the state's already a bootlegger, selling alcohol. You're right. There's huge problems. But no-one can pretend what we're doing now is working."

Past the Falcon Inn. The road dipped down, rose sharply back up as the Moors really started.

"We need to do something," Brady said. "Take the SIM out of your phone."

"Why? You phoned Ty from your phone."

"And how did I track you? By using your number to find Ty's number. So it works the other way round as well. And if Ty escaped – which he did – then they're going to want to know who warned him."

"But that was you."

"Yeah, it was me. But who's sent Ty the most messages?"

"I can't," Maddie said. "Not while the car is moving."

"Why not?"

"I need to find a pin. Or a paper clip. And the car's going up and down too much on this road."

Brady turned off. Up into a lay-by. What had once been the main road. Now it was a place for walkers to park before they set off across the Moors. For reps to stop and eat their sandwiches.

He turned the engine off. Maddie rummaged in her bag.

"I can't find one," she said.

"OK," Brady said. Then, "Sorry about this, Maddie. It's just that... If that bastard's following us up the road. If he tracks your phone. Give me it."

"I can do it at home."

"No." Brady held his hand out. "I can't take any chances. Give me the phone."

Maddie passed it to him. He got out of the car. The rain had stopped. The sun was coming out. It was peaceful. Calm. No traffic for a moment, the silence broken only by a skylark.

He climbed over a stile onto what must have been an old World War II road. It was made of concrete blocks. He dropped Maddie's iPhone onto the concrete. Watched the glass shatter. Stamped down hard on it. Ground his heel from side to side. Just like Gorse had done on Carl's hand.

He heard a noise. Looked up. Two elderly walkers

coming towards him. A husband and wife. Weary-but-happy expressions. Rain still dripping off their water-proofs. The husband looked like a retired bank manager. "Good morning," his wife said. "Lovely day at last."

Brady nodded. "Lovely. Let's hope it stays fine."

The husband glanced down. Saw the shattered phone under Brady's right heel. Smiled at him. "PPI again? Persistent buggers, aren't they? Yes, well, enjoy your day."

Brady bent down. The phone was in three pieces now. He threw them as hard as he could in different directions. Climbed back over the stile and got in the car.

"That was my phone," Maddie said.

"I'll buy you a new one," he replied.

47

They were nearly back. A business plan for drug dealing, a close encounter with a killer, a mobile phone scattered over the North York Moors and they were nearly
home.

"Here," Brady said, passing Maddie his mobile.
"Phone your mum. Tell her to put the kettle on."

"What's your passcode?"

Ash's birthday. What else? "Two – one – zero – three."

And five minutes later they were walking through the
front door.

Hugs, kisses. "I'm sorry, Mum." "I was so worried." "I
know you were." "It doesn't matter. You're home now."

Brady stood back and watched. Then Kate finally
released her daughter. Walked over to him. Put her arms
round his neck. "Thank you," she whispered. "Thank
you."

He hugged her back. "No problem," he said. "But..."

She stepped back, looked up at him, suddenly
anxious. "But what?"

"No, nothing serious," he smiled. "I owe her a mobile phone. And ... she's a good girl, Kate. You can trust her."

Kate nodded. "You're right. Seventeen years and I thought I'd got this parenting thing mastered. Clearly not." She hugged him again. "Let me make you a cup of tea."

Brady shook his head. He'd done his job: it was time to go. "No. You're fine. I need to take Archie out. Get some writing done. And I promised Ash I'd be there when she came home. She needs some help with a school project she's doing."

He kissed Kate again, hugged Maddie, told her to come round and see Ash some time. Told Kate it was no problem again. And left them to talk and hug and cry. And then talk about Bill and hug and cry some more. They needed each other, not him.

He walked out to the car. Yes, he needed to take Archie out. No, Ash didn't need his help. The days when Ash asked for his help were long gone.

He needed to be on his own. To go through Ty's story. To start and put some pieces together.

But first he needed to take his dog out. And more importantly, see his daughter.

When was the last time they ate together? Not this week. The week before? He couldn't remember. Maybe he could get a takeaway and they could watch a film together.

He'd loved those evenings. The three of them on the sofa, Ash snuggled in between him and Grace. A big box of popcorn and a *Mulan* DVD. Or *Pocahontas. Toy Story, The Lion King...*

Then it had just been Grace and Ash, watching old films together. They must have seen *Sleepless in Seattle* half a dozen times.

So what would he watch with Ash? What did she like now? She was 13. So presumably she'd watched... What? What did she watch with her friends? 15 rated? Was that what came after PG? 18? Surely not, Ash was too young.

Whiplash. He'd seen a trailer. Kate had said she'd enjoyed it. Maybe they could watch that one together. And he'd get some spare ribs. Two birds with one stone. Ash and Archie would *both* be happy with spare ribs.

Brady turned left at the roundabout. He'd check with Ash first. Maybe she'd prefer pizza. How long before he had to cross that bridge? 'You want a beer with your pizza, Ash?' A good few years, yet. Besides, she'd drink wine like her mum.

He glanced across the road. Two kids in school uniform coming out of the park. Holding hands. The boy was older, dark haired. The girl looked a lot like Ash.

For Christ's sake. It *was* Ash.

Brady turned his head again. Saw them kiss. Saw the boy slide his hand round her back. Move it lower. Watched his 13 year old daughter push it away.

Looked up. Saw the car in front of him braking at the second roundabout. Slammed his brakes on. Knew it was too late. Heard the noise as the Tiguan hit the back of a grey SUV. Jerked forward in his seat. Felt the seat belt bite across his chest.

Lifted his head up. Looked in the rear view mirror.

Saw his daughter running across the road. She'd seen the car. Abandoned the dark-haired boy.

HE WAS HOME HALF an hour later. The Tiguan wasn't badly damaged. Neither was the other car. Brady had apologised. "Completely my fault. I'm really sorry. I suffer from hay fever. I sneezed."

She'd accepted the explanation. They'd exchanged details. No-one was injured. Just Brady's embarrassment. "I'm sorry again," Brady had said. He'd held out his hand.

She'd shaken it. "Shit happens," she'd said, smiling.

Brady parked the car outside the house. Walked up to his front door. Then he stopped. Asked himself a question.

What the hell are you going to say to her?

48

Brady let go of the door handle. Walked back down the path. Got back into the car.

Five minutes. Take five minutes. Work it out.

"What would you do, Gracie?" he said out loud.

'Phone your sister: ask for advice,' was the obvious answer. But Kate had enough on her plate.

Three things. Don't lose your temper. Don't tell her she's too young. Don't say she can't see him again.

How difficult could it be?

Watch *Whiplash* together? Maybe another night.

HE OPENED THE FRONT DOOR. Archie bounded towards him. Brady bent down and ruffled the dog's head. "Hey up, Archie. Whatever happens, you love me don't you? I'll do your dinner, talk to Ash and then we'll go out."

Roast beef and vegetables flavour. When did dog food stop being dog food? Brady threw a few biscuits in for good measure and put Archie's bowl down. He walked to the bottom of the stairs. "Ash? Are you in?"

"Yes," she shouted back. "Seeing as I'm answering you that's obvious."

Mistake number one. You should have gone up to her bedroom. Let's do this on her territory.

He walked up the stairs. Knocked on Ash's door.

"What?"

"I need to talk to you."

"What about?"

"Two or three things. Can I come in?"

"Suppose so."

Brady pushed the door open. Ash was sitting at her desk, the lid of her laptop closed.

"Can I sit on the bed?"

"No, because Archie will have been jumping all over you and I don't want dog hairs on the bed."

"But you let Archie sleep in here the other day."

"That was different. Bean is coming over. She's allergic."

Brady looked around the room. Did she expect him to stand up? "I need to talk to you, Ash. I can't do it standing up."

"Why not? Loads of people talk standing up."

"Because... Well, because it feels too formal."

Ash sighed. "So you want to go downstairs? What do you want to talk about anyway?"

Did it have to be this difficult?

"Yes, it'll only take five minutes, if that's alright."

She sighed again. Even more theatrically. "I'm just going to text Bean. Tell her I'm in a shit-hot conference."

Brady bit his tongue. He didn't like her swearing.

Treat her like an adult. Whatever you do, treat her like an adult.

It took her ten minutes to text Bean. It would be dark soon. "Sorry, Archie," he said. "It might be up and down the road on the lead."

"What do you want, Dad?"

Where did he start? A suspect who refused to talk was easier than your teenage daughter.

"I ran into the back of someone else," Brady said. "I've damaged the car."

"Yeah, I saw."

"I know you did. That was the reason I crashed. You coming out of the park with... with...

"Josh," Ash said simply.

"Is that his name?"

"Yeah, Dad. Everyone has a name. His is Josh."

"OK. So you're seeing him?"

"Yep."

"How long for?" Long enough to have come in flushed the other day. But clearly not long enough for her father to work out what 'I was late, I was running up the hill' really meant.

"Two weeks."

What did he ask next? How far has it gone? Brady wasn't sure he could cope with the answer. "So when you've told me you've been going to Bean's..."

"Yes, Dad, I've been going to Bean's. Shit, Dad, what is this? The fucking inquisition?"

One of his friends had said it to him. 'Enjoy it while

you can, Mike. She'll get to 13 and she'll swear at you. The first time it happened to me it pierced my heart.'

Brady felt the knife slide coldly in.

"I'm your dad, Ash. I'm just being protective."

"Well don't!"

"Ash, there's no need to shout at me."

"Well how else will you understand anything? I don't need you to be protective and I don't need you to interfere."

"I'm not interfering - "

"Of *course* you're interfering. How can you *not* be interfering? You're spying on me."

"You've only just started at the school…"

"So what am I supposed to do, Dad? Some sort of probation period? Wear a bag over my head until I'm in Year 10? I'm going out."

"No, Ash."

"Yes, Dad. I'm going to Bean's. Like I said I was. Because unlike you I have friends. And a life."

He heard the door slam. The knife in his heart twisted from side to side.

Brady reached for Archie's lead. "How did that happen, Archie? I didn't lose my temper, I didn't tell her she was too young. I didn't say she couldn't see him. And it was still a bloody disaster. Just tell me, Archie, how did that happen?"

49

Brady clipped Archie's lead on. Apologised again for the inadequate exercise. "I'll make it up to you in the morning. Promise I will."

Knew it was pointless but still tried to phone Ash as they were walking. Five times. Five times she didn't answer.

He pulled his collar up against the drizzle. Carried on walking.

"Just come over here, Archie."

He'd meant to walk down to the park. Instead he found himself on West Cliff. Needing... Not to talk to Grace. Just to feel her close by.

He could barely make out the hill in the rain and the fading light. Was she still there? Still listening?

"Just tell me what to do, Grace," he said into the rain. "Because I don't have a bloody clue."

The rain swirled around him. He looked down. It was high tide, the beach completely covered, waves crashing relentlessly into the base of the cliffs. The cliffs that were a mix of rock and stone. Brickworks and drainpipes and dripping water.

One day it'll come down. One day some of the east coast will slide gently into the sea.

He bent down and patted Archie. "Come on, mate, let's go home. Let's go home and sort it out. Work out where the hell we go from here."

Find Ash was the immediate problem. It was a school night. She knew she had to be in by nine. Brady didn't want to think about the implications if she wasn't. Did he ring Bean's house? Would Ash see that as more interference? More 'spying on me?'

It was academic. He didn't have Bean's number.

It had been so simple. Come back home, escape the memories. Write the book. Be a good dad, be there for Ash. Kate on standby if he needed her. A ready-made friend in Patrick.

And now Patrick was dead. Daz Kidby was dead. His sister's husband had cancer. He'd fallen out with Ash. A ruthless drugs gang was tightening its grip on Whitby. No-one seemed interested in stopping it. He'd saved his niece – for now – but there'd be plenty more 17 year olds he couldn't save.

And he'd probably pissed off a psychopath.

"At least you'll never let me down, Archie. And a proper walk in the morning, I promise."

Brady reached for his door key. Had he really left that many lights on?

. . .

He opened the door and walked in. Heard voices. Ash was back – and talking to someone. A voice he didn't recognise.

"Hi, I brought Ash home."

Fiona, Bean's mum.

She was in her 30s. Blonde hair to her shoulders. Clear blue eyes. A dark jacket over a business suit.

"Thank you," Brady said. "I appreciate that. I... We..."

Fiona smiled. "You don't need to say anything. Thirteen's not the easiest age."

"Can I get you a drink? Would you like - "

Fiona shook her head. "No, I have to get back. I just wanted to make sure Ash was safely home."

She picked her car keys up off the table. Turned back to Ash, who'd come out of the kitchen and was standing behind her. "Deal?" she said.

Ash nodded. Fiona gave her a hug. Ash hugged her back. Without any of the self-consciousness ·she had when she hugged him. Brady watched. And realised he felt jealous.

He followed Fiona into the hall. "I can't thank you enough," he said.

She smiled. Reached a hand out and put it on his arm. "Go and talk to her. She's a good kid. But it's a difficult age. And it's nice to meet you at last."

He walked back into the lounge. Ash stood awkwardly in front of him, her head down.

"I'm sorry," she whispered.

Brady stepped forward. Took his daughter in his arms. Bent forward and kissed the top of her head. "You don't have to say that. And if you're sorry, sweetheart, you're nowhere near as sorry as I am."

He hugged her. And then hugged her even harder. "Daddy?" she said.

"What, sweetheart?"

"There's something I need to tell you."

Brady panicked. Josh. Had the relationship gone that far? Was that the deal? She had to tell him?

"What, Ash?"

"You're squashing me."

He laughed and let her go. Ash licked her finger, chalked an imaginary 'I' in the air.

"Shall we just put this one down to experience?"

She nodded.

"I was going to get a film tonight," he said. "I thought we could – you know, like we used to."

"I'd like that," she said. "You'd have to promise to buy some popcorn though. And let me choose the film."

"OK," he said. "But no rom-com. You know I don't do rom-com."

"OK. Saturday night maybe? Bean's going to Center Parcs with her mum and brother."

Brady nodded. "That would be lovely. If you don't mind spending a night with your dad?"

"I'm going to bed," Ash said. "I'm tired. Is it alright if Archie sleeps in my room? I'd like that."

"I thought you said Bean was allergic?"

"Not *that* allergic. And she's not as important as Archie."

"Yeah, sure it is. Make sure he gets a good night's sleep

though, I'm taking him on the Moors tomorrow if it's fine. I owe him a long walk."

Ash walked towards the door. "Ash?" Brady said. "What was your deal with Fiona?"

She paused in the doorway. "That we make friends," she said. "I talked to her. She said you were doing your best. That you were cross because you cared. That it's difficult for you…"

Brady nodded. Felt the tears prick the back of his eyes. "It's OK. Say thank you for me. It's just … well, nothing prepares you."

"Dad?"

"What, love?"

Ash smiled at him. "You should ask Fiona out. Bean and I have talked about it. She's on her own as well. So we think it's a good idea."

50

'I'm taking him on the Moors tomorrow if it's fine.'

It wasn't. Archie's long walk would have to wait.

Which was just as well. Brady had been awake half the night. Turning it over and over in his mind.

The one question he couldn't answer.

Why? Why did Gorse kill Patrick?

He'd thought Ty's story would tell him. It hadn't.

What had Patrick done – or said – or seen – or even hinted he might do – that had threatened them so much?

Patrick ran his business. He had a young wife. They were trying to start a family.

There was simply no need for Patrick to get involved. He *wouldn't* have got involved.

He'd thrown Kidby out of his flat. But that was all. A business decision: no more, no less.

He'd had a cup of tea with Brady. Bumped into him on the Saturday night. But by that time Gorse was trailing him. So Gorse had decided to kill Patrick well before Saturday night.

Why?

Whichever angle Brady came at it from he got the same answer. There wasn't an answer.

There was only one way to find out. Only one person who could tell him.

He walked up the steps and rapped on Enzo's door.

"Look, Enzo. I know you're involved in drugs. I know you're getting forced out by... I don't know, someone from Leeds, Sheffield, maybe even Manchester. I don't care. You can sort it out amongst yourselves. But I do care about who killed Patrick. And you can tell me."

Enzo reached across his desk and picked up an e-cigarette. Brought it to his lips and exhaled a cloud of strawberry scented smoke in Brady's face.

"Gorse killed him," he said through the fog. "But you already knew that."

Brady wasn't going to be intimidated. He stood up and took two steps across the office. Opened the top half of the stable door.

He turned back to Enzo. "Yes, I did. I want to know why."

Enzo took a long time replying. Then he looked up at Brady. "You really want the truth? It won't do you any good."

"Of course I want the truth. And I'll decide whether it does me any good or not."

Enzo was silent again. Brady could hear the sounds of early summer on the seafront. A car driving slowly past.

A mother shouting at her child. The inevitable cries of the seagulls.

He looked straight at Enzo. Saw the same expression he'd seen on Bill's face. The same pleasure in Brady's pain.

Bill savouring the moment before he told him about Kara's trip to London.

Now Enzo. The same certainty that he could say whatever he wanted – because whatever he said, Brady couldn't do anything about it.

"Cock-up." Enzo leaned back in his chair and smiled.

"Cock-up? What the hell do you mean 'cock-up?'"

Enzo smiled again. "Exactly what I say."

Brady willed himself to keep calm. "You're saying Patrick was killed because of a mistake? Mistaken identity? Gorse killed the wrong person? The wrong Goth?"

Enzo shook his head. Another cloud of strawberry smoke. "No. Gorse killed the right Goth. Exactly who he meant to kill."

Brady stood up again. Walked to the door. Rested his hands on the bottom half. Leaned out and looked at the steps running down to the road. Saw Gorse running up them towards him. Saw Patrick lying in an alley across the harbour.

And understood exactly what had happened.

He heard Enzo speaking on the phone. "Tell Stevie to come up to the office, will you? Tell him to bring the bat. Yeah, right now. This minute."

Brady took a deep breath. Turned back to Enzo.

"It was you, wasn't it?"

He heard a door open. One of the arcade mechanics

walked into the office. Big, burly, a baseball bat held tightly in his right hand.

"Don't worry, Enzo, I'm not going to attack you."

But I will have my revenge. Not here. Not now. Maybe not for some time. But revenge, Enzo. Count on it.

Enzo laughed. "No, you're not. You're not going to do anything. Because Stevie is twice your size and half your age. And the case is closed. Kidby confesses, Kidby dies in jail." A third cloud of self-satisfied smoke. "How fucking neat is that?"

"Answer me one question," Brady said.

"Maybe." Enzo glanced at the mechanic. "Lock the door, Stevie. Just in case."

"Why did Gorse kill him? Why not just beat him up? That was what you wanted, wasn't it? You didn't want him killed. You wanted him taught a lesson."

Enzo laughed out loud. "You're a dumb fuck, you really are. Or maybe you just haven't met him yet. Gorse is a hunting dog. They can keep the muzzle on for so long, then ... he needs to hunt. He needs raw meat."

"And that was Patrick?" Brady said. "A good man. With a wife. With a baby on the way. That's what he was? 'Raw meat?'"

Brady stood up and looked straight at Enzo. "You disgust me. Your father would be ashamed of you."

He opened the door and walked out of the office.

"And what can I say?" Enzo yelled after him. "Shit happens."

51

Brady walked across the road.

"Hey up," Dave said. "You're a bit late for breakfast."

He was cleaning the griddle. Three in the afternoon and the demand for bacon sandwiches was over for another day.

"If you've got the time," Brady said, "I need a favour."

"Aye? What's that then?"

"When you've finished..." Brady waved in the direction of the griddle in a gesture Dave hopefully interpreted as, 'I know you have a lot to do.'

"Would you come for a walk with me? I know what happened. I want to get it straight in my mind."

"Five minutes."

"Thanks, Dave. I appreciate it."

Now they were on the beach, standing by the side of the pier. "Low tide," Dave said. "Don't often see it this low. Take your shoes and socks off an' you could paddle out to the storm break."

There was a gap in the harbour wall, directly under

the bridge. "You know what?" Brady said. "All these years in Whitby, I've never really known the right name for it. Storm break? Storm gate?"

Dave laughed. "I reckon the one on the pier's the storm gate. The one they close to save dozy buggers from themselves. Stop them thinking the end of the pier in a storm is a good place to take their holiday photos."

"Makes sense."

"Yeah. And then storm break in the wall. Let the water through. Otherwise the storms hit straight into the harbour wall."

Brady looked out to sea. Late May and the North Sea was flat. So flat a paddle boarder was calmly making his way towards Sandsend.

"Different story in a storm," Dave said. "I come down and watch it sometimes. Rough sea, high tide... It's hypnotic. Like the whole of the North Sea crashes through the break. Over the ledge. And then straight into the rocks."

Brady followed his gaze. The rocks were ten, maybe 15 yards across, slightly higher than his waist. Covered in green algae, the water lapping gently round them. The rocks and the foot bridge were perfectly reflected on the wet beach. He looked through the storm break, saw the pier curving gently round.

They turned and started walking along the beach towards Sandsend. A stray football rolled towards them. Brady trapped it. Kicked it back to a father who was being comprehensively outplayed by his son.

"So what happened?" Dave said.

"Enzo's in trouble. He's doing some small scale drug

dealing. He's got cash - "

"Cash *flow*, you mean. There's a big difference. And Enzo's feeling it."

"Sorry, I forgot your background. Yeah, you're right. So he has to fix his cash flow problems. And like everything he does he screws it up. The people he's buying off – Leeds would be my guess – see an opportunity. They make Enzo a very simple offer. *Gorse* makes Enzo a very simple offer..."

"So who's this Gorse?"

"The enforcer. The rottweiler. Someone who did the jobs the Army never admit to. Now in the private sector. And..."

Did he say it to Dave? There was no-one else to tell.

"...And the person who murdered Patrick."

"Right." Dave was silent for a minute. "So I'll have maybe seen him? When he's been to lean on Enzo?"

"Yes," Brady said, suddenly aware of the load he was sharing. "Yes. I'm sorry."

"I might have made the bugger a bacon sandwich?"

Brady couldn't help laughing. "Yes, you could."

"Probably not something to share with the wife. So when this murderer's eaten a bacon sandwich he goes and leans on Enzo?"

"Yes. And Enzo has no choice. He's maybe met him once. He's already terrified. But he's a sly bastard. He sees a chance as well. He's pissed off with Patrick. Long term, he thinks he's dishonoured his sister. Won't do any business deals with him. Short term..."

"Something happened?" Dave said.

"Yeah. Patrick went round to look at one of the houses

he owns. He wants to sell it. Finds Kidby's growing dope on the window sill. Goes downstairs. Takes a chance. Knocks. Carl answers the door – "

"The lad you told me about?"

"Yeah. And he's not thinking straight. Doesn't realise his landlord has to give him notice if he wants to come in. So Carl lets him in. And Patrick's not a fool. He sees what's going on. Says 'thanks very much.' Goes outside. Sits in his car. And loses his temper. He's calm, he's rational, he's calculating. Just once he loses his temper and it costs him his life. He's heard the stories, he knows who supplying Carl. So he drives down here. Straight in to see Enzo. 'No more drugs in my flats.' Maybe he threatens Enzo with the police."

"And Enzo knows he's safe?"

"Yeah. And he sees the chance of a little petty revenge. Thinks he'll teach Patrick a lesson."

To gloat. To enjoy someone else's pain. 'Nasty black eye you've got there, Patrick. Someone said you fell over...'

"So he hints to Gorse that Patrick's trying to muscle in on the drugs deals?"

"Exactly," Brady said. "Thomas a Becket all over again. Will no-one rid me of this turbulent property developer? Except Gorse isn't planning to copy Henry II and do penance."

"But he must have asked for some evidence? He's only someone's bloody rottweiler. He can't just murder Patrick on Enzo's say-so."

Brady shrugged. "I don't know. Enzo says 'Look, one of our lads lives in his property. He's trying to get him to switch sides...'"

"So Gorse goes back to someone. Says 'we need to make a statement. Show them we're serious?'"

Brady nodded. "And Enzo was right. For once. Whoever controls Gorse knows they have to slip him off the leash. Turn him loose occasionally."

"And it sends a message."

"Yep, it does. Not just Whitby. Scarborough. Middlesbrough. Up and down the coast. There's nothing we won't do. Whoever you are."

"So it's just business then?" Dave said.

"Maybe," Brady said. "What's the drugs trade in Whitby worth? Depending on who you talk to the UK is up to twenty billion quid. Me? I think it's nearer 30. But let's say it's only ten. If Whitby's one per cent of one per cent it's still a million."

"So 50% profit margin. Half a million quid a year."

"Tax free," Brady added.

"So is that why Patrick was killed? For half a million quid a year?"

"No," Brady said. "Patrick was killed because Enzo didn't give a fuck. And because that's what Gorse does. He kills people. And he enjoys it."

They turned round. Started walking back towards Whitby.

"So what are you going to do about it?" Dave said.

"You asked me that once before."

Dave nodded. "And you've found out who killed your friend. But what now? Are you going after this Gorse?"

"No," Brady said. "I won't have to. He's coming after me."

52

"Ash?" Brady put his head tentatively round the bedroom door. "You OK this morning?"

"Uh-huh," she answered sleepily. "Yeah, I'm good."

"OK, I'm taking Archie on the Moors. I owe him a long walk. And it's not raining for once. I'm going to take him to the Hole of Horcum."

"OK. Have fun."

Brady walked across to her. Kissed his fingers and touched them to her cheek. "Make sure you get up in time."

"Don't worry, Bean's coming for me. And Dad..." The quilt was almost covering her face. She squinted up at him.

"What, love?"

"Your beard needs trimming. If you're going to keep it you need to trim it."

He laughed – "What next, Ash? Fashion advice?" – and walked out of the room.

Was that a muttered 'too late' as a parting shot? It

didn't matter. The argument was behind them. The sun was shining and the Hole of Horcum was calling. Five or six miles with Archie, come home, finally, finally, make some progress with the book. It was a perfect morning.

THERE WERE WISPS of mist hanging over the tree tops. Fog lying in the bottom of the valley. More autumn than spring. And a few hundred feet up on the Moors, ten degrees colder than Whitby. Brady zipped his jacket up and opened the tailgate. Clipped the lead on a very impatient dog.

"Come on, pal, you know you need your lead on. Just for two minutes."

He locked the car and they walked across the road. "No, Archie. Leave it," Brady said. There was a rabbit stretched out in the middle of the road, its lifeless eyes staring up into the sky. "Come on, let's go."

Brady walked down the 13 steps to the path. Look down at all the tracks crisscrossing the side of the hill. "I should bring you here more often, Archie."

They turned right and started to walk along the path, the ferns – still wet from last night's rain – growing across the path and soaking Brady's trousers. The path wound gradually downhill as it ran along by the side of the road. Then there was a decision to make.

"What's it to be, Archie? Do we take the high road or the low road? Up onto the Moors or down into Wade the Giant's bowl?"

Brady opted for the Moors. He wanted the space. The fresh air. The view back towards Whitby. "You alright to climb over the stile, Arch? Maybe not?" He opened the gate and they were off...

Two hours later – one of them wishing he'd brought a flask of coffee, the other ready to do it all again – and they were back. It had been perfect. An easy path. Plenty of smells for Archie to explore. The heather promising to come into bloom. A kestrel hovering a hundred yards in front of them...

"Just down here, Archie," Brady said. "Through the gate and then ten minutes back to the car. And we'll come back at the weekend. See if we can persuade Ash to come with us."

They walked down the path towards the gate.

Light travels faster than sound.

They'd done it at school. "So for your homework," Binksy had said, "Work out an experiment to prove that light travels faster than sound."

The beach was the obvious place. Patrick had been carrying an old tin bucket. "Two hundred yards enough?" he'd said.

"Should be," a 16 year old Brady had replied. "Besides, it's freezing. It'll have to be."

He'd stood by the pier. Patrick had walked off towards Sandsend. Stopped when he thought he was 200 yards away. Knowing Patrick he'd have counted the steps. Brady watched as Patrick put the bucket down and then started wandering round the beach. "Why didn't you find a rock first?" he yelled into the wind.

Patrick was back. He'd found one. He waved to

Brady. Brady waved back. Patrick lifted the rock above his head. Then let it fall. Brady saw the rock hit the bucket. A split second later he heard the dull metallic clang.

IT WAS EXACTLY THE SAME.

Brady saw Archie stumble. Pitch forward.

A split second later he heard the shot.

Looked down. Archie lying on his side. Gasping for breath. Brown eyes looking up at him. Questioning.

What's happened? We were having a walk.

Someone had shot his dog.

A farmer? But there were no sheep.

Who then?

Brady looked around. The Moors, the path. The road in front of him. Trees on the other side of it.

No-one.

He bent down. Put his hands under Archie. Lifted him as gently as he could. Felt the blood warm on his hands. Saw it on his jacket. Heard Archie whimper. Lifted him up. Bent his head. Kissed him. "Hang in there, Archie. Ten minutes and we're back at the car."

Walked down the path 50 yards. Knew he had a problem. A serious problem. The gate. He couldn't open the gate. Not without putting Archie down. He couldn't do that. And he couldn't climb the stile.

There was a walker. Middle-aged, walking with his son, coming towards him. "Please," Brady called. "Could you open the gate for me?"

The man looked up. Saw Brady carrying his dog. Did

as he was asked. "Is he alright? We've got a Springer at home..."

Brady shook his head. "No. Thank you. My car's in the car park."

"What's happened?"

A May morning. A beauty spot. He couldn't believe the words he was saying. "My dog has been shot."

And he was past them. Walking back up the path. Next to the road now. A battered camper van passed him. A woman – 30 maybe – in the passenger seat. Saw Brady carrying his dog. Her mouth opened in shock. And they were gone.

The path kept rising. Archie was heavy. Still panting. "Just breathe, Archie. Just keep breathing."

The ferns still wet. Still soaking his legs. But here. The car park. Finally. Brady walked up the steps. Half ran, half stumbled across the road.

Made it back to the car.

As far as he could tell the bullet had hit Archie's shoulder. How much blood had he lost? How much blood was *in* a Springer Spaniel?

What the hell did he do? He couldn't put a tourniquet on Archie's shoulder. All he could do was get to the vet's as fast as he could.

His keys were in his jacket pocket. Somehow he managed to fumble for them without letting go of Archie. He pressed the fob twice and unlocked the car.

Another problem.

How did he open the tailgate? Put Archie down on the ground? How much damage would he do picking him up again? Supposing the bullet had broken his shoulder?

But he couldn't risk dropping him. Couldn't risk causing him pain.

Hold on to Archie. Find a way – any way – to lift the tailgate.

Brady knelt down. Tried to readjust the way he was holding Archie so he could reach the catch. Stupidly remembered watching an ad on TV. Some new SUV. "Seriously," he'd said to Ash. "Who's daft enough to pay money for a car boot that opens automatically?"

"Hang on, Archie. Hang in there, son."

He couldn't reach the catch. He re-adjusted his grip again. Archie whimpered in pain. Louder this time. "Sorry, Arch. I'm sorry."

He tried again. And heard the central locking click. Fuck. Fuck. He'd taken too long. Back to square one. He stood up. Fumbled in his pocket for his keys again. Pressed the fob. Once. Twice. The car was open. He went back down on one knee. Archie was getting heavier...

"You look like you've a problem there. Maybe I can help?"

A Scottish accent. Brady looked up. Jimmy Gorse was standing over him. Black jeans. Black V-neck t-shirt. Black leather jacket.

He was smiling.

Brady had been so intent on carrying Archie back to the car he hadn't seen the dark blue BMW.

Parked near the trees. Parked near the trees that would be perfect cover for someone with a rifle.

He was too stunned to speak. "Here," Gorse said, "Move back slightly. I'll open the car for you." Gorse smiled down at him. "You can lay the pup in the boot. Get yoursel' away to the vet's."

Brady stood up slowly. "You bastard. You fucking bastard. You shot my dog."

Gorse lifted the tailgate. Turned, smiled at him for a third time. "Aye, I did that. I meant to kill him. But I see now this is better. Gives us chance for a wee chat."

Gorse stepped forward. He was maybe two inches shorter than Brady. He reached out his right hand. There was nothing Brady could do. The only way to fight back was to drop Archie on the ground.

The hand closed on his throat. Squeezed, just hard enough to leave him short of breath.

"We've had enough," Gorse said. He was speaking quietly. Gently explaining to someone who hadn't quite grasped the problems he was causing. "Ma boss has had enough. I've had enough. This is your last warning, Brady."

The pressure on his throat increased. "Fuck off. You hear me? Fuck off. Back to Manchester. Or next time it'll be that bonny, wee daughter of yours."

Gorse took his hand away. Stepped back. "Now get yourself away to the vet's. I'm nae expert on dogs. People, aye. Not dogs. What do you think, Brady? Fifty-fifty?"

Brady laid Archie gently in the boot. Thought he should cover him. Keep him warm. There was only one option. He took his jacket off and laid it over his dog. Gently closed the tailgate.

He turned and faced Gorse. "You bastard. You absolute fucking bastard. I'll - "

Gorse laughed. "You'll do what? Get even with me?

Sort me out? Hae a fuckin' word wi' yourself, Brady. You're ten years older than me. Not even half-fit. I'd kill you inside thirty seconds."

Gorse gestured over his shoulder. There was a minibus pulling into the car park, Lady Lumley's School written on the side. "If it wasn't for the school trip I might even do it now. But they'll all hae their phones. Stamping on your fucking face. All over YouTube, eh?"

No warning. Gorse stepped forward. Threw a left-handed punch at Brady's face. Brady instinctively brought his hands up to protect himself. Felt Gorse's right fist slam into his solar plexus, driving the wind out of his body. Brady was on his knees. Slumped against the car. Gasping for breath.

Felt Gorse lean over him. The hand back on his throat, squeezing harder. Much harder.

"There won't be a school trip next time, pal."

Gorse let him go. Walked to his car. Brady heard the door slam shut. The engine start. Forced himself to breathe. Forced himself to stand up. Saw the mist still hanging over the tree tops. Found his car keys. Knew that right now he only had one job.

53

He'd driven down Blue Bank. Through Sleights. Paid no attention to the speed limit.

Run into the vet's. "My dog has been shot."

"What's her name?"

"His. Archie. He was in two weeks ago. When we registered."

The vet was young, brisk, efficient. Veronika. German. Possibly Dutch.

Brady had laid Archie gently on the black table. Veronika had examined the wound. Sucked her breath in. The way a garage mechanic does when he's going to give you bad news.

"He will have lost a lot of blood, Mr Brady. He will need a transfusion. Plasma maybe. Whether there is the right match in Whitby..."

"Please," Brady said. "Just do what you have to. Just save him."

"Is he insured?"

"Yes."

Was Archie insured? A direct debit went out every month. Did Pet Plan cover that? A psychopath shooting your dog to give you a warning?

"Yes, he is. But it doesn't matter. Do whatever it takes. Anything. Please. Just save him."

Veronika smiled briefly. Nodded. "Leave him with us, Mr Brady. He looks a healthy dog. But..." She didn't finish the sentence. Brady blinked away the tears.

Now he was home. He sat on the settee. Realised he was shaking. Archie, Gorse, the hand on his throat.

He hadn't taken it in at the time. The adrenaline of saving Archie.

Now it was wearing off. Now all he could do was wait. And think.

It wasn't just what Gorse had said. It was the implication. The threat. Like an iceberg. It was what lay beneath that terrified him.

Gorse had followed him from the house. Or someone else had followed him and told Gorse where he was. The man who had killed Patrick in cold blood could follow his daughter. Knew where she went to school. Knew who her friends were.

He heard Enzo's voice again. 'He needs raw meat.'

Brady felt helpless. He'd felt helpless sitting by Grace's bed. But Grace had been straightforward. There was a decision to make. One day he'd have to make it.

But protecting his daughter was a whole new level of helpless. He looked out of the window. Imagined a man across the street making a phone call.

And there was another problem. Ash. He had to tell her...

.   .   .

IT WASN'T REALLY a problem though, was it? All he had to do was sit Ash down and explain. Calmly and rationally...

'Look, Ash, there's a bit of bad news. Archie has been shot. He's been shot because – despite several warnings – I carried on investigating Patrick's death. I thought I could solve it. Ride into town on a white horse and sort everything out. Instead I completely screwed it up. And someone – he's a complete psychopath and he might come after you or me – decided to teach me one final lesson by shooting Archie. The dog you love – who sleeps by your bed – has a fifty-fifty chance. The vet says he's a strong dog but he's lost a lot of blood and they don't know if they'll find a match in Whitby. Anyway, how was your day at school?'

That should go well...

He heard her key in the lock. Felt his mouth go dry.

"Dad? You home?"

He stood up. Walked into the hall. "I'm in the lounge. Put your bag down, I need to talk to you."

"What about? Please, Dad, not Josh again. I can't stand another lecture."

Lecture? He'd been trying to discuss it. Brady shook his head. "No, not that."

"Good. Can I get changed first? God, I hate this uniform."

Brady hesitated. He was going to say 'no.' Then he changed his mind. "Yeah, go on then. But be quick. It's important."

Ash started up the stairs. Then she stopped. Came

back into the lounge. "Where's Archie? He knows the sound of my key in the lock. Where is he?"

"Sit down, Ash."

"No. Dad, what's wrong? Something's wrong with Archie."

What could he do except tell her the truth?

"Ash, I don't know how to tell you this - "

She stared at him. "Archie's dead! He's been run over!"

Brady went over to her. Put his hands on her shoulders. Looked into her eyes. "No, he's not. He's at the vet's. I'm really, really sorry, Ash. He's been shot."

She pulled away from him. Stared into his face. "What? What did you say?"

"Archie's been shot. This morning. When I was out on the Moors with him."

"Shot? You mean shot? With a gun?"

Brady nodded. A thought flashed through his mind. A sheep farmer. Dogs were always chasing sheep. Spare her the pain. The fear.

And what had he said to her? "Tell me the truth. Whatever happens tell me the truth."

So there wasn't a sheep farmer.

Ash finally spoke. "Who shot him?"

"The person who killed Patrick."

"And where is he now?"

"He's at the vet's. And they say he's lost a lot of blood, but he's a really strong dog and they'll do everything they can."

"Is he going to die?" Ash whispered as the tears started to roll down her face.

"No, I don't think so." Brady realised he was crying as well. "No, I'm sure he isn't."

"When can we see him?"

"When the vet phones. They have to find the right blood. They have to give Archie a transfusion."

"Like a person?"

Brady nodded. Ash reached a hand up and wiped the tears away. Then she pushed him away and stood up. "I'm going up to my room."

"To get changed?"

"No. I want to be on my own."

"Are you sure? Do you want me to do anything?"

"No. You've done enough. Leave me alone for a minute will you, Dad? Give me some space."

"OK." Brady let her go. Listened to her footsteps going up the stairs. Heard her bedroom door shut.

He sat down. Fought off the urge to phone the vet's.

BRADY CREPT QUIETLY UP the stairs. He had no idea *why* he was creeping upstairs. Ash had said she wanted to be on her own. Why didn't he listen to what she said? She was 13. She knew her own mind.

But he kept tiptoeing up the stairs.

He heard the sobbing when he was half way. Knew it was his fault. Knew everything was his fault. He put his hand on her door, tentatively pushed it open. "Ash?"

She was under the quilt. Completely covered. Still sobbing.

Brady stood there. What did he do? He had no idea.

"Ash?"

"Go away." A muffled response from under the quilt.

"Ash, just talk to me." He sat down on the end of the bed. Reached his hand out to touch her. Took it back. She was just a shape under the quilt. Supposing he touched her in the wrong place?

Grace could have put her hand anywhere. They'd have laughed about it. Two girls together. "Whoops, sorry, Ash. Landed my hand on your bum. Your own fault for being under the quilt."

Her dad couldn't do that.

"Ash, please talk to me."

The quilt stirred. She sat up in bed. Eyes red and puffy, hair dishevelled. "Just go away, Dad. Leave me on my own. I've worked it all out."

"What do you mean you've worked it all out?"

"I've worked out what happened. I know why Archie was shot."

"I told you - "

"No, Dad. You told me what you wanted to tell me."

"Which is what happened."

"Because you thought you could fix everything. And you couldn't. And now Archie will die."

She said it calmly, quietly. And she was right. The knife in his heart? This time it was a sword.

"Do you want me to go back downstairs?"

Ash nodded. Brady did as he was told.

SHE CAME DOWN 15 minutes later. Hair brushed, eyes still puffy, her school bag over her shoulder. Her overnight bag in her right hand.

"What are you doing, Ash?"

"I'm going to Bean's. I've texted her. She's says it's alright."

"Ash, this is madness. You can't just go out to someone else's house because..." Brady was struggling to keep his voice from rising. "Because... Damn it, Ash, we haven't even had an argument."

"What are you going to do, Dad? Stand in the doorway and stop me going out? Lock me in my room and swallow the key?"

"No. Of course I'm not. It's just... Bloody hell, Ash, there must be a better answer than you walking out into the night. What would your mum have said?"

"She'd have understood me," Ash replied, so quietly Brady could only just hear her.

"Ash, sweetheart, I understand you. I'm doing my best - "

And that was the final straw. The dam burst. All over Brady.

"But you're not doing your best are you? You're spying on me. Now Archie's going to die because of you."

"Ash, please. I wish - "

"No, Dad. You know what *I* wish, Dad? Do you *really* know what I wish? I wish the car had hit you and not Mum. I wish you were dead and Mum was alive. Because Mum wouldn't make..." She was crying so much she could barely speak. "She wouldn't just... just... just fuck everything up like you do."

A 12 year old girl, going to say goodbye to her mum. At exactly the time in her life when she needed her mum.

When Dad was becoming more and more irritating,

understanding less and less. When he was getting older, hope-
lessly out of touch. Not even remotely understanding what it
was to be young. And with no hope of ever understanding even
the simplest thing about the life of a nearly-teenage girl.

Brady walked a few steps ahead as they crossed the
hospital car park, Ash and Kate behind him. He glanced back.
Kate had her arm round Ash, neither of them making any
attempt to hold back the tears.

Through reception, past A&E, along the corridor, in the lift
up to the 2nd floor. No-one daring to speak. Brady reached out
and took Ash's hand in the lift. She looked up at him. "Be
strong," she whispered. "That's what Mum would want,
isn't it?"

Brady nodded. He barely trusted himself to speak. "Be
strong," he managed to whisper back.

They'd discussed it beforehand. Kate would go in first.
Then Brady and Ash. Then Kate would take Ash home. And
he'd be left with Dilip Sharma. And Lisa, and one or two other
nurses.

Kate came out of the room. Tears rolling down her face.
Brady took Ash's hand again. "Are you OK, sweetheart?"

She nodded.

Nothing had changed. Nothing from any time they'd been
to visit. The room, the monitors, the heart on the window...

No, that wasn't true. Lisa, maybe one of the other nurses,
had done their best with Grace's hair. Arranged it on the pillow
so it was framing her face. Applied a touch of make-up, a little
colour in her cheeks.

The monitor beeped, the machine breathed, Ash sat down
and held her mother's hand.

"Don't worry, Mum," she said. "Archie and I will take care

of Dad for you." She paused. "And I'll carry on singing. And that song will always be special. Just for you. And I think I might be a vet when I grow up. I just... Well, it looks interesting. And it's helping people. And – "

And then the dam broke and she was sobbing and Brady was doing his best to comfort her. Great, racking sobs that he'd see and hear for the rest of his life. But there was nothing he could do. Nothing he could say. Nothing he could ever do or say that would turn back time. Nothing that would make a car the police had never found hit him and not his wife.

Brady felt physically sick. He knew Ash was right.

54

"You're sure you don't mind?"

He'd conceded defeat. Driven her to Bean's. A silent car journey. Now he was standing in the kitchen, talking to Fiona. "You're absolutely sure?" he said again.

She nodded. Smiled at him. "Give her some space. She'll be fine. And I promise I'll take care of her."

"Thank you. I feel... I feel like I'm abandoning her. Letting her down."

Fiona reached out. Put her hand on Brady's arm. "You're not. You're doing your best, Michael. Go home. Try and sleep. Ring me in the morning. Here." She wrote her mobile number on a piece of paper. "She'll be fine. Really. I promise."

'Go home. Try and sleep. Ring me in the morning.' How many people had said that to him?

Brady glanced at his phone. 3:34. More or less morning.

He was sitting on the sofa, a half drunk glass of

whisky on the table in front of him, the rain drumming against the window.

He hadn't been to bed. No point. Knew he wouldn't be able to sleep. Knew he'd just lie there. Reaching out for Grace. Replaying what Ash had said. Replaying it a hundred times.

A teenage girl needed her mother. Six more years before she went to university. What was he going to do? Phone Kate every time he had a problem? Phone Fiona? Phone the mother of Ash's latest best friend?

'It's Michael Brady. I've a problem with Ash again. Sorry to ring so late at night but I think it's your turn to help me. Oh... and before Ash comes round, could you check there's no-one watching your house? That's another problem I haven't dealt with.'

Brady picked his phone up. Tapped the weather app. Sunrise was in less than an hour.

He knew what he had to do.

THE GORSE SHOULD STILL HAVE BEEN in bloom. The sun should have been coming up out of the sea. The light sparkling and bouncing across the water as the sun rose – optimistically, positively – out of the sea.

It didn't. Sunrise was out there, but it was happening behind a bank of cloud. And it was still raining.

Brady could feel his trousers clinging to him. Wrapping themselves round his legs.

He stood on the cliff top. The same spot where he'd scattered her ashes.

How long ago was that? Six weeks.

Six weeks that had seen his best friend murdered, the wrong person arrested and an innocent man die in jail. That had seen him stumble from mistake to mistake to mistake. When he'd felt a hand ruthlessly tighten on his throat. When he'd laid Archie on the vet's black table.

When he'd put his daughter's life in danger. When he'd come to Whitby to write a book and be a good dad. And failed miserably.

Except that Ash had put it rather more bluntly...

He turned his head upwards. Felt the rain falling on his face. Felt water running down his neck.

The wind stirred slightly. "Hi, Gracie," Brady said. "Thanks for coming. I've missed you. You're the only one I can really talk to."

He unzipped his jacket. Ran the fingers of his right hand through his wet hair, combing it back. Kept his face turned up to the rain. Felt his t-shirt wet against his chest.

What had she said to him?

Take action, Michael. Either you control your life or someone else does.

He nodded. Breathed in deeply. Dragged the salt air into his lungs. Ran his hand through his long hair a second time.

Spoke to where he guessed the sun was rising out of the North Sea. "I love you, Grace. I'll always love you. But I'm going back."

Michael Brady turned and walked back down the cliff path to his car.

Gorse had come for him once.

Fine. Let him come again.

It was time to end this.

55

Two phone calls to make. Brady didn't know which one he was most nervous about.

His daughter first.

"Give her some space."

So he phoned Fiona, not Ash.

"Good morning." He could hear the smile in her voice.

"I daren't ask…"

"She's fine. We talked last night. The three of us. Sitting in front of the fire in our PJs, long after the girls should have gone to bed. So if Ash falls asleep at school today it's probably my fault."

"Thank you," Brady said. "I don't know what else to say. Thank you."

"I should be thanking you. It was lovely. And having Ash here seemed to free up Jess – sorry, Bean – as well."

"I'll come round about five if that's OK?"

"Maybe a little later? I've a conference call at half past four. I think it might run on…"

"Half five then. And thank you again."

And now the second one. He went to his contact list. Opened 'Vet.' Pressed the number. Wasn't superstitious but crossed his fingers.

"Good morning. It's Michael Brady. I brought my dog in yesterday. He'd been... He had a gunshot wound."

"Archie?"

"Yes, that's right." Did she need to check? Did they have more than one dog with a gunshot wound? Had Gorse been wandering round the Moors practising?

"I'll put you through to the vet. One moment, Mr Brady."

There was the click of a phone system that needed updating. The silence that makes you think you've been cut off.

"Mr Brady? Veronika Koval."

The same brisk, efficient voice as yesterday. How much could you tell from four words? Brady thought she sounded positive.

"How is he?"

"He is good, Mr Brady. As good as we could hope for. But..." She paused.

"Yes?"

"He lost a lot of blood. We got some from Middlesbrough. Another hour and... maybe not so good."

"So he's OK?"

"No. He is weak. He will need time to recover. We will need to keep him. A week, maybe ten days. But you still have him, Mr Brady."

"Thank you. Thank you so much." Brady wanted the call to end. He wanted to text Ash. But there was one more question. "His shoulder. Where the bullet hit him..."

"Grazed him. Whoever did this, Mr Brady, he could try another thousand times and not manage such a shot. The bullet passed along the bone, not through it. I think Archie may limp a little as he gets older. For now, he is a lucky boy."

Brady finished the call. Two out of two. More than he dared hope for. He stood up. Clenched his fists. A footballer scoring a goal. A batsman reaching three figures. Ash, five years from now, opening her A-level results.

He punched the air. "Yes!" he said out loud. "Yes!"

Then he sat down and picked up his phone. Wondered for the thousandth time if there was anyone on the planet who texted more slowly. *Archie is on the mend. They'll need to keep him in. But he'll get better. I'll collect you from Bean's around 5:30. Love you, Dad xx*

He still had two more jobs on his list...

56

"You got a job interview or something, sir?"

Brady laughed. "No. Well, maybe, in a manner of speaking."

"So what do you want? Your hair. What grade?"

Brady didn't know. He'd gone to the same barber in Manchester for more than ten years. He sat in the chair. George went to work. He knew what Brady wanted so he didn't ask. He'd sat there and heard people saying, 'Two on top and one at the sides' and assumed that haircuts-by-numbers would never apply to him.

"Short," Brady said.

"How short, sir?"

"Like you said. Like I'm going for a job interview."

"The beard as well? You sure?"

"Certain. Shave it off."

"All of it? Not just a trim?"

"All of it. Like a Gillette ad."

"You're gonna look like a new man. Maybe get a tattoo as well?"

Maybe. But scars are more likely.

The Turkish barber went to work.

"MORNING," Brady said 40 minutes later.

Dave looked up from the hotplate. "Bloody hell," he said. "That's drastic. You look five years younger."

Brady smiled. "Yeah. Might be a bit cold in winter with the wind off the sea. But it feels better. It's me. The real me."

"The usual then?" Dave looked down. "Hang on. Where's the boss?"

"You want the truth? He's at the vets."

"What's up? Nothing bad?"

"You could say. He was shot."

"Shot. With a gun." With Ash it had been a question. With Dave it was a statement. He looked at Brady. "So it's getting serious?"

Brady nodded. "Yes, it's serious."

"Is he going to be alright?"

Brady reached forward, tapped Dave's wooden counter. "The vet thinks so. But they'll need to keep him for a week. But yes. He was incredibly lucky. So fingers crossed. And I've got company this morning."

She was right on time. What Brady now realised was her favourite leather jacket. Blue jeans.

"I had to explain to Alex why a strange man was sending me texts inviting me for breakfast," Frankie Thomson said. Then she looked at Brady more closely. "A very strange man. When did that happen?"

"An hour ago. I was waiting for them to open."

"So what can I do for you, Mr Brady?"

So it was back to 'Mr Brady.' Still, it was an upgrade on the last thing she'd called him.

"Eat a bacon sandwich," he said. "Drink some of Dave's coffee. Listen to what I have to say. Start calling me Mike. Or Michael. Your choice."

"OK." She sounded cautious, Brady thought. Still in charge while Bill was off. Still wanting a quiet life.

Brady bought breakfast and they walked over to the bandstand. Sat down on the seats. "It's never the same, is it?" Brady said.

She followed the direction of his gaze. "No," she said. "The sea, the tide, the light, the weather. Every day is different." She paused. "Makes it hard to leave."

Brady took a bite of his sandwich. "Small town, though. Everyone has to look out for everyone else."

She looked sideways at him. "That's a cryptic comment. You're clearly going to tell me the rest of the story."

"I am, but first of all I want to apologise."

All I've done since I came to Whitby. Stagger from one mistake to the next and then say 'sorry.'

"Last time we spoke," Brady said. "I upset you. You called me - "

"A sanctimonious prick. Don't think you have a monopoly on suffering, Mr Brady."

"Well, whatever it was. I'm sorry."

She raised her eyebrows. "A man who can apologise. A rare species."

"So we're OK?"

She nodded. "Possibly. Tell me your story."

"That day in Kara's kitchen. You let me take the back-pack. You knew it wasn't mine."

Frankie nodded. Didn't speak.

"Why?" Brady asked.

She took a while to reply. "Two reasons," she said. "One, I knew Bill was going to arrest the wrong person. She could have had an alibi signed by the Pope. He'd made his mind up. I thought that was wrong. And two..." She hesitated again. Chose her words carefully. "I could see it was important to you. Not just finding Patrick's killer. You didn't want to be involved: you *needed* to be involved."

"Thank you," Brady said. "I didn't realise it at the time but... yeah, I did."

"So now what?" Frankie asked.

"Gorse shot my dog."

"Is he – "

"No. I was telling Dave. He was incredibly lucky. Maybe he'll limp a bit when he's older but, yeah, he'll be fine."

"So you've had your hair cut and declared war?"

Brady ignored the question. "You didn't ask who Gorse was."

"No. I know who Jimmy Gorse is. Bill knows. Kershaw knows. Everyone knows."

"So why didn't you do something?"

"You know the answer to that as well as I do. Because we're the police. Because we need evidence. And some-times we need approval from a long way up the food chain."

"So not just Whitby?"

Frankie shook her head. "County lines? It's every-where. Up and down the coast. Everywhere."

"I'm going after Gorse," Brady said.

"You realise this is the moment I stop you, Mr Brady? When I warn you that taking the law into your own hands is a very serious matter?"

"But you're not going to." Brady made it a statement, not a question.

"No, I'm not."

"Am I allowed to ask 'why' again?"

"Because I had two sisters. One of them is a paramedic – "

Grey eyes, dark hair. No wonder she'd looked familiar.

"Louise," Brady said.

Frankie nodded. "Louise. My elder sister. The other one – Katie – is dead."

"What happened?"

Frankie held out her mug. "Would you ask Dave to refill this?"

Brady took the mug. Stood up and walked the ten yards back to Dave's kiosk. Understood that she wanted some time with her memories before she told him the story. Began to realise that 'sanctimonious prick' might have been letting him off lightly.

"Thank you," Frankie said as Brady handed her the re-filled coffee.

"Katie was raped," she said simply. "She was coming home from a friend's house. Late October. Just after the clocks changed."

Brady could guess what was coming next. "They caught someone? Then didn't prosecute?"

Frankie nodded. Pursed her lips tightly. Brady could see how much it took to keep her emotions in check.

"Not enough evidence. And then a cock-up with the DNA sample. A complete fiasco from beginning to end. And – obviously – he said it was consensual. Said she wanted rough sex."

Brady stayed silent.

"She was 15. She hadn't even had a boyfriend." Frankie paused. "I can introduce you if you like."

"The person that did it?"

"He works in a bank. Assistant manager now. Just in the main street. We could be there in five minutes. Whitby's a small town. Especially if you go out for a sandwich at lunchtime. I see him once a week."

"Who made the decision?" Brady asked.

"Not to proceed? They never told us. You want my guess? Kershaw."

"And Katie?" Brady said, as gently as he could.

"She was the brightest and best of us. After it happened – after everything she went through – she simply switched off. Like someone had turned a light out. It was New Year's Eve. She took my father's overcoat. Loaded the pockets with stones from the beach. Walked out onto the pier at high tide. They found her the next morning. When they went for a New Year's Day swim."

Her left hand was on the bench between them. Brady reached across and put his hand on hers. "I'm really sorry. Really sorry."

Frankie breathed in. Forced herself to smile. "So that's why I joined the police," she said. "Stopped teaching

Maths and signed up. I thought if I could save just one Katie in my career it would be worth it."

She moved her hand from under Brady's. Turned and looked at him. "And that's the real reason I let you take the backpack. So we have a secret, Brady. And I won't stop you going after Gorse. I can't help. But I won't stop you."

Brady nodded. Then stood up and walked over to the railings. Frankie followed and stood by his side, both of them looking out to sea. "Gorse isn't the answer," Brady said. "But he's part of the answer."

"You're not going to cure the drugs problem. There'll always be a demand. There'll always be a supply."

"I know that. I just think a disorganised shambles is better than a ruthless, efficient machine. You know how old my daughter is. I don't want someone offering her a free sample as she walks out of the school gate."

"You know the risk you're taking?"

Brady walked across to his left. Looked at the pier. Saw it curving out into the sea. Saw Frankie's sister in her father's overcoat. Walking slowly down the parallel lines of the pier's wooden boards, weighed down by the stones in the pockets.

Then what? Did she hesitate? Lean on the railings? Watch the sea? Try to choose the right wave?

"Yes," he said. "I know the risks. I've met Jimmy Gorse. But two people are dead – "

"How?" Frankie said. "That's what I can't work out."

"You're talking about Kidby now?"

She nodded.

"You want my guess? They were in the army together. In Afghanistan. Gorse knew about the PTSD. Found out about Kidby's son. He – or his boss – sees a chance to close the case. Wrap it all up and get back to business. So he makes Darren Kidby an offer. 'You've done time. You can cope. Nice nest egg waiting when you come out. And it means your son carries on playing football. No risk of an injury that ends his career...'"

"And then when he's inside..."

"Yeah. Poor bastard's desperate to control the PTSD. Someone says, 'Try this, mate.'"

"So you have to do something."

"Yes. Because if I don't, where does it end? My dog? My daughter? Someone else's son or daughter? What do I do when one of Ash's friends dies of an overdose? Tell her I could have done something? But it was too risky?"

He turned back to Frankie. Met her gaze.

"Have you got a plan?" she asked.

Brady nodded. Heard the waves lapping gently against the harbour wall. Felt the sun on his face.

"More or less," he said.

57

He should get Fiona something. Something to say 'thank you.' A bottle of wine? He didn't even know if she drank wine. Chocolates? Wasn't that 30 years out of date?

He should buy her flowers. Obviously.

Brady walked over to the display. And stopped. He couldn't. He couldn't buy another woman flowers. He felt... Brady wasn't sure how he felt. 'Unfaithful' was the wrong word. But... uncomfortable.

He'd put his hand on Frankie's. Now he was thinking of buying a woman flowers.

He couldn't. Not yet.

But there were two women he needed to thank. Fiona *and* Veronika. He could buy them both flowers. A single bunch of flowers meant something. Two was just saying 'thank you.' Being polite.

He rang the doorbell. Heard a shout from inside. "Ash, your dad is here."

Ash opened the door.

"Hi, sweetheart."

Ash didn't say anything. Stood there. Looked up at him. Started to smile. "You don't do things by half do you, Dad?"

Fiona appeared behind her. "Hi Michael. Ash is all packed. And she's - " Her turn to look at him. "Oh. That's different. I'd got used to seeing you with a beard. And - "

"Long hair," Brady finished for her. "I decided they weren't me."

Which was one way of putting it.

He hugged Ash, not expecting her to respond in front of other people.

"Would you like to come in, Mike?" Fiona asked. "Like a cup of tea? Or something stronger?"

Brady shook his head. "Do you mind if I say 'no?' I'm really grateful, Fiona, but I need to be somewhere before six."

"I don't mind at all. But let me ask you something. This extra week they've got for half-term..." She hesitated. Looked at Ash. Bean had magically appeared.

"We're going to Center Parcs in the morning. I don't suppose... I don't suppose you'd let Ash come with us? We've got a three bedroom villa and three people. There's plenty of room."

"When are you back?" Brady asked.

"It's Friday to Friday. We couldn't go today because of Jamie's football. So first thing tomorrow."

"Of course she can. If she'd like to. Ash?"

Ash grinned. High-fived Bean. Their plan had clearly worked. "No, Dad," she said. "I don't want to go swimming. And cycling through the woods. And barbecuing. And hanging out with Bean."

Brady laughed. "You'd better come home and pack then." He turned to Fiona. "Let me know how much I owe you."

"Nothing. She's a delight."

"No, I can't have that," Brady said. "She may be a delight, but she's a delight who eats. Let me at least give you some money for food."

Fiona reluctantly agreed. Brady promised to give her the money when he dropped Ash off in the morning.

And it was perfect. Better than perfect. It gave him six days.

"Dad," Ash said as she climbed into the car. "There are two bunches of flowers on the back seat."

"I know. I bought them."

"So who are they for?"

"One of them," Brady said, "Is for Fiona. The other, you'll see..."

He picked up the assortment of – were those chrysanthemums? He had no idea – and walked back up the path. Rang the bell a second time.

Bean answered the door. "Hi Bean, I just need your mum again if she's free."

Fiona walked down the hall drying her hands on a tea-towel. Pushing a stray lock of blonde hair back off her face.

Brady held the flowers out. "I just wanted to say 'thank you' properly."

Fiona took them. "You didn't need to do that. I told you, she was lovely. But thank you."

Brady stood awkwardly on the doorstep. "I'd

forgotten you were going away. They'll be dead by the time you get back."

"Don't be silly. I'll take them with us. I'm not going to leave them behind."

Brady turned to go. "Thank you again. I mean it, I can't tell you how grateful I am. For everything."

Fiona put her hand on his shoulder. "She's a lovely girl, Mike. But... what happened... must have been incredibly difficult for her. Give her time. And space. And I'm always here. And thank you for the flowers." She reached up and kissed him on the cheek. "They're lovely."

"So who's the second bunch for?" Ash demanded.

"You'll see."

58

"This isn't the way home."

"No, it isn't."

"So where are we going?"

"Like I said, you'll see."

Brady turned right by the rugby club, followed the road round to the left. "We're going to the vet's!" Ash said. He could hear the excitement, the relief in her voice.

"Yes. And that's who the other flowers are for. Veronika. She's the vet who's been taking care of Archie. And she said it was OK to come and see him."

Brady pushed the door open, caught sight of the clock above reception. 5:55. Made it, just.

"Hi," he said. "Michael Brady. I spoke to Veronika this afternoon. She said we could see Archie. Just for five minutes."

The receptionist was in her 50s. Dark hair, slightly shorter than shoulder length. A face that had seen thousands of dogs and cats and their owners come through the door. That had delivered its fair share of good and bad news. She smiled.

"You can see him, Mr Brady. And I'm guessing this is your daughter? You can certainly see him, but you can't take him home." She winked at Ash. "We've all fallen in love with him."

The door to the consulting room opened. Veronika came into reception. "Mr Brady? It is good to see you again. And in happier times. As I said to you before, he is a lucky boy. *Er scheint sieben Leben zu haben, wie eine Katze.*"

Brady shook hands and tried to remember his schoolboy German. "This is Ash, my daughter," he said. "And these are to say thank you. And surely it's nine, not seven?"

She laughed. The warmth of her smile surprised him. "You didn't have to do that. It's my job. But thank you. And no, in Germany a cat has only seven lives."

"Can we see him?" Ash said. "We couldn't bear the thought of... Of anything happening to him."

"Suzanne, would you take care of these for me?" Veronika passed the flowers to the receptionist. "Come," she said. "Just to say hello. I think it will be good for Archie to see you."

Archie was sleeping. He had an Elizabethan collar on. "Is that to stop him licking himself?" Ash asked.

"For sure. He has the dressing on the other side. You cannot see it now, but... Ah, he must have heard you."

Right on cue Archie lifted his head. Turned towards them. Looked at them with his big brown eyes. Was it only two days ago? That he'd looked up with those same brown eyes? As Brady stumbled back to the car? Desperate to get Archie to the vets. No idea that Gorse was waiting in the car park.

"Hi, mate," Brady said. "How are you doing?"

Ash put her hand on the glass. "We love you, Archie. We miss you. Get well soon."

He had to prise her away. "I'm *definitely* going to be a vet," she said as she climbed into the car.

BRADY WASN'T LOOKING FORWARD to this. Kate had known him forever. Understood his motivations.

The obvious question first though. "How's Bill doing?"

"Badly. Not medically, psychologically."

Five minutes of discussing his likely treatment. The prognosis. How the girls were reacting.

And then Brady passed his sister an envelope.

"Here," he said. "I want you to have this."

Kate reached a hand across the table. "This looks very formal. What is it?"

"Paperwork. I've been a grown up. I've made a will."

"Why?"

"Because I should, because I'm a single parent with a teenage daughter. Because if anything happens to me it'll save someone a lot of effort. And time. So all the details – bank accounts, Grace's pension – they're all in there."

Kate looked at him sharply. "What's the real reason?"

I'm going to tempt a killer to come after me. Someone who's already had his hand round my throat. Who squeezed. Hard. And I'm going to use the only bait I have. Me.

"There isn't a 'real reason.' I'm being a responsible adult."

"You're frightening me, Michael. It's not just the hair and the beard that's changed."

"You mean I look like a detective again?"

"Yes. And no. You look like... I don't know. Remember when you were growing your beard? I said you looked a bit like an older Chris Hemsworth?"

"Yeah. Once you'd told me who he was."

"Now you don't. You've gone cold, Michael. The warmth has gone out of your eyes. Your expression reminds me of Clint Eastwood. When he rides into town. Before people start dying."

It was Brady's turn to reach across the table. He took her hand. "It'll be fine, Kate. I've got Ash. I've got you. I'm not going to do anything stupid. Like I said. I'm a responsible adult."

Five minutes later Brady was in his car. It was time to talk to an artist.

59

He hadn't expected to be back here. The cottage with the green door. But it was the only way.

Assuming Carl would play his part.

"Good morning," he said. "You must be Carl's grandmother. I'm Michael Brady – the one who collected him from the hospital."

He'd caught her in the middle of baking. Her apron was covered in flour. She held out an equally floury hand. "He mentioned you. Said you'd bought one of his drawings. And thank you. I don't like hospitals. You get to my age and, well... You know you'll be there soon enough."

Brady smiled. She looked a picture of health. He shook the floury hand. "You're more than welcome. Is he in?"

"Yes, he's in the garden. Come in. Would you like a cup of tea?"

"I'd love one," Brady said, placing a hefty wager on a scone to go with it.

He walked through the house and into the back

garden. Carl was sitting in a wooden chair, his phone in his hand. There was a small table at the side of him with his sketch pad and some pencils.

"Morning," Brady said. "How are you doing?"

A small bird flew off from the hedge.

"Bloody hell, all the stealth of a charging rhino. Thanks, David Attenborough. That was a greenfinch. I was photographing it so I could draw it. But good morning. And I'm doing fine. Well, fine-ish."

"How's the finger?"

"The lack of finger you mean? Yeah, not bad. I was back at the hospital yesterday. 'As well as expected,' they said. Next appointment is in two weeks. Not sure I'll ever get used to looking at the gap though."

Carl's grandmother bustled out with the tea. Brady saw he'd lost his bet. Fruit cake, not scones.

"Here we are," she said. "Yorkshire Tea. I hope you like it, Mr Brady."

Brady smiled again. "It's perfect. Thank you." He gestured at Carl. "He's got real talent. Does he get it from you?"

She moved the morning's sketches so she could put the tray down. "From my father," she said. "You'd look at his drawings – portraits, he did – and you'd swear they'd open their mouths and talk. But in those days working class men didn't draw. And then the war came."

She looked at Brady. "Arnhem," she said simply.

And now here she was, he thought, willing Carl to achieve what his great-grandfather never could. "I'm sorry," he said.

"It's a long time ago," she said. "A lot of dirty water under the bridge."

"A lot of dirty water for all of us," Brady said.

A phone alarm went off. "Ah! Thank you, phone. Time to put the bread in."

Brady stood up and walked over to the hedge. Looked across a field to the river. He could just make out the sound of it.

"So..." Carl said.

"So I didn't come here to eat fruit cake and scare birds? Is that what you're saying?"

"Duh, Sherlock."

Brady sat down. "I've got some good news," he said.

"So this is the old good news, bad news crap? I'll have the bad news first if that's OK."

"No. Sorry. It's the good news, potentially very bad news crap."

But I'm sorry, it's the only way.

Brady had been through it a hundred times.

"I want you to phone Gorse," he said.

"That's not potentially bad, Brady, that's potentially shit. Potentially life-ending. I'm assuming it's part of a foolproof master plan where nothing can go wrong?"

The greenfinch was back. Brady decided it was a good omen. And did his best not to make any sudden movements. He waited until Carl had taken his photos.

"No. It's part of a plan that might work. That's full of holes. That relies on Gorse's impatience. On his need for..."

'Raw meat' probably wasn't the right choice of words.

"...On making him lose his temper. Yes, I think it'll work. And it's the only plan I have."

"You want to catch him?"

"Almost," Brady said. "I want the chance of him being caught. I want the police to know that he killed Patrick. I want something that'll compromise him with his own people."

"You're mad," Carl said.

Brady nodded. "Probably. But like I said, it's the only plan I've got."

"What's in it for me? Apart from the chance of a matching pair of hands?"

"Revenge? I'm asking a lot, I know. But maybe you'll get Gorse out of your life once and for all. Maybe you'll make sure that this time next year he isn't stamping on someone else's hand."

Carl took another two photos of the greenfinch. Then he turned and looked at Brady.

"I've seen it with drug addicts," he said. "Just before they shoot up. They have this moment. They pause. They anticipate what's coming. It's like they're... like they're coming home. This is where they belong. I don't know, maybe fucking Picasso had it before he picked up a paint brush. And Gorse has it, Brady. I looked up and saw his face. Then he stamped on my hand. That's what he lives for, Brady. And you want me to help you? To risk that again?"

"Yes," Brady said. He stood up. "I'm sorry. I shouldn't have asked."

Carl looked up at him. Put his bandaged right hand up to shield his eyes from the sun. "Sit down, you dozy bugger. Of course I'll do it. And if you want to know why, two reasons. Revenge. And bollocks to all that 'best served cold' crap. But more than that. Because I'm bloody terrified. And if I don't do it I'll always be bloody terrified."

Twenty years in the police and Brady had seen his share of bravery. He might even have had an odd moment of it himself. But here he was. A 19 year old boy who looked like a medieval squire. Sitting in a North Yorkshire garden with a sketch pad. The bravest person he knew.

"Thank you," he said. "I mean that."

"I know you mean it. But stop being grateful and tell me what you want me to do. Before I change my mind."

"Have you still got his phone number?" So much for a foolproof plan. If Carl had deleted Gorse's number the whole thing fell at the first hurdle.

"Does anyone ever delete a number?" Carl picked his phone up and opened his contacts. "Gorse," he said. "That's all. And look at that. I was too bloody frightened to type his first name."

THEY WERE SITTING in Brady's car. "Press speaker," he said. "I want to listen."

Gorse answered on the third ring. And clearly he hadn't deleted Carl's number either. "Never expected to hear from you again."

"Yeah, you could say."

"So what do you want?"

"Nothing. I've something to tell you."

Brady was impressed. Carl was controlling his nerves better than he'd hoped.

"What's that? Your finger's grown back?"

"No. Enzo's bought another horse."

"What's that to me?"

"He paid a hundred grand for it."

"He hasn't got a hundred grand."

"Not now he hasn't. He will have when he's back in control. He called me. Wants me to work for him."

Brady was even more impressed. A pity the police didn't recruit drug dealers with missing fingers. Not that Carl could have coped with the bureaucracy...

"You're telling me the stupid prick thinks he can take over? And he's already spent the money?"

"Yes."

"You know what'll happen if you're lying."

"That's why I'm not lying."

Gorse was silent. Thirty seconds. His army training kicking in. Taking time to think. The last thing Brady wanted.

"How does a little twat like you know about the horse?"

"My brother's a stable boy. Apprentice jockey. At the stable. In Malton. He rode the horse up the gallops so Enzo could see it."

"Name?"

Carl hesitated for the first time. "The horse? I – I don't know."

"The fucking stable. Where your brother works."

"Drummond. At Norton. Just outside Malton."

"And Enzo wanted you to work for him?"

"Yes."

Gorse was silent again. When he spoke again his tone was lighter. Almost friendly. "This is a career move isn't it?"

"What?"

"I can see what you're thinking, Carly. Enzo goes, there's a vacancy. No problem. We like ambition. Especially since you and I understand each other so well."

And the line went dead.

"Job done?" Carl put his hand on the door handle.

"Job done brilliantly," Brady said. "But is it true?"

"Is what true?"

"Your brother? The jockey."

Carl smiled. "Yeah. He took after my dad. Small and strong. Rode his first winner the other day."

"So if Gorse checks..."

"Yeah," Carl said. "I was telling the truth."

"One more thing," Brady said.

"Now what?"

"I never gave you the good news."

Carl raised his eyebrows. "You've taken out some life cover for me."

"No. I've spoken to a friend of mine. His name's Craig. And he's the admissions tutor for an art school in Manchester. I sent him the picture I bought off you. Well, a copy of it."

"And he said you'd wasted your money."

"I explained the circumstances," Brady said. "Gave him the back story. Slightly edited. He said one drawing is all it takes. 'You can always tell,' were his exact words. He wants to meet you."

Carl didn't say anything. He sat in the passenger seat, looking through the windscreen. Seeing a lot more than the road in front of him. Then he nodded his head towards the house. "You bastard," he said. "You know I've got to tell her. And it'll make her cry."

60

Brady was dressed in black. Black trainers, black jeans, black t-shirt, black hoodie.

You look like a burglar on your first job...

He'd gambled on Carl saying 'yes.' And the package had been waiting for him. Behind the recycling bin. Where else would the courier leave a special ops-grade listening device?

"Hi. It's Brady," he'd said to Mozart, after the phone call had made its mandatory round-the-world trip.

"Mr Brady. Good morning. You are fast becoming my best customer. What can I do for you?"

"I need to bug a conversation."

"Don't tell me you've taken the corporate shilling? You want to bug your competitor's board meeting?"

"You know me better than that. I need something that will attach to a wooden door. We'll be listening across the road. Maybe 30, 40 yards away."

"You don't need me for that, Mr Brady. Tap it into Google. That nice Mr Bezos at Amazon will do it for you.

Do you have Prime? Order in the next ten hours as he likes to say."

Brady smiled to himself. He'd gone from Scholesy's endless sarcasm to Mozart's homespun wit. "You know as well as I do that 'nice Mr Bezos' will keep a record. He'll file me under 'apprentice spies' or something."

"...And you don't want any trace. You'd like a suitably anonymous package. Do you want instructions?"

"Probably. I don't have a police techie to hold my hand any more. And I need the best. I need it to work."

"Of course. Two questions. What colour is the door?"

"It was white. It's been weathered. Cream. Some rust staining from the hinges."

"And how many listening devices?"

It was important Frankie heard the conversation. More than important. "Two. And a spare. Just in case. And we'll need to record."

"Leave it with me. Next day delivery. DHL's Whitby run has become a lot more interesting since you moved in, Mr Brady."

"Thank you."

A RIDICULOUSLY SMALL LISTENING DEVICE. A marginally bigger suction cup. If you weren't looking for it, you'd never see it.

He walked down the Khyber Pass and turned right onto the sea front. A hundred yards and he was opposite Enzo's arcade. He looked at his watch. 3:30. It would be light in half an hour. A teenage couple walked past, not so much hand-in-hand as tongue-in-tongue. They didn't even see him.

Brady pulled his hood up. There was just enough light to see the steps. Enzo's arcade on one side, a shop wall on the other. He walked slowly up them. The last thing he needed was to trip up.

Sensor alarm? Motion alarm? Enzo had clearly decided that feeding his racehorses was more important.

He took the tiny listening device out of his pocket. Chose the top left corner. Pressed it firmly against the door.

Job done. Simple. Eat your heart out, James Bond.

He walked even more carefully back down the stairs. Crossed the road. Took the controls out of his pocket. Flicked the switch to 'on.' The instructions had promised him 100 hours of battery life.

Four days.

He was betting everything on Gorse's impatience.

61

Somehow he'd managed a couple of hours' sleep. And now the spy was gone. Replaced by the salesman.

How was he going to persuade her? The same way he'd persuaded Carl. Tell the truth. Hope he was still talking to the woman who'd eaten the bacon sandwich. Not the woman getting comfortable in Bill Calvert's office.

He sent a text. *I told you I had a plan. I'd like to share it with you.*

"More or less," she said, cradling her coffee cup, "'That's what you said. I'm not sure that 'more or less' *is* a plan, Brady. I'm not even sure I should be meeting you. Much less listening to what you're going to tell me."

Brady nodded. "You're probably right. No, you're definitely right. But..."

"But here I am. Drinking bad coffee and watching the rain. And like I said, I can't help. But I won't stop you."

"I want you to listen to a conversation."

"Let me guess. Which you obtained illegally?"

"It hasn't taken place yet."

Frankie looked into his eyes. "You know I didn't hear that, don't you?"

"Yeah, sorry. I don't want to make you complicit."

"So what else am I not going to hear?"

Brady ran through what he was planning to do. She was looking doubtful when he started. She was looking even more doubtful when he'd finished.

"You're betting a lot on Gorse reacting in a certain way."

"No," Brady said. "I'm betting *everything* on Gorse reacting in a certain way. But there's no other option."

Frankie looked at him across the table. "I'll do what you want. I'll find a way to listen. But officially... You know you're on your own."

"Not quite. I've got Dave."

"Dave? Don't you think he's a bit old?"

"Yes. I'd like a team of young, fit coppers. But like you said, I'm on my own."

Brady stood up. Walked over to the counter and paid for the coffees. They stepped out into the rain.

"You're enjoying this, aren't you?" Frankie said.

"The investigation? Being involved? Or knowing it's nearly over?"

"None of the above. The freedom. Making your own rules."

"You want an honest answer to that? Yes. I spent all my life playing by the rules. Where did it get me? Seeing my wife's head hitting the kerb. Switching her life support machine off."

Brady watched the rain bounce off the roofs of the

filleting sheds. "Yes. I'm not going to have it for much longer. One way or the other. So I'm going to enjoy it while I can."

Frankie pulled her collar up against the rain. Put her hands in her pockets. "Take care," she said. Then she put her hand on his arm. "We've turned a blind eye to the bad guys. Maybe it's time to do the same for the good guys. But I can only do it once."

"I know. And I'll call you. It won't be long."

BRADY WALKED ACROSS THE ROAD. Down the seafront.

Two minutes to walk from the coffee shop to Dave's kiosk.

Long enough to change his mind.

"Don't you think he's a bit old?"

Of course he was too old. Dave had come to Whitby for a quiet life. Make the world's best bacon sandwiches. Go fishing. Two months in Spain in the winter.

He couldn't ask him.

"No demand when it rains?" Brady asked the back of Dave's head.

Dave slowly straightened up. "Jesus," he said. "That hurts. Getting down there to clean the cupboard. My knees are buggered. But..." He gestured at the rain. "I've done the crossword."

"You could go home?"

Dave shook his head. "No, there might be a lad on the pier's missed his lunch. Can't let your regulars down. Anyway, you didn't come here to discuss business."

"No," Brady said. "I was just passing. Thought I'd say 'hello.' Let you know Archie's on the mend."

Dave didn't say anything. He turned to the sink. Rinsed the dishcloth he'd been using to clean the cupboard. Draped it over a tap. Dried his hands on a faded blue towel. Finally turned back to Brady.

"You know what, Mike? I reckon that's the first lie you've told me."

Brady was eight again. Being told off by his father. *"At least have the courage to admit it, Michael..."*

He started to speak. Dave cut him off. "You're going into battle," he said. "You were going to ask for my help. Some time in the last five minutes you changed your mind. Decided I was too old and too knackered."

"No. I decided that I liked you. That I've only known you for two months but – "

"Careful. Remember what you said. Men don't talk about feelings."

Brady laughed. "Yeah. Sorry. You're right. Besides, whoever heard of a lookout that needed reading glasses?"

"So that's what you want me to do?"

"No. That's what I was going to ask. But I don't have the right. I'm – "

Dave held his hand up. "Don't say you're sorry. What's the plan?"

"Set Enzo up. I'm betting on Gorse coming over to straighten him out. I've bugged his office. I'm going to listen to the conversation."

"*We're* going to listen to the conversation. Then what?"

"We've got Gorse on tape."

"How do you know he's going to say the right thing?"

"I don't."

"So you're luring him over here and hoping for the best? That's your plan?"

Brady nodded.

"It's shit," Dave said. "It's the worst plan anyone's – fuck it, Mike, it isn't even a plan. But if you try and do it without me I'll never speak to you again." Dave paused. Looked across the road. "So we have to watch the arcade until he turns up?"

"Yes."

"When's he coming?"

"Soon."

"Tomorrow then. Maybe the day after."

"Tomorrow's my guess. I'm betting on his anger."

"One question, mastermind."

"What's that?"

"Supposing he comes tonight? It's light until nearly ten. The arcade'll stay open."

Brady had to admit defeat. "That'll be my watch then?"

Dave smiled at him. "Piss off home, Michael. Get yourself a good book. Make some sandwiches and a flask of tea. I'll stay here until four. Then you can take over. I'll get you a deckchair. You'll be needing a bucket as well…"

62

A blue and white striped deckchair. Absolutely ideal for an afternoon on the beach. Not so ideal for a night in a bacon sandwich kiosk.

There was a gap in the floorboards. Dave's two bar electric heater was fighting a losing battle against the wind off the sea.

Brady pulled the blanket round him. Stretched his legs. As much as he could in the cramped space. Looked at his watch. 9:30. Checked the bug one more time. No conversation. Was that the note-counting machine whirring in the background? It stopped. A door opened and closed. Enzo had finished cashing up.

It would be tomorrow then.

Brady was certain.

This time tomorrow – well before this time tomorrow – it would be over.

One way or the other.

He'd have justice for Patrick. Revenge for Archie. Security for Carl.

Or not...

"I won't let them down, Grace," he said out loud.

"You're sure, Michael?"

"You know I am, Dilip. We've discussed it. I've thought about it. I've walked the dog and thought about it some more." Brady sighed. *"What can we do? You know it's the only decision we can take."*

"You know that... Once we do this there's no going back?"

"Dilip..." Brady thought of him as a friend now. *"Dilip, you've explained everything. A hundred times."*

"I'm sorry, Michael. I have to ask."

Brady nodded. Sat down where Ash had been sitting. Took Grace's hand in his. *"Just... I'm sorry,"* he said. *"I thought I was ready. I'm sorry, Dilip. Would you give me five more minutes?"*

"Of course. Take as long as you want. Whenever you want us."

He thought he'd said everything he had to say. All the nights of sitting on her bed. But no, he needed to say it all one more time.

"I'll take care of her for you. I promise. And I'll make mistakes but I'll try and learn from them. And I'll try and be cool when she comes home with a boyfriend I don't like. And I'll remember to take Archie to the vet's. And everything else."

The tears were rolling down his cheeks. He made no attempt to stop them. Instead he kicked his shoes off. Gently, carefully, desperate not to disturb anything, he lay on the bed next to her. On his side, on a narrow strip of the bed.

"First date, Gracie. Do you remember? You were wearing that red dress. And I couldn't take my eyes off you. And I've never been able to take my eyes off you."

He touched his fingers to his lips. Traced them gently

across her cheek. Let them rest on her lips. "I'll see you one day, Gracie. Then we'll have eternity together. You and me. And we can look down on Ash and her children. You and me, forever."

Michael Brady kissed his fingers again. Leaned over and pressed them to his wife's lips. Then he swung his legs off the bed. Sat on the side of it. Took the deepest breath he'd ever taken.

Stood up and opened the door.

Saw Dilip waiting for him.

Nodded.

"We're ready," he said.

Somehow – cold, stiff, frightened: in a draughty kiosk on Whitby seafront – Michael Brady slept.

63

You thought it was summer and suddenly it was winter again. The wind was coming straight off the sea, the rain was pouring down. But Dave was as good as his word. He'd been there at seven.

"Cometh the hour, cometh the bacon sandwich," he said. "Or do you want to go home and get changed?"

Brady did. A shave. A hot shower. Clean clothes. Black jeans, black t-shirt. Black zipped jacket. The same clothes he'd worn to plant the bug. The same as Gorse had worn at the Hole of Horcum. Fire with fire. Battle dress.

Now it was three in the afternoon. Still raining, the wind stronger, cars with their headlights on.

"I need the loo," Brady said.

"Just like James Bond, eh? Always needs a pee before he sorts out Spectre."

"You got an umbrella?"

Dave had. Ten yards down the seafront and it had blown inside out.

Brady's phone buzzed when he was in the public toilets.

"They're here," Dave said.

"One minute," Brady replied.

Real life. Just like the movies.

He sent one text – *Gorse is here. I'm at Dave's* – and ran back along the seafront. He was concentrating on getting back. Avoiding the puddles. He'd missed the significance in Dave's two words.

The BMW was parked outside the arcade. "They've just gone in," Dave said.

"What did you say?"

"They've just gone in. Up those stairs."

"They? More than one? Gorse was supposed to be on his own."

Dave shook his head. "He had a young lad with him. Nineteen? Twenty maybe? He didn't look like a volunteer."

Carl. It had to be Carl. Gorse hadn't been convinced. He'd tracked Carl's phone. Knocked on every door until he'd found him. Nan had opened the door. Probably still with flour on her apron. 'Someone else to see you, Carl.'

And Carl had seen Gorse standing in the doorway. Felt his heart sink. Known his only option was to go with him. Known he couldn't have Gorse in his grandmother's house. 'We're just going out for a bit, Nan. Maybe a couple of hours. Back in time for tea...'

Brady reached for the headphones. Turned the receiver on. Checked his phone at the same time. No reply from Frankie.

Even through the rain the sound quality was impressive. Mozart hadn't spared any expense. Just in time he remembered to press 'record.'

"...unexpected pleasure." Enzo was talking. His tone of voice was sarcastic. Not likely to improve Gorse's mood.

Good.

"On my way to Middlesbrough," Gorse replied. "Thought I'd call in. See how things were going."

"Why bring him?" Enzo was obviously referring to Carl.

"He's seen the light," Gorse said. "Realised which side his bread is buttered. He's my apprentice. You know. Master and apprentice. Just like *Star Wars*."

"What happened to your hand?" Enzo asked.

Carl spoke for the first time. "Accident. With a lawnmower."

"You lost a finger?"

"Yep. Could have been worse though."

"Could have been a lot worse," Gorse said. "Dangerous thing, cutting the grass."

There was a moment of silence. Brady guessed Enzo was reaching for his e-cigarette. Did it calm your nerves like the real thing? He'd soon find out.

He checked his phone. Still nothing from Frankie.

"Enough of this pleasant small talk," Gorse said. "We need some figures, Enzo."

"Yeah, yeah," Enzo said. "It's going well."

Calm your nerves? 'No' was the answer. Brady could hear the sudden tension in Enzo's voice. Through the listening device, through the rain, 40 yards across the street and Brady could see him starting to sweat.

There was a loud bang. Gorse had slammed something onto a desk. The flat of his hand, Brady guessed. "Fuck it, Enzo. I have *told* you. 'Going well' is not the answer. How many fucking bags? How much money? Who have you recruited? What we can measure, Enzo, we can improve. We cannot fucking measure 'yeah, it's going well.'"

The ruthless machine taking over from the disorganised shambles...

"Or shall I put someone else in charge?"

Did Gorse look at Carl at that moment? He must have done. "Him?" Enzo said. "You're mad."

"You're fucking right I'm mad. But not with my nine-fingered friend here."

Brady heard the door in Enzo's office open and close.

"What the fuck are you doing?" Enzo's voice. "I told you to go out the other way."

"Yeah, well, I forgot didn't I?"

He recognised the voice. The young girl he'd seen before. Long, brown hair. Pale blue jeans, flat black shoes.

Gorse laughed. "Who's this then, Enzo? Does your wife know?"

Chloe. Was that her name?

It didn't matter. Everything fell apart.

He'd promised Carl. 'It's the best plan I've got.'

A few short words from Chloe and he had no plan at all.

"Carl? What are you doing here? Mum said you were going to art school."

There were ten seconds of silence. Then Gorse spoke.

"What did you say, sweetheart?"

"Ow! Let go! You're hurting my arm."

"I'll hurt more than your fucking arm, you little tart. What did you say?"

"I – I – said I thought Carl was going to art school. Stop it. You're breaking my arm. Stop it. Please."

"How do you know him?"

"We were at school together. My – my mum knows his grandma."

It was so simple. Carl had gone back into the house and told Nan. 'He knows someone. Art college in Manchester. He likes my work. Wants to meet me.'

And the next day Nan had gone shopping. Bursting with pride. Carl was going to do what the War had stopped her father doing. What she'd always known he should do. Bumped into one of her friends. Told her the news. And she'd gone home and told her daughter. 'You'll never guess what. That lad you were at school with.' And her daughter had gone off to see the married man who was paying her for sex on wet afternoons...

"And she told you that fucking Rembrandt was going to art school?"

There was no reply. Chloe must have nodded.

Brady heard a dull thud. A crash. A chair getting knocked over. Someone falling over furniture.

"You. Fuck off. And make sure you never see me again. As for you, you little prick. I - "

"No!" Enzo pleading. "Not in my office. I don't want blood all over my office."

Silence. Gorse was thinking. Weighing up his options.

"The girl's come out," Dave said. "She's coming down the stairs. Shall I - "

"No," Brady said. "Let her go."

Where the hell was Frankie? Where was the bloody cavalry?

Gorse was speaking again. Cold, calm, calculating.

He didn't want Gorse cold and calculating. He wanted him impetuous. Angry. Out-of-control. Likely to make a mistake.

"We're being recorded, aren't we? This whole bloody thing is a set-up."

Another thud. Brady heard Carl moan.

"Someone put you up to this, didn't they? Brady. Fucking Brady. Is he listening now?"

No reply. Another thud. Another moan.

"Is – he – fucking – listening - now?"

Carl must have nodded.

"Good. BRADY! I know you can hear this. I warned you. I shot your dog. That should have been enough. But you won't learn, will you? Like everyone in this fucking shithole, you won't bloody well learn."

There was the sound of movement. More moans from Carl.

"We should go in," Dave said. "Two of us, one of him."

"No," Brady said. "He's going to come out. It's me he wants."

"What about me?" It was Enzo's voice.

"You? You? You fucking pervert? Just fucking sit there and work out what you're going to say to your wife. I'll come back and deal with you later. BRADY!" Gorse was shouting now.

Brady had wanted angry. He'd got angry. And more.

"Take the fucking headphones off, pretty boy. I'm coming out."

"The door's opening," Dave said. "It's Carl. And that fucker Gorse is behind him."

Brady took the headphones off. Stepped out of the kiosk. Breathed in deeply. The air smelled of salt water and rain. He noticed how quiet it was. Just the sound of the rain. For the first time, the seagulls were silent.

The end game.

Here. Now. Inevitable.

"Stay here, Dave. Let me do this."

"No. There's two of us. One of him."

Brady hadn't expected any other reply. "Just stay behind me then."

He walked into the rain. Looked across the road.

Gorse was standing on the pavement at the bottom of the steps. He was holding a clearly terrified Carl in front of him. It looked like Carl's hands were tied behind his back. Gorse had his left hand on Carl's shoulder. His right hand held a long, thin blade. It was resting lightly on Carl's neck.

Brady stopped in the middle of the road. Felt Dave at his side. Put his left arm out to protect him.

"I see you brought another dog, Brady. Let's hope he fares better than the last one."

"There's two of us, Gorse. One of you. Put the knife down. It's over."

"You're a fucking trier, Brady. I'll grant you that. I should've driven that car. I told them – "

"What? What did – "

The implication of what Gorse had said crashed into Brady. Hit him like a tidal wave. He started forward. Felt Dave's hand pulling him back.

And watched. As his life went into slow-motion.

For the second time.

Brady saw the water cascading down the steps behind Gorse. Saw Gorse move his left hand from Carl's shoulder. Grab hold of his hair. Pull his head back. Draw the knife lightly across his throat. The blood trickling down his neck. "Put this knife down, Brady? The one I used to kill your friend? The one I'll use to kill you? Come and take it, pretty boy."

Brady felt someone charge past him. A man who'd spent too many years in the front row of a rugby scrum, whose face had the scars to prove it. Sixty-two years old, bad knees, moved to Whitby for the fishing. A Geordie prop forward. Head down, aiming at Carl's knees. Determined to make one last tackle.

"Dave! No!"

Gorse let go of Carl. Drove his left knee into the back of Carl's leg. Carl crumpled. Gorse side-stepped at the last minute. The knife flashed down. Dave stumbled over

Carl, his momentum carrying him onto the bottom of the steps.

Gorse stepped back. Put distance between them. Held the knife out in front of him. "You were saying, Brady? Two of you, one of me? Maybe not."

He grabbed Carl by his collar, pulled him away.

Brady ran across to Dave. He was lying on his back, half on the steps, half on the pavement.

Brady turned. Gorse was yelling at him through the rain. "Come and find me when he's dead, Brady. Me and this lying piece of shit'll be on the end of the pier. You can watch him die."

Brady saw Gorse lift Carl onto his shoulder. A butcher with a carcass. He set off towards the pier.

Brady tore his jacket off. Bent over Dave. Just like he'd bent over Grace. Put the jacket under Dave's head. Looked down. Saw the blood oozing out of the right side of his chest.

"Dave? Dave? Come on, Dave."

Was this how it had been for Patrick? Feeling the blood running down his back? Kara coming out of the bar? Seeing him lying there?

Slumped in an alley. Slumped on some steps. What difference did it make?

I'm not going to lose another one.

He put his hands on Dave's shirt. Pressed hard.

Heard running feet behind him. Turned. Saw Frankie Thomson. On her own. No back-up.

"I couldn't get away," she said. "There's been an incident – oh fuck."

Brady risked taking one of his hands away. Touched

his fingers to Dave's neck. Found a pulse. Faint. But there. Definitely there.

Frankie was talking into her phone. "Ambulance. Barella's arcade. And immediate back-up. That's immediate. And suspect is armed."

Brady could see the rota pinned up in the canteen.

If there is any back-up in Whitby on a wet Wednesday afternoon.

"Dave," he said. "Dave. Open your eyes. Look at me."

Dave's eyelids fluttered. "It hurts," he said.

Brady looked down at him. Smiled at the man who'd become his friend. "Pain is good, Dave. It's better than the alternative."

"Go after him," Dave whispered. "He knows…"

Brady nodded. "Yeah. He does. And that's why he'll wait. It's me he wants."

Brady stood up.

Frankie reached out. Held his arm. "You can't."

"I can. And I am. It's personal."

And Brady set off through the rain. Towards the end of the pier. Towards Jimmy Gorse. Towards the man who had the information he wanted more than anything else.

The name of the person who had killed his wife.

65

There was nothing.

Simply nothing.

Seats. A rubbish bin. Lifebuoys fastened to the railings.

Everything you needed to eat your fish and chips in the sun.

Nothing Brady could use as a weapon.

And no time to find one. Gorse would wait. But not for ever.

It was high tide. Brady hadn't noticed. Hadn't even looked in the harbour.

Not just high tide. Spring tide. The wind driving the waves onshore. The spray already stinging his eyes.

It had never struck him before. How long the pier was. He started to run. Straight into the wind. Almost impossible.

He reached the lighthouse. And he was in the sea now. Just the pier, the railings between him and the North Sea.

The storm gate was closed. He remembered the words on the plaque. *To save life this storm gate is closed during dangerous conditions.*

A wave slammed into the sea wall. The spray arced up over him. Soaked him even more. He wiped his eyes. Ran his tongue across his lips. Tasted the salt. Saw the huge wave race along the harbour wall, surge through the storm break below him.

This was the moment to turn back. Wait for some uniforms. Say, 'He's down there. At the end of the pier.' Leave it to someone younger, fitter.

Someone without a daughter.

But Gorse was waiting. And he had Carl.

And he knew. He knew who'd killed Grace.

I should've driven that car...

Brady put both hands on top of the storm gate. Swung his right leg up. Got it on top of the gate. Levered the rest of himself up. Felt the wind pushing him backwards. Forced himself over the gate. Slipped as he landed on the wet, wooden planking of the pier.

What had Gorse done with Carl? Thrown him over the gate. Jumped over after him. Yanked him to his feet. Taken his collar again. Marched him out to the end. Out into the sea.

The pier curved round to the right. Rusty white railings. The wooden sleepers at the side. The red lifebuoys. The parallel lines formed by the planks hypnotically pointing the way.

Forwards. You can only go forwards.

Brady looked to his left. The last lifebuoy casing had been opened. The lifebuoy was nowhere to be seen. The rope was missing.

He saw the end of the pier. The green harbour light. The ladder leading up to it. And two figures on the pier. One of them was lying on the wet planks. Twisting from side to side. Arching his back. A fish out of water, flipping helplessly on a boat's deck.

And Jimmy Gorse.

He was stripped to the waist. Even from 20 yards away. Even through the rain and the spray Brady could see a series of angry red scars running across his back. The knife was next to him. Driven into the pier.

For now.

He was fastening the rope from the lifebuoy round Carl's feet. Brady squinted. Saw the other end was tied to the railings.

Ten yards. Brady watched as Gorse bent his legs like a weightlifter. Put his hands under Carl. Kept his back straight. Stood up. A perfect lift.

Five yards.

Gorse turned to Brady. Smiled at him. Just like in the car park.

Casually, calmly he tossed Carl off the end of the pier.

66

Brady stopped. Gorse was leaning back against the railings. Leaning back like he was on holiday. His arms spread out at either side. Like the sun was behind him. Like a man waiting for his wife to take a photo.

"Brady. Perfect," he yelled through the wind. "Just, you, me and..." He bent at the knees, never once taking his eyes off Brady. "...And my wee fish knife."

The harbour light was between them. A ladder leading up to it. Surrounded by railings, rusty spikes at the top of them. A gap in the planks. Another ladder leading down to the second stage of the pier. The harbour light resting on four wooden legs, the bottom two feet of them clad in metal surrounds. Rusty iron bolts sticking out. Brady saw himself on the floor. Saw Gorse laughing. Driving his head back into one of the bolts.

It would be over quickly. Fights in real life never lasted long. Two, three punches. A kick. Someone was beaten in the first thirty seconds. A minute at the most.

"The police are on their way," Brady shouted. "You're trapped. It's over."

"It's never over, Brady."

I should've driven that car...

No, it wasn't.

Gorse moved to his left. Brady did the same, keeping the gap, the ladder between them.

Gorse has to make a move. Has to. Delay. Delay him until Frankie gets here. Until the back-up arrives.

A wave crashed into the pier sending spray over both of them. Gorse slipped. Quickly regained his balance. Held the knife out in front of him. Carried on circling to his left. Yelled through the rain. "Your daughter, Brady. Your bonny, wee daughter. She'll be next for ma knife."

And now Brady had his back to the sea. They'd switched positions. More spray crashed over him.

Idiot. You fucking idiot.

Delay. Delay him until you're trapped against the railings, Brady.

It wasn't man to man. It wasn't him and Gorse. There were three of them in the fight. And now the North Sea was on Gorse's side.

He risked a glance to his right. Saw Carl suspended from the lifebuoy rope. Swinging from side to side. Hard to judge the distance. But not in the water.

Where the hell was Frankie? Where were the police? The paramedics must be with Dave by now.

I should've driven that car...

Gorse had stopped circling. Stood, legs apart, knees slightly bent.

Balanced. Poised. Coiled.

"You want to know, Brady?" Gorse was shouting at the top of his voice. Making himself heard over the sea and the wind.

"You want to know who was driving that car? I bet you fucking do."

Gorse shook his head from side to side. A bull ready to charge. Ran his left hand through his hair. Wiped rain and spray off his forehead.

"Nae fucking chance."

The wave hit Brady in the back. He heard the sound of it hitting the wall. A giant fist punched into him. Suddenly he was down on his hands and knees. Gorse had stepped back, avoided the worst of the wave.

The bull charged. One, two, three steps forward, lightning quick. The knife flashed down. Brady twisted. Desperate. Rolled to his left. Onto his back. Kicked out. Felt his foot connect with Gorse's hand. Saw the knife spiral away.

But Gorse was on him. A fist slammed into his face. Another fist. Brady knew his nose was broken. Gorse's hand closed round his throat. Dragged his head up. Until their faces were two inches apart. Gorse stared straight into his eyes.

"You're going to die, Brady. Here. Now. On this pier. And you'll never fucking know."

Gorse let go of Brady's throat. Stood up. Stepped to his right. Kicked Brady once, twice in the ribs. Drove all the wind, all the resistance, out of him.

Brady lay on the pier. Tried to raise his head. Couldn't.

I'm sorry, Grace. I won't be there for Ash. I'm sorry. Frankie? You were too late...

Gorse stood over him. Raised his right foot. The right foot that had stamped down on Carl's hand. Heavy shoes. Brady hadn't noticed them before. Black. Dripping with water. Now. Here it came. Gorse lifted his right foot even higher.

'Stamping on your fucking face.'

It was just like Carl had said.

'They have this moment. They pause. They anticipate what's coming. It's like they're coming home. And Gorse has it, Brady.'

He'd seen it once. Playing football at school. Someone flying into a tackle. Leg out, studs up. Missing the ball. Making contact with the defender's knee. At exactly the right angle. The leg bending backwards at 45 degrees. The scream of pain.

Gorse had all his weight on his left leg. Brady brought his right leg up. Drove it forward. Drove it straight into Gorse's knee. A perfect tackle. He saw the leg bend backwards. Heard Gorse scream.

"That's for my fucking dog, you bastard."

Now there were two of them lying on the pier.

And the sound of running feet. Brady managed to raise his head. Frankie Thomson. And one man in uniform. The cavalry. At last.

The uniform was holding something. A taser.

"You're done, Gorse. You're fucked. You're beaten. Tell me the name. Who killed my wife?"

Gorse looked up. Saw the police. Saw the taser. Knew it was over.

Lay on the pier. Looked at him through the rain.

"Fuck you, Brady," he said. "Fuck you."

Gorse reached his hands above his head. Grabbed the bottom bar of the railings. Pulled himself towards them.

"No!" Frankie yelled. Rushed forward. "No! We'll fire."

Too late. Gorse had gone.

Brady twisted over. Gasped in pain. Pulled himself to the railings. Looked down into the sea. Saw a huge wave pick Gorse up. Throw him into the sea wall. Scrape him along the wall. Toss him helplessly through the storm break.

Into the rocks on the other side.

Taking revenge for Patrick. For Carl. For Dave. For Archie.

But not for Grace.

The guy in uniform was running. Frankie was shouting into her phone. Brady couldn't hear.

He collapsed back onto the pier.

Tasted the blood in his mouth. Felt the spray hit him. Felt the rain.

Felt the tears start to run down his face.

67

"Good morning, Mr Brady."

Brady looked up. It hurt. A lot. "Dr Van der Bijl. Good to see you."

Van der Bijl looked down at him. "I thought I told you to avoid life's darker corners, Mr Brady?"

Brady smiled. Then changed his mind. That was even more painful. "Wetter," he said. "Not darker."

Van der Bijl nodded. "I heard. Well, some of it."

"What's the score?" Brady said. "I didn't really take it in last night."

"Two broken ribs. One cracked. Your nose was broken, we've re-set that. And a hairline fracture of your cheekbone. A few stitches. And the bruising will be spectacular. Are you familiar with Freddy Krueger, Mr Brady? He'll be living in your bathroom mirror for a week or two."

"What about Dave? And Carl?"

Van der Bijl shook his head. "There I can't help you. I'm assuming they're both in James Cook. I'm sure one of your visitors will have news. But you should rest. You've a lot of healing to do."

Brady let his head fall back on the pillow. What day was it? Was Ash due back from Center Parcs today? He had no idea.

He closed his eyes. Saw Dave lying on the steps. Saw Carl hanging above the sea. Saw Gorse's knee bending backwards. Knew beyond any doubt how lucky he'd been...

He must have fallen asleep. The door opened. "Michael?" a nurse said. "You've got a visitor. Not strictly visiting time. But I could hardly say no."

"I pulled rank," Frankie Thomson said.

"Grapes?" Brady asked hopefully.

She sat down in the chair. "I thought you'd rather have news."

He nodded. "Good news. I hope."

"Yes," she said. "There are no more dead bodies. On our side. That's what you want to know isn't it?"

"Yes. More than anything. And how they're doing."

"Dave lost a lot of blood. But no permanent damage. The bacon sandwich stall will be closed for a while. But given time, he'll be fine."

"For good," Brady said.

Frankie looked puzzled. "For good," Brady repeated. "He's not going to spend the day looking at the spot where he almost died. I'll have to bring Archie into the police canteen."

"He's alright?"

"Archie? I think I'm due to collect him soon. If today's Thursday. Then Monday."

"You can't walk a Springer if your ribs are broken."

"Try telling Archie that."

Frankie stood up, looked around the room. "You want a glass of water or anything?"

Brady shook his head. "Are you playing for time here, Frankie? Tell me about Carl."

"You mind if I sit on the bed?"

"No. I'd prefer it. Hurts to twist my head to look at you."

She sat at the end of the bed. "OK. Superficially, he's fine. Well, as fine as anyone who's been thrown head first into the North Sea can be. Plenty of bruising but nothing broken. But – I only talked to the doctor briefly – the psychological scars are going to run deep."

Brady didn't reply. Carl must have been convinced he was going to die. *He'd* been convinced he was going to die. But only briefly. Carl had all the way down the pier to think about it. All the time Gorse was tying him up. The headlong fall into the sea.

"My fault," he finally said. "All my fault."

"No," Frankie said. "As much my fault as yours. This fucking incident we had - "

Brady held his hand up. "Tell me another time. It'll keep. What about Gorse?"

"Keillor waded in."

"The one with the taser? And – "

"Yeah. Dan Keillor. The taser and too much information on Bill Calvert's operation. You remember. But he's brave. Stripped off, walked into the sea and retrieved the body."

"It was definitely Gorse?"

"Definitely Gorse. Definitely dead."

Brady felt no satisfaction. No sense of triumph.

He tried to sit up in bed. Found something else that was too painful.

"I had a text from Kate," he said. "Bill. It's confirmed."

Frankie nodded. "I heard."

They were both silent. Both knowing there was something else.

"I'm coming back," Brady said eventually.

"I heard that too."

"I had a conversation with Kershaw. Before the shit hit the fan. There's a vacancy. Now Bill can't come back…"

Frankie looked at him. "So I should get used to calling you 'boss?'"

"No," Brady said. "You should do what you've been doing. You're good. Really good. And I won't be there for ever. One other thing," he added.

"What's that?"

"He knew. Gorse knew who killed my wife."

Frankie looked past him, out of the window. Took time to choose her words carefully. "You have to let it go," she said. "It figures. It's a small world. Especially for people like that. But you have to let it go. Move on with your life."

"I - "

The door opened. No nurse, no knock. Ash stood there. Looking tanned and – was it possible? – even taller than a few days ago.

"Dad! You're a hero!"

She almost ran to him. Then stopped short. "Oh. A battered hero. I guess I probably shouldn't hug you."

She looked more closely. "They didn't tell us you were so badly... Does it hurt?"

Brady smiled. Beamed at her. Like he was seeing her for the first time. "Yes. A lot. But not so much that I can't hug you. Come here."

He held his arms out. Did his best to move his face out of harm's way and held her. His daughter: sassy, argumentative, assertive. Still his little girl one minute, a young woman the next.

"I love you, Ash," he said into her hair.

"I love you too, Dad."

He let her go. Realised he'd forgotten his manners. "Ash, this is Frankie. Someone I'm going to be working with. Frankie, my daughter, Ash."

Frankie stood up, an inch or two taller than Ash. "I'll leave you to take care of him, Ash. And lovely to meet you. And if he gives you any trouble, just hug him." She winked at Ash, gave Brady what passed for a wave and opened the door.

"She's nice," Ash said. "Almost as nice as Fiona."

"Did Fiona bring you? And I thought you were back tomorrow?"

Ash nodded. "The police called us. So we came back early. And she's outside."

"You can't do that. Tell her to come in. I have to say thank you. And hear all about Center Parcs. But warn her about what I look like."

Ash stood up. Moved towards the door.

"And I assume I have to come next time?" Brady said.

"Obviously. And you have to race me down the rapids."

68

Michael Brady turned round. "Come on, Archie, just to the top of this hill."

Archie reluctantly left the remains of a barbecue and trotted after them.

"You OK?" Brady asked.

"Yeah," Ash said. "I'm good. I'm sad. But I'm good."

Brady put his arm round her shoulder and pulled her to him as they walked. "Me too. I know what you mean. Just over there," he said, pointing to the right.

"It looks more like the surface of the moon every time we come," Ash said.

Brady laughed. "Wait until winter. A cold, frozen, muddy moon."

"Duh, Dad. It can't be frozen *and* muddy can it?"

"Sorry, Ash. You can put me in the old people's home next week."

They stood on the cliff edge. Brady looked down at the sea. It was flat. Calm and peaceful. Two kayaks glided past: a family on holiday.

The sun shone down from a cloudless sky. They could have been in Greece.

He turned and gazed back to Whitby. Saw the pier. Pushed the image of Jimmy Gorse out of his mind. Concentrated on his daughter. "She'd have been so proud of you, Ash. I can't tell you how much."

"And you, Dad. What you did."

"Just work, sweetheart."

The red and white fishing boat was back, even lower at the back than he remembered. That was an appointment he needed to keep. And Dave had said he probably wouldn't be seasick. "Not after your second or third time anyway…"

"Dad?"

"What, love?"

"She wouldn't want you to be lonely, you know. Not for ever."

"I'm not lonely. I've got you. And Archie. Especially when he's rolled in a dead fish and you won't go near him."

"You know what I mean."

"Yeah, I do. But time enough."

Dare he risk it? Brady decided to. "How's it going with you anyway? Josh?"

"That loser? I dumped him last week."

"Oh. OK." He knew better than to ask any more.

They stood in silence for a few more minutes. Both with their memories.

But they couldn't stand on the cliff top for ever.

"Come on then," Brady said. "Archie needs his tea. He's got his 'feed me' face."

He turned and walked back to the cliff path. Ash put her arm in his. A very happy Springer Spaniel followed them.

Time to drive back to Whitby.

Time to carry on rebuilding their lives.

Time for DCI Michael Brady to go back to work.

REVIEWS & FUTURE WRITING PLANS

Thank you for reading *Salt in the Wounds*. I really hope you enjoyed it.

If you did, could I ask a favour? Would you please review the book on Amazon?

Reviews are important to me for three reasons. First of all, good reviews help to sell the book. Secondly, there are some review and book promotion sites that will only look at a book if it has a certain number of reviews and/or a certain ratio of 5* reviews. And lastly, reviews are feedback. Some writers ignore their reviews: I don't.

So I'd appreciate you taking five minutes to leave a review and thank you in advance to anyone who does so.

What next?

The immediate aim is to have the second Michael Brady book out before Christmas 2020. That will also be available from Amazon.

I'll then write and publish the next four books in the series over the course of the following year. I am also going to write two novellas, looking at Brady's early career. Plus, of course, the story of the case that led to Grace's death.

If you'd like to receive regular updates on my writing – and previews of these books – you can join my mailing list. You can find a link to do that on my website: www.-markrichards.co.uk

ABOUT ME

Way back in 2003 I was at a meeting of Scarborough Writers' Circle.

At the time I had a business in financial services – clients, suits, stripy ties. But I also had a small voice inside me: 'Let me out,' it said. 'I'm a writer.'

The speaker that night was the editor of the local paper. "We'd quite like a humorous weekly column if anyone thinks they can write one," he said. That was the start of my writing career – a light-hearted look at family life from a dad's point of view, which ultimately became the 'Best Dad' books you can find on my Amazon page.

But writing was very much second-best to the day job, until – in 2009 – my brother died of cancer.

When Mike died it was one of those pivotal moments in life: a time when you realise that you either pursue your dream – do what you've always wanted to do – or you forget about it for good.

So I sold my business, sent my stripy ties to the

charity shop and started writing. I've worked full-time as a writer since then. Starting from scratch I built a business as a freelance copywriter and content writer – something I still do for a small number of clients.

Then, in the spring of 2016, I had the latest in a long line of mid-life crises and invited Alex – my youngest son – to come for a walk with me. I wanted to do a physical challenge before I was too old for a physical challenge and – despite never having done any serious walking in my life – asked Alex if he wanted to walk 90 miles on the Pennine Way, one of the UK's toughest national trails.

The walk took us five days, and the result was *Father, Son and the Pennine Way* – the challenges we faced, the experiences we shared and what we learned about ourselves and each other. The book is also, sadly, the sorry tale of how I became the first person to walk a mile of the Pennine Way in his underpants...

Pennine Way now has more than 300 reviews on Amazon, the overwhelming majority of them at 5*. 'Brilliantly written, insightful, brutally honest and laugh out loud funny.' And my personal favourite among the reviews: 'I was laughing so hard at this book my husband went off to sleep in the spare room.'

The book is available on your Kindle for £2.99, or in paperback for £7.99. You can find it on Amazon.

Father, Son and the Pennine Way was followed by *Father Son and Return to the Pennine Way* – picking up where the first book left off – in 2018 and *Father, Son and the Kerry Way* – 125 miles around South West Ireland – in 2019.

You can find all my books on my website, or on my Amazon author page.

While there'll be another father/son book out next year, I'll now be increasingly concentrating on fiction. *Salt in the Wounds* is the first book in the Michael Brady series, and I'm planning to write two more crime series after that.

JOIN THE TEAM

If you enjoy my writing, and you would like to be more actively involved, I have a readers' group on Facebook. The people in this group act as my advance readers, giving me feedback and constructive criticism. Sometimes you need someone to say, 'that part of the story just doesn't work' or 'you need to develop that character more.'

In return for helping, the members of the group receive previews, updates and exclusive content and the chance to take part in the occasional competitions I run for them. If you'd like to help in that way, then look for 'Mark Richards: Writer' on Facebook and ask to join.

ACKNOWLEDGMENTS

A number of people helped with this book. Let me start by thanking my wife for the original inspiration: she had the idea about Enzo, and it went on from there.

One part of writing the book I really enjoyed was the research. I'd like to thank Terri Duddy and Michelle Lucianne for all their help with 'Low Grange' prison. Two serving police officers were especially helpful in correcting my mistakes – and in giving me ideas for the rest of the series – but they specifically asked not to be named. I'd also like to thank Mark Yates for walking me step by step through the paramedic scene.

As usual I've worked with a battle hardened team of professionals: Tom Sanderson, who designed the front cover for me, Kevin Partner who converted my Word file into something that works on your Kindle, and Linnhe Harrison for her help with the website and the publicity. And my long-time collaborator, Paul Wilson, for his insight into Whitby's Goths.

I'd also like to thank the members of my reader group

on Facebook who acted as advance readers for me, commenting on early drafts and making plot suggestions. So my thanks to Phyllis Elias, Philip Wood, Julie Jackson, Maggie Baldwin, Tamar Reay, Hazel Cummings, Alison Southward, Gina Crees, Steph Cooke, Dawn Sawyer, Ruth Beale, Shirley Harrall, Deborah Eastwood, Kim Miller, Helene Griffiths-Adams, Sarah Boorman, Sepp Lindner, Lynne Cordingley, Rosaline Hillyard and Micki McCarthy.

But let me end where I began. My wife, Beverley, helped me with the plotting, encouraged me to keep writing and – most importantly – put up with the numerous times I was staring into space and thinking about Brady instead of responding to something she'd said. This is a better book because of her input and I'm hugely grateful.

...As I am to Alex. He read an early draft and made one very perceptive comment which, again, made it a better book. Perhaps my favourite part of writing the book was our discussions round the dinner table as Bev, Alex and I talked about the plot and the characters. Usually over another gin...

Mark Richards
September 2020

Made in the USA
Middletown, DE
10 April 2023

28602388R00236